P9-BZZ-696

Dear Reader,

Happy holidays! In celebration of the season, Silhouette Books gives you the gift of romance in this heartwarming anthology of stories by three of your favorite authors.

The collection begins with a classic story by *New York Times* bestselling author Debbie Macomber. In "Let It Snow," a woman on her way home for the holidays finds herself stranded with a very cranky—and very handsome—bachelor. And once she glimpses the warmth beneath his hard heart, it's no wonder she's wishing the sudden snowstorm that hits will keep them together a little longer—maybe even forever!

Next, join Morgan Trayhern and his family for an unforgettable "Five Days of Christmas." In this emotional story, *USA Today* bestselling author Lindsay McKenna shows the healing power of love when Morgan's matchmaking wife brings together an emotionally wounded mercenary and a pretty widow. It's a brand-new MORGAN'S MERCENARIES story you won't forget.

Finally, the Murdock family gets a very beautiful—very *pregnant*—visitor in "Twins under the Tree," a brand-new TWINS ON THE DOORSTEP story from national bestselling author Stella Bagwell. We know you'll enjoy this delightful story of a woman about to give birth to twins and the rugged rancher who stands by her side—and loses his heart to the new mom and her babies.

We hope you enjoy the gift of these stories. Best wishes to you and your family from all of us here at Silhouette Books.

Happy reading!

The Editors at Silhouette Books

DEBBIE MACOMBER

has always enjoyed telling stories, first to her baby-sitting charges and then to her own four children. As a full-time wife and mother and an avid romance reader, she dreamed of one day sharing her stories with a wider audience. In the autumn of 1982 she sold her first book, and that was only the beginning. Today Debbie is a *New York Times* bestselling author with over 60 million copies of her books in print worldwide.

LINDSAY McKENNA

A homeopathic educator, Lindsay teaches at the Desert Institute of Classical Homeopathy in Phoenix, Arizona. When she isn't teaching alternative medicine, she is writing books about love. She feels love is the single greatest healer in the world and hopes that her books touch her readers on all levels. Coming from an Eastern Cherokee medicine family, Lindsay was taught ceremony and healing ways from the time she was nine years old. She creates flower and gem essences in accordance with nature and remains closely in touch with her Native American roots and upbringing.

STELLA BAGWELL

has written more than forty books for Silhouette. She always loved reading romances, but it wasn't until an allergic reaction to hair spray ended her career as a hairdresser that she found the urge to write one. Stella married her high school sweetheart at the age of seventeen and has one son. She and her husband have recently moved to Texas. After more than thirty years of marriage, Stella feels love is the thing that makes life most precious and worthwhile.

Debbie
Macomber
Lindsay McKenna
Stella Bagwell

Midnight Clear

Published by Silhouette Books
America's Publisher of Contemporary Romance

If you purchased this book without a cover you should be aware
that this book is stolen property. It was reported as "unsold and
destroyed" to the publisher, and neither the author nor the
publisher has received any payment for this "stripped book."

 SILHOUETTE BOOKS

MIDNIGHT CLEAR

Copyright © 2001 by Harlequin Books S.A.

ISBN 0-373-48451-8

The publisher acknowledges the copyright holders
of the individual works as follows:

LET IT SNOW
Copyright © 1986 by Debbie Macomber

THE FIVE DAYS OF CHRISTMAS
Copyright © 2001 by Lindsay McKenna

TWINS UNDER THE TREE
Copyright © 2001 by Stella Bagwell

All rights reserved. Except for use in any review, the reproduction
or utilization of this work in whole or in part in any form by any
electronic, mechanical or other means, now known or hereafter
invented, including xerography, photocopying and recording, or in
any information storage or retrieval system, is forbidden without
the written permission of the editorial office, Silhouette Books,
300 East 42nd Street, New York, NY 10017 U.S.A.

All characters in this book have no existence outside the imagination of
the author and have no relation whatsoever to anyone bearing the same
name or names. They are not even distantly inspired by any individual
known or unknown to the author, and all incidents are pure invention.

This edition published by arrangement with Harlequin Books S.A.

® and TM are trademarks of Harlequin Books S.A., used under
license. Trademarks indicated with ® are registered in the United States
Patent and Trademark Office, the Canadian Trade Marks Office and in
other countries.

Visit Silhouette at www.eHarlequin.com

Printed in U.S.A.

CONTENTS

LET IT SNOW   9
Debbie Macomber

THE FIVE DAYS OF CHRISTMAS   111
Lindsay McKenna

TWINS UNDER THE TREE   241
Stella Bagwell

LET IT SNOW

Debbie Macomber

For Joyce Beaman
Fellow author, fortune cookie collector
and, above all, dear friend.

Dear Reader,

Back in 1986, I was approached by my friends at Silhouette to write a Christmas story to be published together with novellas by three other authors for Silhouette's very first Christmas anthology.

Never having written a story of this length before, I searched for just the right idea. Then it happened. I was trapped in Portland, Oregon, because of fog. (These were the days before planes could land in fog and long before cell phones and personal 800 numbers.) It was only supposed to be an overnight trip. This was December, and I had a husband and four children who needed me at home. I was a woman on a mission—I wanted out of there! But alas, I was stuck. Eventually the airline rented buses and we made the drive north to Seattle. What should have been a thirty-minute flight ended up taking all day. I staggered into the house, so glad to be home, only to be met by a family convinced I'd spent the day having fun without them. From this experience, "Let It Snow" was born. The fog became a snowstorm, and the mission became getting home in time for Christmas. And the romance in my story (though not, of course, in my real-life experience!)—two strangers who agree to share the expense of a rental car.

The overwhelming success of *Silhouette Christmas Stories* stunned everyone. I'm very proud to have been a part of it, and I am delighted that my story, "Let It Snow," is being made available again in this new collection. I hope you enjoy "Let It Snow."

Merry Christmas, and God bless you and yours.

Debbie Macomber

Chapter 1

"Ladies and gentlemen, this is your captain speaking."

Shelly Griffin's fingers compressed around the armrest until her neatly manicured nails threatened to cut into the fabric of the airplane seat. Flying had never thrilled her, and she avoided planes whenever possible. It had taken her the better part of a month to convince herself that she'd be perfectly safe. She told herself that the Boeing 727 would take off without incident from San Francisco and land unscathed ninety minutes later in Seattle. Flying, after all, was said to be relatively riskless. But if it wasn't Christmas, if she wasn't so homesick and if she'd had more than four days off, she would have done anything to get home for the holidays—except fly.

"Seattle reports heavy snow and limited visibility," the captain continued. "We've been rerouted to Portland International until the Seattle runways can be cleared."

A low groan filled the plane.

Shelly relaxed. Snow. She could handle snow. She wasn't overjoyed with the prospect of having to land twice, but she was so close to home now that she would have willingly suffered anything to see a welcoming smile light up her father's eyes.

In an effort to divert her thoughts away from impending tragedy, Shelly studied the passengers around her. A grandmotherly type slept sedately in the seat beside her. The man sitting across the aisle was such a classic businessman that he was intriguing. Almost from the moment they'd left San Francisco, he'd been working out of his briefcase. He hadn't so much as cracked a smile during the entire flight. The captain's announcement had produced little more than a disgruntled flicker in his staid exterior.

Shelly had seen enough men like him in her job as a reporter in the federal court to catalog him quickly. Polished. Professional. Impeccable. Handsome, too, Shelly supposed, if she was interested, which she wasn't. She preferred her men a little less intense. She managed to suppress a tight laugh. Men! What men? In the ten months she'd been living in the City by the Bay, she hadn't exactly developed a following. A few interesting prospects now and again but nothing serious.

As the Boeing 727 slowly made its descent, Shelly's fingers gripped the armrest with renewed tension. Her gaze skimmed the emergency exits as she reviewed affirmations on the safety of flying. She mumbled them under her breath as the plane angled sharply to the right, aligning its giant bulk with the narrow runway ahead.

Keeping her eyes centered on the seat in front of her, Shelly held her breath until she felt the wheels gently bounce against the runway in a flawless landing. A burst of noise accompanied the aircraft as it slowed to a crawl.

The oxygen rushed from Shelly's lungs in a heartfelt sigh of relief. Somehow the landings were so much worse than the takeoffs. As the tension eased from her rigid body, she looked around to discover the businessman slanting his idle gaze over her. His dark eyes contained a look of surprise. He seemed amazed that anyone could be afraid of flying, and he was utterly indifferent to her apprehension. The blood mounted briefly in her pale features, and Shelly decided she definitely didn't like this cheerless executive.

The elderly woman sitting next to her placed a hand on Shelly's forearm. "Are you all right, dear?"

"Of course." Relief throbbed in her voice. Now that they were on the ground, she could feign the composure that seemed to come so easily to the other passengers.

"I hope we aren't delayed long. My daughter's taking off work to meet my flight."

"My dad's forty minutes from the airport," Shelly murmured, hoping that he'd called the airline to check if her flight was on time. She hated the thought of him anxiously waiting for her.

The other woman craned her neck to peek out the small side window. "It doesn't seem to be snowing much here. Just a few flakes floating down like lazy goose feathers."

Shelly grinned at the verbal picture. "Let's hope it stays that way."

She remained seated while several of the other passengers got up and left the plane. The business-man was among those who quickly vacated their seats. From what the captain had said, they wouldn't be in Portland long, and Shelly didn't want to take a chance of missing the flight.

After checking her watch every ten minutes for forty minutes, Shelly was convinced that they'd never leave Oregon. The blizzard had hit the area, and whirling snow buffeted the quiet plane with growing intensity. Her anxieties mounted with equal force.

"This is the captain speaking." His faint Southern drawl filled the plane. "Unfortunately, Seattle reports that visibility hasn't improved. They're asking that we remain here in Portland for another half hour, possibly longer.''

Frustration and disappointment erupted from the passengers seated on the plane, and they all began speaking at once.

"This is the captain again," the pilot added, his low drawl riddled with wry humor. "I'd like to remind those of you who are upset by our situation that it's far better to be on the ground wishing you were in the sky than to be in the sky *praying* you were on the ground.''

Shelly added a silent amen to that! As it was, she was beginning to feel claustrophobic trapped inside the plane. Unsnapping her seat belt, she stood, reached for her purse and headed down the narrow aisle toward the front of the plane.

"Do I have time to make a phone call?''

"Sure," the flight attendant answered with a cordial smile. "Don't be long, though. The conditions in Seattle could change quickly.''

"I won't," Shelly promised and made her way into the airport terminal.

It wasn't until she was sorting through her purse for change that she noted the unsympathetic businessman from her flight had the phone booth adjacent to hers.

"This is Slade Garner again," he announced with the faintest trace of impatience creeping into his voice. "My plane's still in Portland.''

A pause followed while Shelly dumped the contents of her coin purse into her hand and scowled. She didn't have change for the phone.

"Yes, yes, I understand the snow's a problem on your end as well," he continued smoothly. "I doubt that I'll make it in this afternoon. Perhaps we should arrange the meeting for first thing tomorrow morning. Nine o'clock?" Another pause. "Of course I realize it's the day before Christmas."

Rummaging in her purse for a quarter, Shelly managed to dredge up a token for the cable car, a dried peach pit and a lost button.

Pressing her lips tightly together, she mused what a coldhearted tycoon this businessman had to be to insist upon a meeting so close to Christmas. Instantly she felt guilty because her thoughts were so judgmental. Of course he'd want to keep his appointment. He certainly hadn't taken this flight for his health. Her second regret was that she had intentionally eavesdropped on his conversation, looking for excuses to justify her dislike of him. Such behavior was hardly in keeping with the Christmas spirit.

Pasting on a pleasant smile, Shelly stepped forward when Slade Garner replaced the receiver. Abruptly he turned around.

"Excuse me." His gaze refused to meet hers, and for a second Shelly didn't think that he'd heard her.

"Yes?" His expression was bored, frustrated.

"Have you got change for a dollar?" She unfolded a crisp one-dollar bill, anticipating the exchange.

Slade uninterestedly checked the contents of his

pocket, glaring down at the few coins in his palm. "Sorry." Dispassionately he tucked them back in his pocket and turned away from her.

Shelly was ready to approach someone else when Slade turned back to her. His dark brows drew together in a frown as something about her registered in his preoccupied thoughts. "You were on the Seattle flight?"

"Yes."

"Here." He handed her a quarter.

The corners of Shelly's mouth curved up in surprise. "Thanks." She was convinced that he hadn't heard her as he briskly walked away. Shelly didn't know what difference it made that they'd shared the same plane. Without analyzing his generosity any further, she dropped the coin in the slot.

After connecting with the operator, Shelly shifted her weight from one foot to the other while the phone rang, waiting for her father to answer.

"Dad."

"Merry Christmas, Shortcake."

Her father had bestowed this affectionate title on Shelly when she was a young teen and her friends had sprouted around her. To her dismay Shelly had remained a deplorable five foot until she was seventeen. Then within six months she had grown five inches. Her height and other attributes of puberty had been hormonal afterthoughts.

"I'm in Portland."

"I know. When I phoned Sea-Tac, the lady at the

reservation desk told me you'd been forced to land there. How are you doing?''

"Fine." She fibbed about her dread of flying. "I'm sorry about the delay."

"That's not your fault."

"But I hate wasting precious hours sitting here when I could be with you."

"Don't worry about it. We'll have plenty of time together."

"Have you decorated the tree yet?" Since her mother's death three years before, Shelly and her father had made a ritual of placing the homemade ornaments on the tree together.

"I haven't even bought one. I thought we'd do that first thing in the morning."

Shelly closed her eyes, savoring the warmth of love and security that the sound of her father's voice always gave her. "I've got a fantastic surprise for you."

"What's that?" her father prompted.

"It wouldn't be a surprise if I told you, would it?"

Her father chuckled and Shelly could visualize him rubbing his finger over his upper lip the way he did when something amused him.

"I've missed you, Dad."

"I know. I've missed you, too."

"Take care."

"I will." She was about to hang up. "Dad," she added hastily, her thoughts churning as her gaze focused on a huge wall advertisement for a rental car agency. "Listen, don't go the the airport until I phone."

"But—"

"By the time you arrive, I'll have collected my things and be waiting outside for you. That way you won't have to park."

"I don't mind, Shortcake."

"I know, but it'll work better this way."

"If you insist."

"I do." Her brothers claimed that their father was partial to his only daughter. It was a long-standing family joke that she was the only one capable of swaying him once he'd made a decision. "I do insist."

They said their goodbyes, and after Shelly disconnected the line, she checked for the quarter that had slipped into the change slot. Feeling light-hearted and relieved, she flipped it in the air with a flick of her thumb and caught it with a dexterity that surprised her. Instead of heading down the concourse toward the plane, she ventured in the opposite direction, taking the escalators to the lower level and the rental car agencies.

To her surprise Shelly found that she wasn't the only one with alternate transportation in mind. The businessman who had loaned her the quarter was talking with a young man at the first agency. Shelly walked past him to the second counter.

"How much would it cost to rent a car here and drop it off in Seattle?" she asked brightly.

The tall, college-aged woman hardly looked up from the computer screen. "Sorry, we don't have any cars available."

"None?" Shelly found that hard to believe.

"Lots of people have had the same idea as you," the clerk explained. "A plane hasn't landed in Seattle in hours. No one wants to sit around the airport waiting. Especially at Christmas."

"Thanks, anyway." Shelly scooted down to the third agency and repeated her question.

"Yes, we do," the clerk said with a wide grin. "We only have one car available at the moment." She named a sum that caused Shelly to swallow heavily. But already the idea had gained momentum in her mind. Every minute the plane remained on the ground robbed her of precious time with her father. And from what he'd told her, the snow was coming down fast and furiously. It could be hours before the plane was able to take off. She freely admitted that another landing at another airport in the middle of the worst snowstorm of the year wasn't her idea of a good time. As it was, her Christmas bonus was burning a hole in her purse. It was a good cause. Surely there was some unwritten rule that stated every favorite daughter should spend Christmas with her father.

"If she doesn't take the car, I will." Slade Garner spoke from beside Shelly. A wide, confident smile spread across his handsome features.

"I want it," she cried. His aura of self-assurance bordered on arrogance.

"I have to get to Seattle."

"So do I!" she informed him primly. In case he mentioned that he'd loaned her the quarter, she pulled it from her jacket pocket and handed it to him.

"I've got an important meeting."

"As a matter of fact, so do I." Turning back to the counter, Shelly picked up a pen and prepared to fill in the rental form.

"How much?" Slade asked. His features tightened with unrelenting resolve that negated his manly appeal.

"I beg your pardon?"

"How much do you want for the car?" His hand slipped into the pocket of his suit coat, apparently prepared to pay her price.

Squaring her shoulders with angry frustration, Shelly exchanged looks with the clerk. "Get your own car."

"There's only one car available. This one."

"And I've got it," she told him with a deceptively calm smile. The more she saw of this man, the more aggravating he became.

His jaw tightened. "I don't think you understand," he said and breathed out with sharp impatience. "My meeting's extremely important."

"So is mine. I'm—"

"You could share the car," the clerk suggested,

causing both Shelly and Slade to divert their shocked gazes to the impromptu peacemaker.

Shelly hesitated.

Slade's brows arched. "I'll pay the full fee for the car," he offered.

"You mention money one more time and the deal's off," she shot back hotly.

"Don't be unreasonable."

"I'm not being unreasonable. You are."

Slade rubbed a hand along the back of his neck and forcefully expelled his breath. "Have we or have we not got a deal?"

"I'm not going to Seattle."

He gave her a sharp look of reproach. "I just heard you say Seattle."

"I'm headed for Maple Valley. That's in south King County."

"Fine. I'll drop you off and deliver the car to the rental place myself."

That would save her one hassle. Still, she hesitated. Two minutes together and they were already arguing. Shelly wondered how they'd possibly manage three hours cooped up in the close confines of a car.

"Listen," he argued, his voice tinged with exasperation. "If I make it into Seattle this afternoon, I might be able to get this meeting over with early. That way I can be back in San Francisco for Christmas."

Quickly he'd discerned the weakest link in her

chain of defenses and had aimed there. Christmas and home were important to her.

"All right," she mumbled. "But I'll pay my share of the fee."

"Whatever you want, lady."

For the first time since she'd seen him, Slade Garner smiled.

Chapter 2

"What about your luggage?" Slade asked as they strolled down the concourse toward the plane.

"I only have one bag. It's above my seat." Honey-brown hair curled around her neck, and she absently lifted a strand and looped it over her ear. A farm girl's wardrobe didn't fit in with the formal business attire she needed in San Francisco so Shelly had left most of her clothes with her father. Now she realized that having packed light was a blessing in disguise. At least there wouldn't be the hassle of trying to get her suitcase back.

Shelly's spirits buoyed up; she was heading home and she wasn't flying!

"Good. I only have a garment bag with me."

Shelly hesitated. "I have another bag filled with presents."

Slade's gaze briefly scanned hers. "That shouldn't be any problem."

When he sees the monstrosity, he might change his mind, Shelly mused good-naturedly. In addition to a variety of odd-sized gifts, she had brought her father several long loaves of sourdough bread. The huge package was awkward, and Shelly had required the flight attendant's assistance to place it in the compartment above her seat. Normally Shelly would have checked a bundle that size with the airline. But with the long loaves of bread sticking out like doughy antennas, that had been impossible.

The plane was nearly empty when they boarded, confirming her suspicion that the delay was going to be far longer than originally anticipated. Checking her watch, she discovered that it was nearly noon. The other passengers had probably gone to get something to eat.

Standing on the cushioned seat beside hers, Shelly opened the storage compartment.

"Do you need help?" Slade asked. A dark gray garment bag was folded neatly over his forearm.

"Here." Shelly handed him her one small bag. She heard him mumble something about appreciating a woman who packed light and smiled to herself.

Straining to stretch as far as she could to get a good grip on her package, she heard Slade grumble.

"Look at what some idiot put up there."

"Pardon?"

"That bag. Good grief, people should know better than to try to force a tuba case up there."

"That's mine and it isn't a tuba case." Extracting the bag containing the bread, she handed it down to him.

Slade looked at it as if something were about to leap out and bite him. "Good heavens, what is this?"

What is it! Bread had to be the most recognizable item in the world. And to have it shaped in long, thin loaves wasn't that unusual, either!

"A suitcase for a snake," she replied sarcastically.

The beginnings of a grin touched his usually impassive features as he gently moved in front of her. "Let me get that thing down before you fall."

Shelly climbed down from the cushioned seat. "Suitcase for a snake, huh?" Unexpectedly Slade Garner smiled, and the effect on Shelly was dazzling. She had the feeling that this man didn't often take the time to laugh and enjoy life. Only minutes before she'd classified him as cheerless and intense. But when he smiled, the carefully guarded facade cracked and she was given a rare glimpse of the intriguing man inside. And he fascinated her.

By the time they'd cleared their tickets with the airline, the courtesy car from the rental agency had arrived to deliver them to their rented vehicle.

"I put everything in my name," Slade said on a serious note. The snow continued to fall, creating a picturesque view.

"That's fine." He'd taken the small suitcase from

her, leaving her to cope with the huge sack filled with Christmas goodies.

"It means I'll be doing all the driving."

One glance at the snowstorm and Shelly was grateful.

"Well?" He looked as though he expected an argument.

"Do you have a driver's license?"

Again a grin cracked the tight line of his mouth, touching his eyes. "Yes."

"Then there shouldn't be any problem."

He paused, looking down on her. "Are you always so witty?"

Shelly chuckled, experiencing a rush of pleasure at her ability to make him smile. "Only when I try to be. Come on, Garner, loosen up. It's Christmas."

"I've got a meeting to attend. Just because it happens to fall close to a holiday doesn't make a whit's difference."

"Yeah, but just think, once you're through, you can hurry home and spend the holidays with your family."

"Right." The jagged edge of his clipped reply was revealing, causing Shelly to wonder if he had a family.

As they deposited their luggage in the trunk of the rented Camaro, Shelly had the opportunity to study Slade. The proud, withdrawn look revealed little of his thoughts; there was an air of independence about him. Even with a minimum of contact, she realized that he must possess a keen and agile mind. He was a man of contrasts—pensive yet decisive, cultured while maintaining a highly organized facade.

Standing in the fallen snow, the young man at the rental agency handed Slade a map of the city and pointed him in the direction of the nearest freeway entrance ramp.

After studying the map thoroughly, Slade handed it to Shelly. "Are you ready?"

"Forward, James," she teased, climbing into the passenger seat and rubbing her bare hands together to generate some warmth. When she'd left San Francisco that morning, she hadn't dressed for snow.

With a turn of the key, Slade started the engine and adjusted the heater. "You'll be warm in a minute."

Shelly nodded, burying her hands in her jacket pockets. "You know, if it gets much colder, we might get snow before we reach Seattle."

"Very funny," he muttered dryly, snapping his seat belt into place. Hands gripping the wheel, Slade hesitated. "Do you want to find a phone and call your husband?"

"I'm visiting my dad," she corrected. "I'm not married. And no. If I told him what we're doing, he'd only worry."

Slade shifted gears and they pulled onto the road. "Do you want to contact…your wife?"

"I'm not married."

"Oh." Shelly prayed that the small expression

wouldn't reveal her satisfaction at the information. It wasn't often that she found herself so fascinated by a man. The crazy part was that she wasn't entirely sure she liked him, but he attracted her.

"I'm engaged," he added.

"Oh." She swallowed convulsively. So much for that. "When's the wedding?"

The windshield wipers hummed ominously. "In approximately two years."

Shelly nearly choked in an effort to hide her shock.

"Both Margaret and I have professional and financial goals we hope to accomplish before we marry." He drove with his back stiff, his expression sullen. "Margaret feels we should save fifty thousand dollars before we think about marriage and I agree. We both have strong feelings about having a firm financial foundation."

"I can't imagine waiting two years to marry the man I loved."

"But then you're entirely different from Margaret."

As far as Shelly was concerned, that was the nicest thing anyone had said to her all day. "We do agree on one thing, though. I feel a marriage should last forever." But for Shelly love had to be more spontaneous and far less calculated. "My parents had a marvelous marriage," she said, filling the silence. "I only hope that, when I marry, my own will be as happy." She went on to elaborate how her parents had met one Christmas and were married two months later on Valentine's Day. Their marriage, Shelly told him complacently, had been blessed with love and happiness for nearly twenty-seven years before her mother's unexpected death. It took great restraint not to mention that her parents had barely had twenty dollars between them when they'd taken their vows. At the time her father had been a student of veterinary medicine with only two years of schooling behind him. They'd managed without a huge bank balance.

From the tight lines around his mouth and nose, Shelly could tell that Slade found the whole story trite.

"Is your sweet tale of romance supposed to touch my heart?"

Furious, Shelly straightened and looked out the side window at the snow-covered trees that lined the side of Interstate 5. "No. I was just trying to find out if you had one."

"Karate mouth strikes again," he mumbled.

"Karate mouth?" Shelly was too stunned at Slade's unexpected display of wit to do anything more than repeat his statement.

"You have the quickest comeback of anyone I know." Admiration flashed unchecked in his gaze before he turned his attention back to the freeway.

Shelly was more interested in learning about Margaret so she tried to keep the conversation away from herself. "I imagine you're anxious to get back to spend Christmas with Margaret." She regretted her earlier judgmental attitude toward Slade. He had good reason for wanting this meeting over.

"Margaret's visiting an aunt in Arizona during the holidays. She left a couple of days ago."

"So you won't be together." The more she heard of Margaret, the more curious Shelly became about a woman who would agree to wait two years for marriage. "Did she give you your Christmas gift before she left?" The type of gift one gave was always telling.

Slade hesitated. "Margaret and I agreed to forgo giving gifts this year."

Shelly had barely managed to control her tongue when he had spouted off about his long engagement, but this was too much. "Not exchange gifts? That's terrible."

"We have financial goals," Slade growled irritably. "Wasting money on trivialities simply deters us from our two-year plan. Christmas gifts aren't going to advance our desires."

At the moment Shelly sincerely doubted that good ol' Margaret and Slade had "desires."

"I bet Margaret's just saying she doesn't want a gift," Shelly offered. "She's probably secretly hoping you'll break down and buy her something. It doesn't have to be something big. Any woman appreciates roses."

Her companion gave an expressive shrug. "I thought flowers would be a nice touch myself, but Margaret claims they make her sneeze. Besides, roses at Christmas are terribly expensive. A waste of money, really.''

"Naturally," Shelly muttered under her breath. She was beginning to get a clearer picture of this stuffy fellow and his ever-so-practical fiancée.

"Did you say something?" A hint of challenge echoed in his cool tones.

"Not really." Leaning forward, she fiddled with the radio dial, trying to find a station that was playing music. "What's Margaret do, by the way?"

"She's a systems analyst."

Shelly arched both eyebrows in mute comment. This was the type of occupation that she expected from a nuts-and-bolts person like Margaret. "What about children?"

"What about them?"

Shelly realized that she was prying, but she couldn't help herself. "Are you planning a family?"

"Of course. We're hoping that Margaret can schedule a leave of absence in eight years."

"You'll be near forty!" The exclamation burst from her lips before Shelly could hold it back.

"Forty-one, actually. Do you disapprove of that, too?"

Shelly swallowed uncomfortably and paid an inordinate amount of attention to the radio, not understanding why she couldn't get any music. "I apologize, I didn't mean to sound so judgmental. It's just that—"

"It's just that you've never been goal oriented."

"But I have," she argued. "I've always wanted to be a court reporter. It's a fascinating job."

"I imagine that you're good at anything you put your mind to."

The unexpected compliment caught her completely off guard. "What a nice thing to say."

"If you put your mind to it, you might figure out why you can't get the radio working."

Her gaze flickered automatically from Slade to the dial. Before she could comment, he reached over and twisted a knob. "It's a bit difficult to pick up the transmission waves when the radio isn't turned on."

"Right." She'd been too preoccupied with asking about Margaret to notice. Color flooded into her cheeks at her own stupidity. Slade flustered her and that hadn't happened in a long time. She had the feeling that, in a battle of words, he would parry her barbs as expertly as a professional swordsman.

Soft, soothing music filled the car. Warm and snug, Shelly leaned back against the headrest and cushioned seat and hummed along, gazing at the flakes of falling snow.

"With the snow and all it really feels like Christmas," she murmured, fearing more questions would destroy the tranquil mood.

"It's caused nothing but problems."

"I suppose, but it's so lovely."

"Of course it's lovely. You're sitting in a warm chauffeur-driven car with the radio playing."

"Grumble, grumble, grumble," she tossed back lightly. "Bah, humbug!"

"Bah, humbug," he echoed, and to her astonishment Slade laughed. The sound of it was rich and full and caused Shelly to laugh with him. When the radio played a Bing Crosby Christmas favorite, Shelly sang along. Soon Slade's deep baritone joined her clear soprano in sweet harmony. The lyrics spoke of dreaming, and Shelly's mind conjured up her own longings. She was comfortable with this man when she'd expected to find a dozen reasons to dislike him. Instead, she discovered that she was attracted to someone who was engaged to another woman. A man who was intensely loyal. This was the usual way her life ran. She was attracted to Slade, but she didn't know where this feeling would lead. She wasn't entirely sure that her insights about him were on base. As uncharitable as it sounded, she may have formed these feelings simply because she considered him too good for someone like Margaret.

Disgusted with herself, Shelly closed her eyes and rested her head against the window. The only sounds were the soft melodies playing on the radio and the discordant swish of the windshield wipers. Occasionally a gust of wind would cause the car to veer slightly.

A gentle hand on her shoulder shook her. "Shelly."

With a start she bolted upright. "What's wrong?"

Slade had pulled over to the shoulder of the freeway. The snow was so thick that Shelly couldn't see two feet in front of her.

"I don't think we can go any further," Slade announced.

Chapter Three

"We can't stay here," Shelly cried, looking at their precarious position beside the road. Snow whirled in every direction. The ferocity of the storm shocked her, whipping and howling around them. She found it little short of amazing that Slade had been able to steer the car at all. While she'd slept, the storm had worsened drastically.

"Do you have any other suggestions?" he said and breathed out sharply.

He was angry, but his irritation wasn't directed at her. Wearily she lifted the hair from her smooth brow. "No, I guess I don't."

Silence seeped around them as Slade turned off the car's engine. Gone was the soothing sound of Christmas music, the hum of the engine and the rhythmic swish of the windshield wipers. Together they sat waiting for the fury to lessen so that they could start up again. Staring out at the surrounding area between bursts of wind and snow, Shelly guessed that they weren't far from Castle Rock and Mount St. Helens.

After ten minutes of uneasiness, she decided to be the first to break the gloom. "Are you hungry?" She stared at the passive, unyielding face beside her.

"No."

"I am."

"Have some of that bread." He cocked his head toward the back seat where she'd stuck the huge loaves of sourdough bread.

"I couldn't eat Dad's bread. He'd never forgive me."

"He'd never forgive you if you starved to death, either."

Glancing down at her pudgy thighs, Shelly sadly shook her head. "There's hardly any chance of that."

"What makes you say that? You're not fat. In fact, I'd say you were just about perfect."

"Me? Perfect?" A burst of embarrassed laughter slid from her throat. Reaching for her purse, she removed her wallet.

"What are you doing?"

"I'm going to pay you for saying that."

Slade chuckled. "What makes you think you're overweight?"

"You mean aside from the fat all over my body?"

"I'm serious."

She shrugged. "I don't know. I just feel chubby. Since leaving home, I don't get enough exercise. I couldn't very well bring Sampson with me."

"Sampson?"

"My horse. I used to ride him every day."

"If you've gained any weight, it's in all the right places."

His gaze fell to her lips, and Shelly's senses churned in quivering awareness. He stared into her dark eyes and blinked as if not believing what he saw. For her part, Shelly studied him with open curiosity. His eyes were smoky dark, his face blunt and sensual. His brow was creased as though he was giving the moment grave consideration. Thick eyebrows arched heavily over his eyes.

Abruptly he pulled his gaze away and leaned forward to start the engine. The accumulated snow on the windshield was brushed aside with a flip of the wiper switch. "Isn't that a McDonald's up ahead?"

Shelly squinted to catch a glimpse of the world-famous golden arches. "Hey, I think it is."

"The exit can't be far."

"Do you think we can make it?"

"I think we'd better," he mumbled.

Shelly understood. The car had become their private cocoon, unexpectedly intimate and highly sensual. Under normal circumstances they wouldn't have given each other more than a passing glance.

What was happening wasn't magic but something far more exhilarating.

With the wipers beating furiously against the window, Slade inched the car to the exit, which proved to be less than a half mile away.

Slowly they crawled down the side road that paralleled the freeway. With some difficulty Slade was able to find a place to park in the restaurant's lot. Shelly sighed with relief. This was the worst storm she could remember. Wrapping her coat securely around her, she reached for her purse.

"You ready?" she blurted out, opening the car door.

"Anytime."

Hurriedly Slade joined her and tightly grasped her elbow as they stepped together toward the front entrance of the fast-food restaurant. Pausing just inside the door to stamp the snow from their shoes, they glanced up to note that several other travelers were stranded there as well.

They ordered hamburgers and coffee and sat down by the window.

"How long do you think we'll be here?" Shelly asked, not really expecting an answer. She needed reassurance more than anything. This Christmas holiday hadn't started out on the right foot. But of one thing she was confident—the plane hadn't left Portland yet.

"Your guess is as good as mine."

"I'd say two hours, then," she murmured, taking a bite of her Big Mac.

"Why two hours?"

"I don't know. It sounds reasonable. If it's longer than that, I might start to panic. But, if worse comes to worst, I can think of less desirable places to spend Christmas. At least we won't starve."

Slade muttered something unintelligible under his breath and continued eating. When he finished, he excused himself and returned to the car for his brief-case.

Shelly bought two more cups of coffee and propped her feet on the seat opposite her. Taking the latest issue of *Mad Magazine* from her purse, she was absorbed in it by the time he returned. Her gaze dared him to comment on her reading material. Her reading *Mad Magazine* was a long-standing joke between Shelly and her father. He expected it of her and read each issue himself so that he could tease her about the contents. Since moving, she'd fallen behind by several months and wanted to be prepared when she saw her dad again. She didn't expect Slade to understand her tastes.

He rejoined her and gave her little more than a conciliatory glance before reclaiming his seat and briskly opening the *Wall Street Journal.*

Their reading choices said a lot about each other, Shelly realized. Rarely had she seen two people less alike. A lump grew in her throat. She liked Slade.

He was the type of man she'd willingly give up *Mad Magazine* for.

An hour later a contented Shelly set the December issue aside and reached in her purse for the romance novel that she kept tucked away. It wasn't often that she was so at ease with a man. She didn't feel the overwhelming urge to keep a conversation going or fill the silence with chatter. They were comfortable together.

Without a word she went to the counter and bought a large order of fries and placed them in the middle of the table. Now and then, her eyes never leaving the printed page, she blindly reached for a fry. Once her groping hand bumped another, and her startled gaze collided with Slade's.

"Sorry," he muttered.

"Don't be. They're for us both."

"They get to be addictive, don't they?"

"Sort of like reading the *Wall Street Journal*?"

"I wondered if you'd comment on that."

Shelly laughed. "I was expecting you to mention my choice."

"*Mad Magazine* is something I'd expect from you." He said it in such a way that Shelly couldn't possibly be offended.

"At least we agree on one thing."

He raised his thick brows in question.

"The French fries."

"Right." Lifting one from the package, he held it out for her.

Shelly leaned toward him and captured the fry in her mouth. The gesture was oddly intimate, and her smile faded as her gaze clashed with Slade's. It was happening again. That heart-pounding, room-fading-away, shallow-breathing syndrome. Obviously this... feeling...had something to do with the weather. Maybe she could blame it on the season of love and goodwill toward all mankind. Shelly, unfortunately, seemed to be overly infected with benevolence this Christmas. Experiencing the sensations she was, heaven only knows what would happen if she spied mistletoe.

Slade raked his hand through his well-groomed hair, mussing it. Quickly he diverted his gaze out the window. "It looks like it might be letting up a little."

"Yes, it does," she agreed without so much as looking out the window. The French fries seemed to demand her full attention.

"I suppose we should think about heading out."

"I suppose." A glance at her watch confirmed that it was well into the afternoon. "I'm sorry about your appointment."

Slade looked at her blankly for a moment. "Oh, that. I knew when I left that there was little likelihood that I'd be able to make it today. That's why I made arrangements to meet tomorrow morning."

"It's been an enjoyable break."

"Very," he agreed.

"Do you think we'll have any more problems?"

"We could, but there are enough businesses along

the way that we don't need to worry about getting stranded.''

''In other words, we could hit every fast-food spot between here and Seattle.''

Slade responded with a soft chuckle. ''Right.''

''Well, in that case, bring on the French fries.''

By the time they were back on the freeway, Shelly noted that the storm had indeed abated. But the radio issued a weather update that called for more snow. Slade groaned.

''You could always spend Christmas with me and Dad.'' Shelly broached the subject carefully. ''We'd like to have you. Honest.''

Slade tossed her a disbelieving glare. ''You don't mean that?''

''Of course I do.''

''But I'm a stranger.''

''I've shared French fries with you. It's been a long time since I've been that intimate with a man. In fact, it would be best if you didn't mention it to my dad. He might be inclined to reach for his shotgun.''

It took a minute for Slade to understand the implication. ''A shotgun wedding?''

''I am getting on in years. Dad would like to see me married off and producing grandchildren. My bro-thers have been lax in that department.'' For the moment she'd forgotten about Margaret. When she remembered, Shelly felt her spirits rush out of her with all the force of a deflating balloon. ''Don't worry,'' she was quick to add. "All you need to do is tell Dad about your fiancée and he'll let you off the hook.'' Somehow she managed to keep her voice cheerful.

"It's a good thing I didn't take a bite of your hamburger.''

"Are you kidding? That would have put me directly into your last will and testament.''

"I was afraid of that,'' he said, laughing good-naturedly.

Once again Shelly was reminded of how rich and deep the sound of Slade's laughter was. It had the most overwhelming effect on her. She discovered that, when he laughed, nothing could keep her spirits down.

Their progress was hampered by the swirling snow until their forward movement became little more than a crawl. Shelly didn't mind. They chatted, joked and sang along with the radio. She discovered that she enjoyed Slade's wit. Although a bit dry, under that gruff, serious exterior lay an interesting man with a warm but subtle sense of humor. Given any other set of circumstances, Shelly would have liked to get to know Slade Garner better.

"What'd you buy your dad for Christmas?''

The question came so unexpectedly that it took Shelly a moment to realize that he was speaking to her.

"Are you concerned that I wrapped up soup to go with the bread?''

Slade scowled, momentarily puzzled. "Ah, to go with the sourdough bread. No, I was just curious."

"First, I got him a box of his favorite chocolate-covered cherries."

"I should have known it'd be food."

"That's not all," she countered a bit testily. "We exchange the usual father-daughter gifts. You know. Things like stirrup irons, bridles and horse blankets. That's what Dad got me last Christmas."

Slade cleared his throat. "Just the usual items every father buys his daughter. What about this year?"

"Since I'm not around Sampson, I imagine he'll resort to the old standbys, like towels and sheets for my apartment." She was half hoping that, at the mention of her place in San Francisco, Slade would turn the conversation in that direction. He didn't, and she was hard-pressed to hide her disappointment.

"What about you?"

"Me?" His gaze flickered momentarily from the road.

"What did you buy your family?"

Slade gave her an uncomfortable look. "Well, actually, I didn't. It seemed simpler this year just to send them money."

"I see." Shelly knew that that was perfectly acceptable in some cases, but it sounded so cold and un-caring for a son to resort to a gift of money. Undoubtedly, once he and Margaret were married, they'd shop together for something more appropriate.

"I wish now that I hadn't. I think my parents would have enjoyed fresh sourdough bread and chocolate-covered cherries." He hesitated for an instant. "I'm not as confident about the stirrups and horse blankets, however."

As they neared Tacoma, Shelly was surprised at how heavy the traffic had gotten. The closer they came to Maple Valley, the more anxious she became.

"My exit isn't far," she told him, growing impatient. "Good grief, one would expect people to stay off the roads in weather like this."

"Exactly," Slade echoed her thoughts.

It wasn't until she heard the soft timbre of his chuckle that she realized he was teasing her. "You know what I mean."

He didn't answer as he edged the car ahead. Already the night was pitch-dark. Snow continued to fall with astonishing regularity. Shelly wondered when it would stop. She was concerned about Slade driving alone from Maple Valley to Seattle.

"Maybe it would be better if we found a place to stop and phoned my dad."

"Why?"

"That way he could come and pick me up and you wouldn't—"

"I agreed to deliver you to Maple Creek, and I intend to do exactly that."

"Maple Valley," she corrected.

"Wherever. A deal is a deal. Right?"

A rush of pleasure assaulted her vulnerable heart. Slade wasn't any more eager to put an end to their adventure than she was.

"It's the next exit," she informed him, giving him the directions to the ten-acre spread that lay on the outskirts of town. Taking out a pen and paper, she drew a detailed map for Slade so that he wouldn't get lost on the return trip to the freeway. Under the cover of night, there was little to distinguish one road from another, and he could easily become confused.

Sitting upright, Shelly excitedly pointed to her left. "Turn here."

Apparently in preparation for his departure to the airport, her father had shoveled the snow from the long driveway.

The headlights cut into the night, revealing the long, sprawling ranch house that had been Shelly's childhood home. A tall figure appeared at the window and almost immediately the front door burst open.

Slade had barely put the car into Park when Shelly threw open the door.

"Shortcake."

"Dad." Disregarding the snow and wind, she flew into his arms.

"You little... Why didn't you tell me you were coming by car?"

"We rented it." Remembering Slade, she looped an arm around her father's waist. "Dad, I'd like you to meet Slade Garner."

Don Griffin stepped forward and extended his hand. "So you're Shelly's surprise. Welcome to our home. I'd say it was about time my daughter brought a young man home for her father to meet."

Chapter 4

Slade extended his hand to Shelly's father and grinned. "I believe you've got me confused with sourdough bread."

"Sourdough bread?"

"Dad, Slade and I met this morning on the plane." Self-conscious, Shelly's cheeks brightened in a pink flush.

"When it looked like the flight wasn't going to make it to Seattle, we rented the car," Slade explained further.

A curious glint darkened Don Griffin's deep blue eyes as he glanced briefly from his daughter to her friend and ran a hand through is thick thatch of dark hair. "It's a good thing you did. The last time I phoned the airport, I learned your plane still hadn't left Portland."

"Slade has an important meeting first thing to-morrow." Her eyes were telling Slade that she was ready to make the break. She could say goodbye and wish him every happiness. Their time together had been too short for any regrets.

"There's no need for us to stand out here in the cold discussing your itinerary," Don inserted and motioned toward the warm lights of the house.

Slade hesitated. "I should be getting into Seattle."

"Come in for a drink first," Don invited.

"Shelly?" Slade sought her approval. The un-asked question in his eyes pinned her gaze.

"I wish you would." *Fool,* her mind cried out. It would be better to sever the relationship quickly, sharply and without delay before he had the oppor-tunity to touch her tender heart. Her mind shouted fool, but her heart refused to listen.

"For that matter," Don continued, seemingly oblivious to the undercurrents between Slade and Shelly, "stay for dinner."

"I couldn't. Really." He made a show of glancing at his wristwatch.

"We insist," Shelly added. "After hauling this bread from here to kingdom come, the least I can offer you is a share of it."

To her astonishment Slade grinned, his dark eyes crinkling at the edges. The smile was both sponta-neous and personal—a reminder of the joke between them. "All right," he agreed.

"That settles it, then." Don grinned and moved to

the rear of the car while Slade extracted Shelly's suit-case and the huge sack.

"What's all this?"

"Presents."

"For me?"

"Well, who else would I be bringing gifts for?"

"A man. It's time you started thinking about a husband."

"Dad!" If her cheeks had been bright pink pre-viously, now the color deepened into fire-engine red. In order to minimize further embarrassment, Shelly returned to the car and rescued the long loaves of sourdough bread. Her father managed the huge "tuba case" full of gifts while Slade carried the one small carry-on bag.

The house contained all the warmth and welcome of home. Shelly paused in the open doorway, her gaze skimming over the crackling fireplace and the large array of family photos that decorated the mantel above the hearth. Ol' Dan, their seventeen-year-old Labrador, slept on the braided rug and did little more than raise his head when Don and Slade entered the house. But on seeing Shelly, the elderly dog slowly came to his feet and with some difficulty ambled to her side, tail wagging. Shelly set the bread aside and fell to her knees.

"How's my loyal, mangy mutt?" she asked, af-fectionately ruffling his ears and hugging him. "You keeping Dad company these days?"

"Yeah, but he's doing a poor job of it," Don complained loudly. "Ol' Dan still can't play a decent game of chess."

"Do you play?" Slade's gaze scanned the living room for a board.

"Forty years or more. What about you?"

"Now and again."

"Could I interest you in a match?"

Slade was already unbuttoning his overcoat. "I'd enjoy that, sir."

"Call me Don, everyone does."

"Right, Don."

Within a minute the chessboard was out and set up on a tray while the two men sat opposite each other on matching ottomans.

Seeing that the contest could last a long while, Shelly checked the prime rib roasting in the oven and added large potatoes, wrapping each in aluminum foil. The refrigerator contained a fresh green salad and Shelly's favorite cherry pie from the local bakery. There were also some carrots in the vegetable drawer; Shelly snatched a couple and put them in her pocket.

Grabbing her Levi jacket with its thick wool padding from the peg on the back porch and slipping into her cowboy boots, Shelly made her way out to the barn.

The scent of hay and horses greeted her, and Shelly paused, taking in the rich, earthy odors. "Howdy, Sampson." She spoke to her favorite horse first.

The sleek, black horse whinnied a welcome as Shelly approached the stall and accepted the proffered carrot without pause.

"Have you missed me, boy?"

Pokey, an Appaloosa mare, stuck her head out of her stall, seeking her treat. Laughing, Shelly pulled another carrot from her pocket. Midnight, her father's horse and Sampson's sire, stamped his foot, and Shelly made her way down to his stall.

After stroking his sleek neck, Shelly took out the grooming brushes and returned to Sampson. "I suppose Dad's letting you get fat and lazy now that I'm not around to work you." She glided the brush down the muscled flank in familiar fashion. "All right, I'll admit it. Living in San Francisco has made me fat and lazy as well. I haven't gained any weight, but I feel flabby. I suppose I could take up jogging, but it's foggy and rainy and—"

"Shelly?"

Slade stood just inside the barn, looking a bit uneasy. "Do you always carry on conversations with your horse?"

"Sure. I've talked out many a frustration with Sampson. Isn't that right, boy?"

Slade gave a startled blink when the horse answered with a loud snort and a toss of his head, as if agreeing with her.

"Come in and meet my favorite male," Shelly invited, opening the gate to the stall.

Hands buried deep in his pockets, Slade shook his head. "No, thanks."

"You don't like horses?"

"Not exactly."

Having lived all her life around animals, Shelly had trouble accepting his reticence. "Why not?"

"The last time I was this close to a horse was when I was ten and at summer camp."

"Sampson won't bite you."

"It's not his mouth I'm worried about."

"He's harmless."

"So is flying."

Surprised, Shelly dropped her hand from Sampson's hindquarters.

Slade strolled over to the stall, a grin curving up the edges of his mouth. "From the look on your face when we landed, one would assume that your will alone was holding up the plane."

"It was!"

Slade chuckled and tentatively reached out to rub Sampson's ebony forehead.

Shelly continued to groom the horse. "Is your chess match over already?"

"I should have warned your father. I was on the university chess team."

Now it was Shelly's turn to look amused. She paused, her hand in midstroke. "Did you wound Dad's ego?"

"I might have, but he's regrouping now. I came

out to meet the horse you spoke of so fondly. I wanted to have a look before I headed for Seattle.''

"Sampson's honored to make your acquaintance."

I am, too, her heart echoed.

Slade took a step in retreat. "I guess I'll get back to the house. No doubt your dad's got the board set for a rematch."

"Be gentle with him," Shelly called out, trying to hide a saucy grin. Her father wasn't an amateur when it came to the game. He'd been a member of the local chess club for several years, and briefly Shelly wondered at his strategy. Donald Griffin seldom lost at any game.

An hour later Shelly stamped the snow from her boots and entered the house through the back door, which led into the kitchen. Shedding the thick coat, she hung it on the peg and went to check the roast and baked potatoes. Both were done to perfection, and she turned off the oven.

Seeing that her father and Slade were absorbed in their game, Shelly moved behind her father and slipped her arms around his neck, resting her chin on the top of his head.

"Dinner's ready," she murmured, not wanting to break his concentration.

"In a minute," Don grumbled.

Slade moved the bishop, leaving his hand on the piece for a couple of seconds. Seemingly pleased, he released the piece and relaxed. As though sensing her gaze on him, he lifted his eyes. Incredibly dark eyes locked with hers as they stared at each other for long, uninterrupted moments. Shelly felt her heart lurch as she basked in the warmth of his look. She wanted to hold on to this moment, forget San Francisco, Margaret, the snowstorm. It became paramount that she capture this magic with both hands and hold on to it forever.

"It's your move." Don's words cut into the stillness.

"Pardon?" Abruptly Slade dropped his eyes to the chessboard.

"It's your move," her father repeated.

"Of course." Slade studied the board and moved a pawn.

Don scowled. "I hadn't counted on your doing that."

"Hey, you two, didn't you hear me? Dinner's ready." Shelly was shocked at how normal and unaffected her voice sounded.

Slade got to his feet. "Shall we consider it a draw, then?"

"I guess we better, but I demand a rematch someday."

Shelly's throat constricted. There wouldn't be another day for her or Slade. They were two strangers who had briefly touched each other's lives. Ships passing in the night and all the other clichés she had never expected would happen to her. But somehow Shelly had the feeling that she would never be the same again. Surely she wouldn't be so swift to judge another man. Slade had taught her that, and she would always be grateful.

The three chatted easily during dinner, and Shelly learned things about Slade that she hadn't thought to ask. He was a salesman, as she'd suspected. He specialized in intricate software programs for computers and was meeting with a Seattle-based company, hoping to establish the first steps of a possible distribution agreement. It was little wonder that he'd considered this appointment so important. It was. And although he didn't mention it, Shelly was acutely aware that if this meeting was successful, Slade would be that much closer to achieving his financial and professional goals—and that much closer to marrying dull, dutiful Margaret.

Shelly was clearing the dishes from the table when Slade set his napkin aside and rose. "I don't remember when I've enjoyed a meal more, especially the sourdough bread."

"A man gets the feel of a kitchen sooner or later," Don said with a crusty chuckle. "It took me a whole year to learn how to turn on the oven."

"That's the truth," Shelly added, sharing a tender look with her father. "He thought it was easier to use the microwave. The problem was he couldn't quite get the hang of that, either. Everything came out the texture of beef jerky."

"We survived," Don grumbled, affectionately loop-ing an arm around Shelly's shoulder. The first eighteen months after her mother's death had been the most difficult for the family, but life goes on, and almost against their wills they'd adjusted.

Slade paused in the living room to stare out the window. "I can't ever remember it snowing this much in the Pacific Northwest."

"Rarely," Don agreed. "It's been three winters since we've had any snow at all. I'll admit this is a pleasant surprise."

"How long will it be before the snowplows are out?"

"Snowplow, you mean?" Don repeated with a gruff laugh. "King County is lucky if they have more than a handful. There isn't that much call for them." He walked to the picture window and held back the draperies with one hand. "You know, it might not be a bad idea if you stayed the night and left first thing in the morning."

Slade hesitated. "I don't know. If I miss this meeting, it'll mean having to wait over the Christmas holiday."

"You'll have a better chance of making it safely to Seattle in the morning. The condition of the roads tonight could be treacherous."

Slade slowly expelled his breath. "I have the distinct feeling you may be right. Without any streetlights Lord knows where I'd end up."

"I believe you'd be wise to delay your drive. Besides, that will give us time for another game of chess."

Slade's gaze swiveled to Shelly and softened. "Right," he concurred.

The two men were up until well past midnight, engrossed in one chess match after another. After watching a few of the games, Shelly decided to say good-night and go to bed.

She lay in her bed in the darkened room, dreading the approach of morning. In some ways it would have been easier if Slade had left immediately after dropping her off. And in other ways it was far better that he'd stayed.

Shelly fell asleep with the insidious hands of the clock ticking away the minutes to six o'clock when Slade would be leaving. There was nothing she could do to hold back time.

Without even being aware that she'd fallen asleep, Shelly was startled into wakefulness by the discordant drone of the alarm.

Tossing aside the covers, she automatically reached for her thick housecoat, which she'd left at her father's. Pausing only long enough to run a comb through her hair and brush her teeth, she rushed into the living room.

Slade was already dressed and holding a cup of coffee in his hands. "I guess it's time to say good-bye."

Chapter 5

Shelly ran a hand over her weary eyes and blinked. "You're right," she murmured, forcing a smile. "The time has come."

"Shelly—"

"Listen—"

Abruptly they each broke off whatever it was that they had planned to say.

"You first," Slade said and gestured toward her with his open hand.

Dropping her gaze, she shrugged one shoulder. "It's nothing really. I just wanted to wish you and Margaret every happiness."

His gaze softened and Shelly wondered if he knew what it had cost her to murmur those few words. She did wish Slade Garner happiness, but she was convinced that he wouldn't find it with a cold fish like Margaret. Forcefully she tossed her gaze across the room. For all her good intentions, she was doing it again—prejudging another. And she hadn't even met good ol' Margaret.

His eyes delved into hers. "Thank you."

"You wanted to say something," she prompted softly.

Slade hesitated. "Be happy, Shelly."

A knot formed in her throat as she nodded. He was telling her goodbye, really goodbye. He wouldn't see her again because it would be too dangerous for them both. Their lives were already plotted, their courses set. And whatever it was that they'd shared so briefly, it wasn't meant to be anything more than a passing fancy.

The front door opened and Don entered, brushing the snow from his pant legs. A burst of frigid air accompanied him and Shelly shivered.

"As far as I can see you shouldn't have a problem. We've got maybe seven to ten inches of snow, but there're plenty of tire tracks on the road. Just follow those."

Unable to listen anymore, Shelly moved into the kitchen and poured herself a cup of hot black coffee. Clasping the mug with both hands, she braced her hip against the counter and closed her eyes. Whatever was being said between Slade and her father had no meaning. She was safer in the kitchen where she wouldn't be forced to watch him walk out the door.

The only sound that registered in her mind was the clicking noise of the front door opening and closing.

Slade had left. He was gone from the house. Gone from her life. Gone forever. Shelly refused to mope. He'd touched her and she should be glad. For a time she'd begun to wonder if there was something physically wrong with her because she couldn't respond to a man. Slade hadn't so much as kissed her, and she'd experienced a closeness to him that she hadn't felt with all the men she'd dated in San Francisco. Without even realizing it, Slade had granted her the priceless gift of expectancy. If he was capable of stirring her restless heart, then so would another.

Humming softly, Shelly set a skillet on the burner and laid thick slices of bacon across it. This was the day before Christmas, and it promised to be full. She couldn't be sad or filled with regrets when she was surrounded by everything she held dear.

The door opened again and Don called cheerfully. "Well, he's off."

"Good."

"He's an interesting man. I wouldn't mind having someone like him for a son-in-law." Her father entered the kitchen and reached for the coffeepot.

"He's engaged."

Don snickered and there was a hint of censure in his voice when he spoke. "That figures. The good men usually are snatched up early."

"We're about as different as any two people can be."

"That's not always bad, you know. Couples often complement each other that way. Your mother was the shy one, whereas I was far more outgoing. Our lives would have been havoc if we'd both had the same personalities."

Silently Shelly agreed, but to admit as much verbally would reveal more than she wished. "I suppose," she murmured softly and turned over the sizzling slices of bacon.

Shelly was sliding the eggs easily from the hot grease onto plates when there was a loud pounding on the front door.

Shelly's gaze clashed with that of her father's.

"Slade," they said simultaneously.

Her father rushed to answer the door, and a breathless Slade stumbled into the house. Shelly turned off the stove and hurried after him.

"Are you all right?" The tone of her voice was laced with concern. Her heart pounding, she checked him for any signs of injury.

"I'm fine. I'm just out of breath. That was quite a hike."

"How far'd you get?" Don wanted to know.

"A mile at the most. I was gathering speed to make it to the top of an incline when the wheels skidded on a patch of ice. The car, unfortunately, is in a ditch."

"What about the meeting?" Now that she'd determined that he was unscathed, Shelly's first concern was the appointment that Slade considered so important to him and his company.

"I don't know."

"Dad and I could take you into town," Shelly offered.

"No. If I couldn't make it, you won't be able to, either."

"But this meeting is vital."

"It's not important enough to risk your getting hurt."

"My truck has been acting up so I took it in for servicing," Don murmured thoughtfully. "But there's always the tractor."

"Dad! You'll be lucky if the old engine so much as coughs. You haven't used that antique in years." As far as Shelly knew, it was collecting dust in the back of the barn.

"It's worth a try," her father argued, looking to Slade. "At least we can pull your car out of the ditch."

"I'll contact the county road department and find out how long it'll be before the plows come this way," Shelly inserted. She didn't hold much hope for the tractor, but if she could convince the county how important it was that they clear the roads near their place, Slade might be able to make the meeting.

Two hours later, Shelly, dressed in dark cords and a thick cable-knit sweater the color of winter wheat, paced the living room carpet. Every few minutes she paused to glance out the large living room window for signs of either her father or Slade. Through some miracle they'd managed to fire up the tractor, but how much they could accomplish with the old machine was pure conjecture. If they were able to rescue Slade's car out of the ditch, then there was always the possibility of towing the car up the incline.

The sound of a car pulling into the driveway captured her attention, and Shelly rushed onto the front porch as Slade was easing the Camaro to a stop. He climbed out of the vehicle.

"I called the county. The road crew will try to make it out this way before nightfall," Shelly told him, rubbing her palms together to ward off the chill of the air. "I'm sorry, Slade, it's the best they could do."

"Don't worry." His gaze caressed her. "It's not your fault."

"But I can't help feeling that it is," she said, following him into the house. "I was the one who insisted you bring me here."

"Shelly." His hand cupped her shoulder. "Stop blaming yourself. I'll contact Bauer. He'll understand. It's possible he didn't make it to the office, either."

Granting him the privacy he needed to make his phone call, Shelly donned her coat and walked to the end of the driveway to see if she could locate her father. Only a couple of minutes passed before she saw him. Proudly he steered the tractor, his back and

head held regally so that he resembled a benevolent
king surveying all he owned.

Laughing, Shelly waved.

Don pulled to a stop alongside her. "What's so
funny?"

"I can't believe you, sitting on top of a 1948 Har-
vester like you owned the world."

"Don't be silly, serf," Don teased.

"We've got a bit of a problem, you know." She
realized that she shouldn't feel guilty about Slade,
but she did.

"If you mean Slade, we talked about this unexpected delay. It might not be as bad as it looks. To
his way of thinking, it's best not to appear overeager
with this business anyway. A delay may be just the
thing to get the other company thinking."

It would be just like Slade to say something like
that, Shelly thought. "Maybe."

"At any rate, it won't do him any good to stew
about it now. He's stuck with us until the snowplows
clear the roads. No one's going to make it to the
freeway unless they have a four-wheel drive. It's impossible out there."

"But, Dad, I feel terrible."

"Don't. If Slade doesn't seem overly concerned,
then you shouldn't. Besides, I've got a job for you
two."

Shelly didn't like the sound of that. "What?"

"We aren't going to be able to go out and buy a
Christmas tree."

Shelly hadn't thought of that. "We'll survive without one." But Christmas wouldn't be the same.

"There's no need to. Not when we've got a good ten acres of fir and pine. I want Slade and you to go out and chop one down like we used to do in the good old days."

It didn't take much to realize her father's game. He was looking for excuses to get Slade and her together.

"What's this, an extra Christmas present?" she teased. From all the comments that Don had made about Slade, Shelly knew that her father thought highly of him.

"Nonsense. Being out in the cold would only irritate my rheumatism."

"What rheumatism?"

"The one in my old bones."

Shelly hesitated. "What did Slade have to say about this?"

"He's agreeable."

"He is?"

"Think about it, Shortcake. Slade is stuck here. He wants to make the best of the situation."

It wasn't until they were back at the house and Slade had changed into her father's woolen clothes and heavy boots that Shelly believed he'd fallen so easily in with her father's scheme.

"You don't have to do this, you know," she told him on the way to the barn.

"Did you think I was going to let you traipse into the woods alone?"

"I could."

"No doubt, but there isn't any reason why you should when I'm here."

She brought out the old sled from a storage room in the rear of the barn, wiping away the thin layer of dust with her gloves.

Slade located a saw, and Shelly eyed him warily.

"What's wrong now?"

"The saw."

"What's the matter with it?" He tested the sharpness by carefully running his thumb over the jagged teeth and raised questioning eyes to her.

"Nothing. If we use that rusty old thing, we shouldn't have any trouble bringing home a good-sized rhododendron."

"I wasn't planning to mow down a California redwood."

"But I want something a bit larger than a poinsettia."

Slade paused and followed her outside the barn. "Are you always this difficult to get along with?"

Jerking the sled along behind her in the snow, Shelly shouted, "There's nothing wrong with me. It's you."

"Right," he growled.

Shelly realized that she was acting like a shrew, but her behavior was a defense mechanism against the attraction she felt for Slade. If he was irritated with her, it would be easier to hold back her feelings for him.

"If my presence is such an annoyance to you, I can walk into town."

"Don't be silly."

"She shouts at me about cutting down rhododendrons and I'm silly." He appeared to be speaking to the sky.

Plowing through the snow, Shelly refused to look back. Determined, she started up a small incline toward the woods. "I just want you to know I can do this on my own."

His hand on her shoulder halted her progress, paralyzing her. "Shelly, listen to me, would you?"

She hesitated, her gaze falling on the long line of trees ahead. "What now?"

"I like the prospect of finding a Christmas tree with you, but if you find my company so unpleasant, I'll go back to the house."

"That's not it," she murmured, feeling ridiculously like an adolescent. "I have fun with you."

"Then why are we arguing?"

Against her will she smiled. "I don't know," she admitted.

"Friends?" Slade offered her his gloved hand.

Shelly clasped it in her own. She nodded wordlessly at him.

"Now that we've got that out of the way, just how large of a tree were you thinking of?"

"Big."

"Obviously. But remember it's got to fit inside the house so that sixty-foot fir straight ahead is out."

"But the top six feet isn't," she teased.

Chuckling, Slade draped his arm across her shoulder. "Yes, it is."

They were still within sight of the house. "I don't want to cut down something obvious."

"How do you mean?"

"In years to come I don't want to look out the back window and see a hole in the landscape."

"Don't be ridiculous. You've got a whole forest back here."

"I want to go a bit deeper into the woods."

"Listen, Shortcake, I'm not Lewis and Clark."

Shelly paused. He'd used her father's affectionate term for her. "What'd you call me?"

"Shortcake. It fits."

"How's that?"

His gaze roamed over her, his eyes narrowing as he studied her full mouth. It took everything within Shelly not to moisten her lips. A tingling sensation attacked her stomach, and she lowered her gaze. The hesitation lasted no longer than a heartbeat.

His breath hissed through his teeth before he asked, "How about this tree?" His fingers gripped the top of a small fir that reached his waist.

Shelly couldn't keep from laughing. "It should be illegal to cut down anything that small."

"Do you have a better suggestion?"

"Yes."

"What?"

"That tree over there." She marched ahead, pointing out a seven-foot pine.

"You're being ridiculous. We wouldn't be able to get that one through the front door."

"Of course we'd need to trim it."

"Like in half," he mocked.

Shelly refused to be dissuaded. "Don't be a spoilsport."

"Forget it. This tree would be a nice compromise." He motioned toward another small tree that was only slightly bigger than the first one he'd chosen.

Without hesitating, Shelly reached down and packed a thick ball of snow. "I'm not willing to compromise my beliefs."

He turned to her, exasperation written all over his tight features. Shelly let him have it with the snowball. The accuracy of her toss astonished her, and she cried out with a mixture of surprise and delight when the snowball slammed against his chest, spraying snow in his face.

His reaction was so speedy that Shelly had no time to run. "Slade, I'm sorry," she said, taking a giant step backward. "I don't know what came over me. I didn't mean to hit you. Actually, I was aiming at that bush behind you. Honest."

For every step she retreated, he advanced, packing a snowball between his gloved hands.

"Slade, you wouldn't." She implored him with open arms.

"Yes, I would."

"No," she cried and turned, running for all she was worth. He overtook her almost immediately, grabbing her shoulder. Shelly stumbled and they both went crashing to the snow-covered ground.

Slade's thick torso pressed her deeper into the snow. "Are you all right?" he asked urgently, fear and concern evident in the tone of his voice as he tenderly pushed the hair from her face.

"Yes," she murmured, breathless. But her lack of air couldn't be attributed to the fall. Having Slade this close, his warm breath fanning her face, was responsible for that. Her breasts felt the urgent pressure of his chest, and even through the thick coats Shelly could feel the pounding rhythm of his heart echoing hers.

"Shelly." He ground out her name like a man driven to the brink of insanity. Slowly he slanted his mouth over hers, claiming her lips in a kiss that rocked the very core of her being. Their lips caressed while their tongues mated until they were both panting and nearly breathless.

Her arms locked around his neck, and she arched against him desperately, wanting to give him more and more.

"Shelly." His hands closed around her wrists, jerking them free of his nape. He sat up with his back to her. All she could see was the uneven rise and fall of his shoulders.

"Don't worry," she breathed out in a voice so weak that it trembled. "I won't tell Margaret."

Chapter 6

"That shouldn't have happened." Slade spoke at last.

"I suppose you want an apology," Shelly responded, standing and brushing the snow from her pants. In spite of her efforts to appear normal, her hands trembled and her pulse continued to hammer away madly. From the beginning she'd known that Slade's kiss would have this effect upon her, and she cursed her traitorous heart.

He swiveled, shocked that she would suggest such a thing. "I should be the one to apologize to you."

"Why? Because you kissed me?"

"I'm engaged."

"I know." Her voice rose several decibels. "What's in a kiss, anyway? It wasn't any big deal.

Right?'' *Liar,* her heart accused, continuing to beat erratically. It'd been the sweetest, most wonderful kiss of her life. One that would haunt her for a lifetime.

"It won't happen again," Slade said without looking at her. He held his body stiffly away from her. His facade slipped tightly into place, locking his expression right before her eyes. Shelly was reminded of the man she'd first seen on the plane—that polished, impeccable businessman who looked upon the world with undisguised indifference.

"As I said, it wasn't any big deal."

"Right," he answered. The light treatment that she gave his kiss didn't appear to please him. Standing, he stalked in the direction of the trees and stopped at the one he'd offered as a compromise earlier. Without soliciting her opinion, he began sawing away at its narrow base.

Within minutes the tree toppled, crashing to the ground and stirring up the snow. Shelly walked over, prepared to help him load the small fir onto the sled, but he wouldn't let her.

"I'll do it," he muttered gruffly.

Offended, she folded her arms and stepped back, feeling awkward and callow. She'd feel better if they could discuss the kiss openly and honestly.

"I knew it was going to happen." She'd been wanting him to kiss her all day.

"What?" he barked, heading in the direction of

the house, tugging the sled and Christmas tree behind him.

"The kiss," she called after him. "And if I was honest, I'd also admit that I wanted it to happen. I was even hoping it would."

"If you don't mind, I'd rather not talk about it."

Slade was making her angrier every time he opened his mouth. "I said *if* I was being honest, but since neither of us is, then apparently you're right to suggest we drop the issue entirely."

Slade ignored her, taking giant steps so that she was forced into a clumsy jog behind him. The north wind whipped her scarf across her mouth, and Shelly tucked it more securely around her neck. She turned and took several steps backward so that the bitter wind buffeted her back instead of her face.

Unexpectedly her boot hit a small, protruding rock, and Shelly momentarily lost her balance. Flinging her arms out in an effort to catch herself, she went tumbling down the hill, somersaulting head over feet until she lay sprawled, spread-eagled, at the base of the slope.

Slade blistered the wind with expletives as he raced after her, falling to his knees at her side, his eyes clouded with emotion. "Do you have to make a game out of everything?"

She'd nearly killed herself, and he accused her of acrobatics in the snow. She struggled to give him a sassy comeback, but the wind had been knocked from her lungs and she discovered that she couldn't speak.

"Are you all right?" Slade looked concerned for the first time.

"I don't know," she whispered tightly. Getting the appropriate amount of oxygen to her lungs seemed to require all her energy.

"Don't move."

"I couldn't if I wanted to."

"Where does it hurt?"

"Where doesn't it would be a more fitting question." Belying her previous answer, she levered herself up with one elbow and wiggled her legs. "I do this now and then so I can appreciate how good it feels to breathe," she muttered sarcastically.

"I said don't move," Slade barked. "You could've seriously injured something."

"I did," she cried, "my pride." Slowly coming to her feet, she mockingly bowed before him and said, "Stay tuned for my next trick when I'll single-handedly leap tall buildings and alter the course of the mighty Columbia River."

"You're not funny."

"I was desperately trying to be."

"Here." He tucked a hand under her elbow. "Let me help you back to the house."

"This may come as a shock to you, but I'm perfectly capable of walking on my own."

"Nothing you do anymore could shock me."

"That sounds amazingly like a challenge."

Slade's indifference almost melted away as he stared down at her with warm, vulnerable eyes. "Trust me, it isn't." He claimed her hand, lacing his fingers with hers. "Come on, your father's probably getting worried."

Shelly sincerely doubted it. What Slade was really saying was that things would be safer for them back at the house. Temptation could more easily be kept at bay with someone else present.

He placed his hand at the base of her neck, and they continued their short sojourn across the snowy landscape.

The house looked amazingly still and dark as they approached. A whisper of smoke drifted into the clear sky from the chimney as though the fire had been allowed to die. Shelly had expected to hear Andy Williams crooning from the stereo and perhaps smell the lingering scent of freshly popped popcorn.

Instead, they were greeted by an empty, almost eerie silence.

While Slade leaned the tree against the side of the house, Shelly ventured inside. A note propped against the sugar bowl in the middle of the kitchen table commanded her attention. She walked into the room and picked it up.

Sick horse at the Adler's. Call if you need me.

Love,
Dad.

She swallowed tightly, clenching the paper in her hand as the back door shut.

"Dad's out on a call," she announced without turning around. "Would you like a cup of coffee? The pot's full, although it doesn't look too fresh. Dad must have put it on before he left. He knew how cold we'd be when we got back." She realized she was chattering and immediately stopped. Not waiting for his response, she reached for two mugs.

"Coffee sounds fine." Slade's voice was heavy with dread. The same dread that Shelly felt pressing against her heart. Her father was the buffer they needed and he was gone.

Shelly heard Slade drag out a kitchen chair, and she placed the mug in front of him. Her thick lashes fanned downward as she avoided his gaze.

Reluctantly she pulled out the chair opposite his and joined him at the table. "I suppose we should put up the tree."

Slade paused. "We might."

From all the enthusiasm he displayed, they could have been discussing income taxes. Shelly's heart ached. She was embarrassed at having made the suggestion. No doubt good ol' Margaret had hers flocked and decorated without ever involving Slade.

Her hands compressed around the mug, burning the sensitive skin of her palms.

"Well?" he prompted.

"I think I'll wait until Dad's back. We—every year since Mom died, we've done it together. It's a

fun time." The walls of the kitchen seemed to be
closing in on them. With every breath Shelly drew,
she became more aware of the man sitting across
from her. They'd tried to pretend, but the kiss had
changed everything. The taste of him lingered on her
lips, and unconsciously she ran her tongue over them,
wanting to recapture that sensation before it disappeared forever.

Slade's eyes followed her movement, and he
abruptly stood, marching across the kitchen to place
his half-full mug in the sink.

"I'll tend the fire," he offered, hastily leaving the
room.

"Thank you."

After emptying her own mug in the sink, Shelly
joined him, standing in the archway between the
kitchen and living room.

Slade placed a small log in the red coals, and instantly flames sizzled over the dry bark. Soon the fire
crackled and hissed at the fresh supply of wood with
ardent, hungry flames.

"I wonder what's happening with the road crew,"
Slade said.

"They could be here any time."

Together they moved toward the phone, each in-
tent on collecting the needed information. In their
eagerness they collided. Shelly felt the full impact of
the unexpected contact with Slade. Her breath caught
someplace between her lungs and her throat but not
from any pain.

"Shelly." His arms went around her faster than a shooting star. "Did I hurt you?"

One hand was trapped against his broad chest while the other hung loosely at her side. "I'm fine," she managed, her voice as unsteady as his. Still, he didn't release her.

Savoring his nearness and warmth, Shelly closed her eyes and pressed her head to his chest, listening to the beat of his heart beneath her ear.

Slade went utterly still until his arms tightened around her, and he groaned her name.

Nothing that felt this wonderful and good could be wrong. Shelly knew that in her heart, but her head buzzed with a nagging warning. Even though her eyes were closed, she could see flashing red lights. Slade had held and kissed her only once and had instantly regretted it. He'd even refused to talk about it, closing himself off from her.

Yet the arguments melted away like snow in a spring thaw when she was in his arms. His lips moved to her hair, and he breathed in deeply as though to capture her scent.

"Shelly," he pleaded, his voice husky with emotion. "Tell me to stop."

The words wouldn't form. She knew that she should break away and save them both the agony of guilt. But she couldn't.

"I want you to hold me," she whispered. "Just hold me."

Automatically his arms anchored her against him,

and his lips nuzzled her ear, shooting tingles of pleasure down her spine. From her ear he found her cheek, her hair. For an eternity he hesitated.

The phone jingled and they broke apart with a suddenness that rocked Shelly. Slade's hand on her shoulder steadied her. Brushing the hair from her face, she drew in a steadying breath.

"Hello." Her voice was barely above a whisper when she answered.

"Shelly? Are you all right? You don't sound like yourself."

"Oh, hi, Dad." She glanced up guiltily at Slade. His returning look was heavy with consternation. He brushed a hand through his own hair and walked to the picture window. "We got the tree."

"That's good." Don Griffin paused. "Are you sure everything's fine?"

"Of course I'm sure," she answered, somewhat defensively. "How are things with the Adlers?"

"Not good. I may be here a while. I'm sorry to be away from you, but Slade's there to keep you company."

"How...long will you be?"

"A couple of hours, three at the most. You and Slade will be all right, won't you?"

"Oh, sure."

But her father didn't sound any more convinced than Shelly felt.

Five minutes later Shelly replaced the receiver. The air in the room seemed to vibrate with Slade's presence. He turned around and held her gaze. "I've got to get to Seattle."

What he was really saying was that he had to get away from her. "I know," she told him in a tortured whisper. "But how?"

"How'd your dad get to that sick horse?"

"The Adler's neighbor, Ted Wilkens, has a four-wheel drive. I suppose he came for Dad."

"Would it be possible for him to take me into Seattle?"

Shelly hadn't thought of that. "I'm not sure. I don't think he'd mind. I'll call."

"It's Christmas Eve." Slade sounded hesitant.

"They're that kind of people," she said, reaching for the phone. Slade paced the small area in front of her while she talked to Connie Wilkens.

"Well?" Slade studied her expectantly as she hung up the phone.

"Ted's out helping someone else, but Connie thinks he'll be back before dark. She suggested that we head their way, and by the time we arrive, Ted should be home."

"You're sure he won't mind?"

"Positive. Ted and Connie are always helping others."

"Good people—like you and your dad," Slade murmured softly.

Shelly laced her fingers together in front of her. "Yes. We're neighbors, although they're a good four miles from here. And friends." She scooted down in front of Ol' Dan and petted him in long, soothing strokes. "I told Connie that we'd start out soon."

Slade's brow furrowed as her words sank in. "But how? The tractor?"

"I couldn't run that thing if my life depended on it."

"Me, either. Shelly, we can't trek that distance on foot."

"I wasn't thinking of walking."

"What other way is there?"

A smile grew on her soft features until it touched her eyes, which sparkled with mischief. "We can always take the horses."

Chapter 7

"You have to be kidding!" Slade gave her a look of pure disbelief.

"No," Shelly insisted, swallowing a laugh. "It's the only possible way I know to get there. We can go up through the woods where the snow isn't as deep."

Rubbing a hand over his eyes, Slade stalked to the far side of the room, made an abrupt about-face and returned to his former position. "I don't know. You seem to view life as one big adventure after another. I'm not used to…"

"Pokey's as gentle as a lamb," she murmured coaxingly.

"Pokey?"

"Unless you'd rather ride Midnight."

"Good grief, no. Pokey sounds more my speed."

Doing her best to hold back a devilish grin, Shelly led the way into the kitchen.

"What are you doing now?"

"Making us a thermos of hot chocolate."

"Why?"

"I thought we'd stop and have a picnic along the way."

"You're doing it again," he murmured, but she noticed that an indulgent half smile lurked just behind his intense dark eyes. Slade was a man who needed a little fun in his life, and Shelly was determined to provide it for him. If she was only to touch his life briefly, then she wanted to bring laughter and sunshine with her. Margaret would have him forever. But these few hours were hers, and she was determined to make the most of them.

"It'll be fun," she declared enthusiastically.

"No doubt Custer said the same thing to his men," Slade grumbled, following her out to the barn.

"Cynic," Shelly teased, holding open the barn door.

Reluctantly he followed her inside.

"How do you feel about a lazy stroll in the snow, Pokey?" she asked as she approached the Appaloosa's stall, petting the horse's nose. "I know Sampson's ready anytime."

"Don't let her kid you, Pokey," Slade added from behind Shelly. "Good grief, now you've got me doing it."

"Doing what?"

"Talking to the animals."

"They often show human characteristics," Shelly defended both their actions. "It's only natural to express one's feelings to 'almost' humans."

"In which case we're in trouble. Pokey is going to have a lot to say about how I feel when I climb on her back."

"You'll be fine."

"Sure, but will Pokey?"

"You both will. Now stop worrying."

When Shelly brought out the riding tack, Slade walked around the small barn, hands buried deep in his pockets. He did what he could to help Shelly saddle the two horses. Mostly he moved around her awkwardly, looking doubtful and ambivalent.

When she'd finished, she led the horses out of the barn. Holding on to the reins, she motioned for Slade to mount first. "Will you need any help?" she asked. Slade looked so different from the staid executive she'd met in Portland that she had trouble remembering that this was the same man. The one facing her now was clearly out of his element and nothing like the unflappable man on the airplane.

"I don't think so," he said, reaching for the saddle and trying to follow Shelly's directions. Without much difficulty he swung his bulk onto Pokey's back. The horse barely stirred.

Looking pleased with himself, Slade smiled down

at Shelly. "I suppose you told her to be gentle with me."

"I did," she teased in return. Double-checking the cinch, she asked, "Do you need me to adjust the stirrups or anything?"

"No." Slade shifted his weight slightly and accepted the reins she handed him. "I'm ready anytime you are."

Shelly mounted with an ease that spoke of years in the saddle. "It's going to be a rough ride until we get under the cover of the trees. Follow me."

"Anywhere."

Shelly was sure that she'd misunderstood him. "What did you say?" she asked, twisting around.

"Nothing." But he was grinning, and Shelly found him so devastatingly appealing that it demanded all her willpower to turn around and lead the way.

She took the path that led them through the woods. Gusts of swift wind blew the snow from the trees. The swirling flakes were nearly as bad as the storm had been. Even Pokey protested at having to be outside.

"Shelly," Slade said, edging the Appaloosa to Sampson's side. "This may not have been the most brilliant idea. Maybe we should head back."

"Nonsense."

"I don't want you catching cold on my account."

"I'm as snug as a bug in a rug."

"Liar," he purred softly.

"I want you to have something to remember me by." She realized she must sound like some lovesick romantic. He would be gone soon, and she must realize that she probably would never see him again.

"Like what? Frostbite?"

Shelly laughed. The musical sound of it was carried by the wind and seemed to echo in the trees around them. "How can you complain? This is wonderful. Riding along like this makes me want to sing."

Slade grumbled something unintelligible under his breath.

"What are you complaining about now?"

"Who says I'm complaining?"

Shelly grinned, her head bobbing slightly with the gentle sway of Sampson's gait. "I'm beginning to know you."

"All right, if you insist upon knowing. I happen to be humming. My enthusiasm for this venture doesn't compel me to burst into song. But I'm doing the best I can."

Holding this contented feeling to her breast, Shelly tried not to think about what would happen when they reached the Wilkens's. She was prepared to smile at him and bid him farewell. Freely she would send him out of her life. But it had been easier before she'd been in his arms and experienced the gentle persuasiveness of his kiss. So very much easier.

Together, their horses side by side, they ambled along, not speaking but singing Christmas songs one after the other until they were breathless and giddy. Their voices blended magically in two-part harmony. More than once they shared a lingering gaze. But Shelly felt her high spirits evaporating as they neared the landmark that pointed out the first half of their short journey.

"My backside is ready for a break," Slade announced unexpectedly.

"You aren't nearly as anxious to scoff at my picnic idea now, are you?" Shelly returned.

"Not when I'm discovering on what part of their anatomy cowboys get calluses." A grin slashed his sensuous mouth.

They paused in a small clearing, looping the horses' reins around the trunk of a nearby fir tree.

While Shelly took the hot chocolate and cookies from her saddlebags, Slade exercised his stiff legs, walking around as though he were on a pair of stilts.

"We'll have to share a cup," she announced, holding out the plastic top of the thermos to Slade. She stood between the two horses, munching on a large oatmeal cookie.

Slade lifted the cup to his lips and hesitated as their eyes met. He paused, slowly lowering the cup without breaking eye contact.

Shelly's breath came in shallow gasps. "Is something wrong?" she asked with difficulty.

"You're lovely."

"Sure." She forced a laugh. "My nose looks like a maraschino cherry and—"

"Don't joke, Shelly. I mean it." His voice was gruff, almost harsh.

"Then thank you."

He removed his glove and placed his warm hand on her cold face, cupping her cheek. The moment was tender and peaceful, and Shelly swallowed the surging emotion that clogged her throat. It would be the easiest thing in the world to walk into his arms, lose herself in his kiss and love him the way he deserved to be loved.

As if reading her thoughts, Sampson shifted, bumping Shelly's back so that she was delivered into Slade's arms. He dropped the hot chocolate and hauled her against him like a man reaching out a desperate hand in need.

"I told myself this wouldn't happen again," he whispered against her hair. "Every time I hold you, it becomes harder to let you go."

Shelly's heart gave a small leap of pleasure at his words. She didn't want him to let her go. Not ever. Everything felt right between them. Too right and too good.

How long he held her, Shelly didn't know. Far longer than was necessary and not nearly long enough. Each second seemed elongated, sustaining her tender heart for the moment she must bid him farewell.

Not until they broke apart did Shelly notice that it was snowing again. Huge crystal-like flakes filled the sky with their icy purity.

"What should we do?" Slade asked, looking doubtful.

Her first instinct was to suggest that they return to the house, but she hesitated. Delaying the inevitable became more difficult every minute.

"We're going back," he said, answering his own question.

"Why?"

"I'm not leaving you and your father to deal with the horses. It's bad enough that I dragged you this far." Placing his foot in the stirrup, he reached for the saddle and mounted the Appaloosa. "Come on, before this snow gets any worse."

"But we can make it to the Wilkens's."

"Not now." He raised his eyes skyward and scowled. "It's already getting dark."

Grumbling, she tugged Sampson's reins free of the tree trunk and lifted her body onto his back with the agile grace of a ballerina.

The house was in sight when Slade spoke again. "After you call the Wilkens's, I need to contact Margaret. She's waiting for my phone call. I told her I'd call Christmas Eve."

Shelly's heart constricted at the mention of the other woman's name. Unless Shelly asked about his fiancée, Slade hadn't volunteered any information about Margaret. Now he freely thrust her between them.

"Naturally, I'll use my credit card."

He seemed to feel her lack of response was due to

the expense. Shelly almost preferred to think that. "Naturally," she echoed.

"She's a good woman."

Shelly didn't know who he was trying to convince. "I don't think you'd love a woman who wasn't."

"I've known Margaret a lot of years."

"Of course you have." And he'd only known Shelly a few days. She understood what he was saying. It was almost as if he were apologizing because Margaret had prior claim to his loyalties and his heart. He needn't; she'd accepted that from the beginning.

When they left the cover of the woods, Shelly spoke, managing to keep her voice level and unemotional. "You use the phone first," she said, surprised that her voice could remain so even. "I'll take care of the horses so you can make your call in private."

"I won't talk long."

Shelly didn't want him to tell her that. "Don't cut the conversation short on my account."

He wiped his forearm across his brow. The movement brought her attention to the confusion in his eyes. "I won't."

At the barn Shelly dismounted slowly, lowering both booted feet to the ground. She avoided his gaze as she opened the barn doors and led the horses through. The wind followed her inside the dimly lit area. The cold nipped at her heels.

With a heavy heart she lifted the saddle from

Pokey's back before she noticed Slade's dark form blocking the doorway. Her hands tightened around the smooth leather of the saddle. "Is there a problem?"

"No."

After leading Pokey to her stall, Shelly turned back to Slade only to find that he'd left.

Taking extra time with the horses, she delayed entering the house as long as possible. Removing the gloves from her hands one finger at a time, she walked in the back door to discover Slade sitting in the living room staring blindly into the roaring fire. She walked quickly to the phone and called the Wilkens's. Connie was glad to hear from her. After a full day driving neighbors around in the snow, Ted was exhausted. Shelly assured her friend that Slade had changed his mind anyway.

"I don't know about you," she called out cheerfully after hanging up the phone, "but I'm starved." The tip of her tongue burned with questions that pride refused to let her ask. Shelly possessed the usual female curiosity about Margaret and what Slade had said, if anything, about his current circumstances.

"How about popcorn with lots of melted butter?"

Slade joined her, a smile lurking at the edges of his full mouth. His eyes were laughing, revealing his thoughts. He really did have wonderful eyes and, for a moment, Shelly couldn't look away.

"I was thinking of something more like a triple-decker sandwich," Slade inserted.

"You know what your problem is, Garner?" It was obvious he didn't so she took it upon herself to tell him. "No imagination."

"Because I prefer something meatier than popcorn?"

Shelly pretended not to hear him; her head was buried in the open refrigerator. Without comment she brought out a variety of fixings and placed them on the tabletop.

Peeling off a slice of deli ham, she tore it in two and gave Slade half. "How about a compromise?"

He looked dubious, sure she was about to suggest a popcorn sandwich. "I don't know..."

"How about if you bring in the tree while I fix us something to eat?"

"That's an offer I can't refuse."

Singing softly as she worked, Shelly concocted a meal neither of them was likely to forget. Sandwiches piled high with three different kinds of meat, sliced dill pickles and juicy green olives. In addition, she set out Christmas cookies and thick slices of fudge that her father had sitting around the kitchen.

Slade set the tree in the holder, dragged it through the front door and stood it in the corner. "The snow's stopped," he told her when she carried in their meal.

"That's encouraging. I was beginning to think we'd be forced to stay until the spring thaw." Shelly wouldn't have minded, and her smile was a mixture of chagrin and ruefulness.

Sitting Indian style in front of the fireplace, their backs resting against the sofa, they dug into the sandwiches. But Shelly discovered that she had little appetite. Never had she been more aware of a man. They were so close that, when she lowered her sandwich to the plate, her upper arm brushed against his. But neither made any effort to move. The touch, although impersonal, was soothing. She paused, wishing to capture this moment of peacefulness.

"This has been a good day," Slade murmured, his gaze following hers as he stared out the living room window.

"It's certainly been crazy."

Slade's hand reached for hers, entwining their fingers. "I don't know when I've enjoyed one more." His dark gaze flickered over her and rested on her mouth. Abruptly he glanced away, his gaze moving to the piano at the far side of the room. "Do you play?"

Shelly sighed expressively. "A little. Dad claimed that my playing is what kept the mice out of the house."

A dark brow lifted with a touch of amusement. "That bad?"

"See for yourself." Rising, she walked to the piano, lifted the lid of the bench seat and extracted some Christmas music.

Pressing her fingers to the ivory keys, the discordant notes were enough to make her wince and cause Ol' Dan to lift his chin and cock his head curiously. He howled once.

"I told you I wasn't any good," she said with a dramatic sigh. Staring at the musical notes a second time, she squinted and sadly shook her head.

Slade joined her. Standing directly behind her, he laid his hands on her shoulders, leaning over to study the music.

"This may be the problem," she stated seriously. Dimples formed in her cheeks as she tried not to smile. Turning the sheet music right side up, she leaned forward to study the notes a second time and tried again. This time the sweet melody flowed through the house.

Chuckling, Slade's hands compressed around her shoulders, and spontaneously he lowered his mouth to her cheek. "Have I told you how much fun you are?"

"No, but I'll accept that as a compliment."

"It was meant as one."

Shelly continued to play, hitting a wrong note every once in a while and going back to repeat the bar until she got it right. Soon Slade's rich voice blended with the melody. Shelly's soprano tones mixed smoothly with his, although her playing faltered now and again.

Neither of them heard the front door open. "Merry Christmas Eve," Don announced, looking exhausted. His pants were caked with mud and grit.

Shelly rested her hands above the keys. "Welcome home. How's the Adler's horse?"

Don wiped a weary hand over his face. "She'll make it."

"What about you?"

"Give me a half hour and I'll let you know."

"There's a sandwich in the kitchen if you're hungry."

"All I want right now is a hot bath." He paused to scratch Ol' Dan's ears. "Keep playing. You two sound good together."

"I thought we were scattering the mice to the barn," Slade teased.

Don scratched the side of his head with his index finger. "Say that again?"

"He's talking about my piano playing," Shelly reminded her father.

"Oh, that. No, by herself Shelly doesn't appear to have much talent. I don't suppose you play?" He directed the question to Slade.

"As a matter of fact, I do."

"You do?" Shelly was stunned. "Why didn't you say something earlier? Here." She slid off the bench. "Trade places."

Slade claimed her position and his large, masculine hands ran over the keys with a familiarity that caused Shelly's heart to flutter. His hands moved over the keys with deep reverence and love. Stroking, enticing the instrument until the crescendo of the music practically had the room swaying. Music, wrapped deep in emotion, so overwhelmingly breath-taking that Shelly felt tears gather in the corner of her eyes. Slade didn't play the piano; he made love to it.

When he'd finished, he rested his hands in his lap and slowly expelled his breath.

Shelly sank into the cushioned chair. "Why didn't you tell me you could play like that?"

A smile brightened his eyes. "You didn't ask."

Even Don was awestruck and, for the first time in years, at a complete loss for words.

"You could play professionally. You're magnificent." Shelly's soft voice cracked with the potency of her feelings.

"I briefly toyed with the idea at one time."

"But..."

"I play for enjoyment now." The light dimmed in his gaze, and the sharp edge of his words seemed to say that the decision hadn't come easy. And it certainly was not one he was willing to discuss, even with her.

"Will you play something else?" Don requested, not moving.

From his look Slade appeared to regret admitting that he played the piano. Music was his real love, and he'd abandoned it. Coming this close again was pure torture for him. "Another time, perhaps."

There wouldn't be another time for them. "Please," Shelly whispered, rising and standing behind him. She placed her hands on his shoulder in a silent plea.

Slade's hand covered hers as he looked into her imploring gaze. "All right, Shelly. For you."

For half an hour he played with such intensity that his shoulders sagged with exhaustion when he'd finished.

"God has given you a rare and priceless gift," Don said, his voice husky with appreciation. He glanced down at his mud-caked clothes. "Now, if you'll excuse me, I'll take a bath before I start attracting flies."

Shelly could find no words to express herself. As Don left the room, she moved to Slade's side, sitting on the bench beside him.

Lovingly her fingers traced the sculptured line of his jaw as the tears blurred her vision. The tightness in her chest made her breathing shallow and difficult.

Slade's hand stopped her. Lifting her fingers to his lips, he gently kissed the inside of her palm. Shelly bit her bottom lip to hold back all the emotion stored in her heart.

A lone tear escaped and trickled down her pale cheek. With his thumb Slade gently brushed it aside. His finger felt cool against her heated skin. He bent down and found her mouth with his. Without speaking a word, Shelly realized that Slade was thanking her. With her he'd allowed his facade to crumble. He opened his heart and revealed the deep, sensitive man inside. He was free now, with nothing more to hide.

Wrapping her arms around him, she kissed him in return, telling him the only way she could how much she appreciated the gift.

"Merry Christmas, Shortcake," Don greeted on the tail end of a yawn.

Shelly stood in front of the picture window, her hands cupping her coffee mug. Her gaze rested on the sunrise as it blanketed the morning with the bright hues of another day. She tried to force a smile when she turned to her father, but it refused to come. She felt chilled and empty inside.

"Where's Slade?" Don asked.

"The snowplows came during the night," she whispered through the pain. "He's gone."

Chapter Eight

"Gone? Without saying goodbye?" A look of disbelief marred Don's smooth brow.

"He left a note." Shelly withdrew it from her pocket and handed it to her father. The message was no more than a few lines. He thanked them for their hospitality and wished Shelly and her father much happiness. He said goodbye. Without regrets. Without second thoughts. Without looking back.

Don's gaze lifted from the note and narrowed as he studied his daughter. "Are you okay?"

"I'm fine."

He slowly shook his head. "I've never seen you look at a man the way you looked at Slade. You really liked him, didn't you?"

I love him, her heart cried. "He's a wonderful

man. I only hope Margaret and that computer firm realize their good fortune.''

"They don't, you know,'' Don whispered, coming to her side. He slipped an arm over her shoulder and hugged her close. She offered him a feeble smile in return.

"He might come back.''

Shelly knew differently. "No.'' He'd made his choice. His future had been charted and defined as precisely as a road map. Slade Garner was a man of character and strength. He wouldn't abandon Margaret and all that was important to him for a two-day acquaintance and a few stolen kisses. He'd shared his deepest desires and secrets with her, opened his heart and trusted her. Shelly couldn't have wished for more. But she did. She wanted Slade.

Christmas day passed in a blur. She flew back to San Francisco the following afternoon, still numb, still aching, but holding her head up high and proud.

Her tiny apartment in the Garden District, although colorful and cheerfully decorated, did little to boost her drooping spirits.

Setting her suitcase on the polished hardwood floor, she kicked off her shoes and reached for the phone.

"Hi, Dad.'' Taking the telephone with her, she sank into the overstuffed chair.

"How was the flight?''

"Without a hitch."

"Just the way you like them." Don chuckled, then grew serious. "I don't suppose—"

"No, Dad." Shelly knew what he was asking. Don seemed to feel that Slade would be in San Francisco waiting for her. Shelly knew better. Slade wouldn't want to think of her. Already he'd banished any thought of her to the furthest corner of his mind. Perhaps what they'd shared was an embarrassment to him now.

Shelly spoke to her father for a few minutes longer, but neither had much to say. When they'd finished, she sat with the telephone cradled in her lap, staring blindly at the wallpaper.

For her part, Shelly worked hard at putting her life back on an even keel. She went to work each day and did her utmost to forget the man who had touched her so profoundly.

Her one resolution for the New Year was simple: Find a man. For the first time since moving to San Francisco, Shelly was lonely. Oh, there were friends and plenty of invitations, but nothing to take away the ache in her soul.

Two days before the New Year, Shelly stepped off the bus and on impulse bought flowers from a vendor on the street corner. One of her shoes had caused a blister on her heel, and she removed the offending pump once inside her apartment building.

The elderly woman who lived across the hall opened her door as Shelly approached. "Good afternoon, Mrs. Lester,'' Shelly said, pulling a red carnation from the bouquet of flowers and handing it to her neighbor.

"Now, isn't that a coincidence.'' Mrs. Lester chuckled. "I've got flowers for you.''

Shelly's heart went still.

"The delivery boy asked me to give them to you.'' She reached back inside, then handed Shelly a narrow white box. "Roses, I suspect.''

"Roses?'' Shelly felt the blood drain from her face. She couldn't get inside her apartment fast enough. Closing the door with her foot, she walked across the room and set the box on a table. Inside she discovered a dozen of the most perfect roses she'd ever imagined. Each bud was identical to the others, their color brilliant. They must have cost a fortune.

Although she went through the box twice, she found no card. It would only be conjecture to believe that Slade had sent them. Unlikely, really. He wouldn't be so cruel as to say goodbye only to invade her life again. Besides, he'd claimed roses were expensive. She couldn't argue with that. They were.

The thought had just formed when the doorbell rang, and a delivery boy handed her a second long narrow box, identical to the first.

"Sign here.'' He offered her his ballpoint pen.

Shelly scribbled her name across the bottom of the delivery order and carried the second box to the kitchen table. Again she'd received a gift of a dozen red roses, and again there was no card.

No sooner had she arranged the flowers in her one and only tall vase when the doorbell chimed a third time. It was a delivery boy from another flower shop with a dozen roses.

"Are you sure you have the right address?" she questioned.

"Shelly Griffin?" He read off her street and apartment number and raised expectant eyes to her.

"That's me," she conceded.

"Sign here."

Again Shelly penned her name. And for a third time there was no card.

Having no vase to arrange them in, she emptied her jar of dill pickles onto a plate, rinsed out the container and used that. These she carried into the living room.

Whoever was sending her the roses was either very rich or else extremely foolish, she thought.

Hands pressed against her hips, she surveyed the small apartment and couldn't decide if it resembled a flower shop or a funeral parlor.

When the doorbell chimed again, she sighed expressively. "Not again," she groaned aloud, turning the dead bolt and opening the door.

But instead of opening it to a delivery boy as she expected, Shelly came face-to-face with Slade. He was so tall, dark and so incredibly good-looking that her breath became trapped in her lungs.

"Slade."

"Hello, Shelly." His eyes delved into hers, smiling and warm. "Can I come in?"

"Oh, of course." Flustered, she stepped aside.

"Do you realize you only have on one shoe?"

She looked down at her nylon-covered foot. "I forgot. You see, they're new and I wore them for the first time today so when—" She stopped abruptly. "Why are you here?" she demanded. With her hands behind her back, she leaned against the closed front door desperately wanting to believe everything she dared not even think about.

"I've missed you."

She closed her eyes to the tenderness that lapped over her in gentle waves. Few words had ever been sweeter. "How did the meeting go?"

"Fine. Better than expected."

"That's nice." Her gaze studied him, still unsure.

"I got a hefty bonus for my part in it, but I may have offended a few friends."

"How's that?"

"They were hoping I'd accept a promotion."

"And you aren't?" This sounded like something Margaret would love.

"No, I resigned this afternoon."

"Resigned? What did...Margaret have to say about that?"

"Well—" he took a step toward her, stopping just short of her but close enough to reach out and touch her if he desired "—Margaret and I aren't exactly on speaking terms."

"Oh?" Her voice went incredibly weak.

"She didn't take kindly to some of my recent decisions."

I'll just bet, Shelly mused. "And what are those decisions...the most recent ones?"

"I decided to postpone the wedding."

Shelly couldn't fault his fiancée for being upset about that. "Well, I can't say that I blame her. When—when's the new date?"

"Never."

"Never?" Shelly swallowed tightly. "Why not?"

"Why?" He smiled. "Because Margaret doesn't walk around with one shoe missing. Or haul sourdough bread across the country or laugh or do any of the things that make life fun."

Speechless, Shelly stared at him, love shining from her eyes.

"Nor does she believe I'll ever make a decent living as a pianist," Slade continued, "Hell, I'm over thirty now. It could be too late."

"But...?"

"But—" he smiled and reached for her, bringing her into the loving circle of his arms "—I'm going to give it one hell of a try. I'm no prize, Shelly Griffin. I don't have a job, and I'm not even sure the conservatory will renew their offer, but for the first time in a lot of years, I've got a dream."

"Oh, Slade," she whispered and pressed her forehead to his broad chest. "I would consider it the greatest honor of my life to be a part of that dream."

"You couldn't help but be," he whispered, lifting her mouth to his. "You're the one who gave it to me."

* * * * *

THE FIVE DAYS
OF CHRISTMAS

Lindsay McKenna

To my editor, Lynda Curnyn,
who is a bright, guiding light in my life.
Authors rarely get great editors,
and she is one of them. Morgan and his family
are forever grateful for her love of them.

Dear Reader,

It was a thrill to create this wonderful Christmas story involving Morgan Trayhern and his family! Just as they are to you, Morgan and the people who work for Perseus are like extended family to me. This story was a joy to write.

Many of you have asked about Morgan's son, Jason, and you will be able to visit with him in this story, as well as many of the men and women you've met in other MORGAN'S MERCENARIES novels, along with their expanding families. Of course, the real mover and shaker at work behind the scenes of this story is Laura Trayhern, who created the Five Days of Christmas celebration for the employees of Perseus—and is doing a little matchmaking this holiday!

In this story we get to meet a very tired mercenary, Colt Hamlin, who has simply seen too much on his last mission to Kosovo. He's resting up—actually, hiding out— in Montana. Until Laura Trayhern coaxes him out of hiding by matchmaking him with her son's high school teacher, Abbie Clemens. Abbie had lost her mercenary husband a year earlier, so in another way she's emotionally hiding, too. But Laura has a sixth sense about the two of them and makes sure they meet and have to work together during the Five Days of Christmas celebration.

Sit back, relax, prop up your feet and enjoy their story, and say hello once again to Morgan, Laura and their family. I hope you enjoy reading this story as much as I did penning it.

Warmly,

Lindsay McKenna

Chapter 1

December 20

"Morgan, you can't say no," Laura pleaded as she stood in her husband's large office at Perseus headquarters, hidden deep in the Rocky Mountains of Montana. Though his office, which was next to the war room, where so many mercenary and military missions were launched, was officially closed for the holidays, Laura had come to talk to her husband as he wrapped things up. The Five Days of Christmas celebration she ran every year was at the top of her agenda. But there was one important detail she felt had to be taken care of first.

Now, as she watched him scowl and rummage

through several top-secret military reports on his desk, love for him welled up in her heart. With silver flecking the temples of his black, short hair, Morgan was getting even more handsome with age.

He lifted his head, and his blue eyes softened as he looked at his wife—at her blond hair in tempting disarray around her slim shoulders, her arms crossed and those soft lips of hers set in a petulant pout. She wore a bright red, cowl neck mohair sweater, dark green slacks and simple oxfords. A piece of green holly with red berries was fastened in her hair. Sighing, he ran his hand across his chin. "Listen, I've tried everything to get Colt out of our safe-house condo. He's hurting, Laura."

Uncrossing her arms, she perched her hip on the side of Morgan's desk and gave him a beseeching look. "I know his mission over in Kosovo was successful. So why is he holed up?"

"It was successful," Morgan agreed, leaning back in his leather chair. Just gazing into Laura's tender eyes made him feel better. She was his anchor. She always had been. And even now, after carrying four beautiful children in that petite but oh-so-strong body of hers, she looked just as young and vibrant as when he'd met her so many years ago. "Colt's suffering from mild PTSD—post-traumatic stress disorder—according to Dr. Jennifer Ramirez, our staff physician."

"Well, if that's so, then all the more reason to get him out of there and back with normal people and society." She stretched out her hand. "Morgan, you know what PTSD is. You've suffered from it for years because of your experience over in Vietnam and later, after you were kidnapped. The last thing you needed was to be alone at times like that. Colt Hamlin has worked for you for seven years now and I agree that he needs downtime. But with people." With a mischievous grin, Laura said, "He can help me with the Five Days of Christmas celebration."

Groaning, Morgan sat up, folded his hands on his desk and raised one eyebrow. "You've got that look in your eye, sweetheart. You're making me nervous."

With a lilting laugh, Laura reached out and covered his massive, hairy hand with her own much smaller one. "Now, darling…"

"Now I know I'm in trouble."

"Colt is, actually," she replied playfully. Patting his hand one last time, Laura eased off the desk. "I have a plan, Morgan. One that I think can help Colt and help me."

"Uh-oh…"

"Don't be such a fussbudget about this. Hear me out, will you?"

One corner of his mouth crooked. "That look in your eyes is still there. You have a plan. I feel like I should already be waving a white flag of surrender…."

Chuckling, Laura said, "Listen, you know Abbie

Clemens, the biology teacher over at the high school? The teacher that Jason loved so much?"

Morgan nodded. "Sure I do. She's helping you with the Christmas celebration, right?"

Laura's smile deepened. "Yes, she is. What I want to do is lure Colt out of hiding and ask him to help Abbie. She takes care of all the decorations for these five days, and I've got my hands full with all I've got to do."

"You're matchmaking—again...." Morgan gave his wife a warm look. He couldn't stop the smile from edging his mouth. Laura stood there, her shoulders back, her smile effusive and her eyes glimmering with happiness.

"Well..." she murmured coyly, "I just feel it's time Abbie got back into the mainstream of life. Her husband died two years ago in the line of duty while working with Perseus. It's the least we can do to help her, Morgan. She's ready to let go of her past."

"And you think bringing snarling, grouchy Colt Hamlin into her life is a *good* thing? Are you a sadist?"

Laughing at his good-natured jab, Laura moved around the room. "I know he's grumpy right now. I just happen to feel Abbie will be like a healing ointment to his emotional wounds. And if she can handle petulant, hormone-driven eleventh-graders, I'm sure she can deal with Colt." Laura pirouetted, taking in his office as she spun around. There were maps of the world on the walls, photographs of their four children, whom Morgan doted upon, and a pair of crossed Marine Corps ceremonial swords to attest to his time spent in that branch of the service.

Morgan watched his wife move with grace around the windowless room. His office was in the basement of the Perseus complex, hidden beneath a Victorian home. Because of the nature of his super-secret work, Morgan did not want to be found by his enemies...and he'd made many over the last fifteen years. He also wished to protect his growing family. Once, several years before, Laura, their oldest son, Jason, and Morgan himself had been captured by drug dealers who wanted to get even after Morgan's mercenaries destroyed their trade in several key regions of South America.

Frowning, Morgan recalled that horrible experience. Laura had suffered badly at the hands of her captors. His son Jason, although very young when it happened, had been scarred, it seemed, for life. Before the kidnapping, Jason had been an outgoing young boy. Afterward, he'd become withdrawn, a loner, angry and rebellious...even to this day. If it hadn't been for Abbie Clemens, who was like a second mother to Jason, Morgan doubted that his son would have gained an appointment to the U.S. Naval Academy to follow in the Trayhern family's two-hundred-year-old tradition of military service.

Guilt ate at Morgan. His family had suffered needlessly because of his own arrogance, his confidence in Perseus and its ability to protect his family...and

the families of people who worked for him around
the world. It had been a lesson he never wanted to
repeat, so he'd gone underground—literally disappeared—so that no terrorists, no drug dealers, however powerful, could hunt Perseus down and take out
their rage and revenge. Moving to the very small
town of Philipsburg, Montana, deep in the heart of
the Rocky Mountains, had been a brilliant tactical
decision. Here, Perseus staff were relatively safe, although none of them let down their guard completely.

As Laura turned and smiled winningly at him,
Morgan knew his goose was cooked. He could never
say no to her. He loved her too much to deny her
anything. Besides, what she was asking was more
than reasonable. She was right: Colt needed to be
pried out of hiding. Being with people would help
him heal.

"Well? What do you think? Can you phone Colt?
Tell him you need him, Morgan? Fib a little and tell
him you're overwhelmed with work and that you
usually do this running around for me in preparation
for the Five Days of Christmas celebration, but you
can't this time. Colt will understand that. And he'll
help if you ask him."

Giving her a wry look and then gesturing to the
mission plans on his desk, Morgan growled, "I don't
think I'll have to fib one iota about being overwhelmed with work."

Laura came over, slid her arms around his massive

shoulders and placed a warm, lingering kiss on his crooked mouth. In response, he lifted her and settled her on his lap. With a sigh, she placed her brow against his and whispered, "I love you, Morgan Trayhern."

"You love me because you can wheedle anything you want out of me, whenever you want it," he chuckled as he lifted his chin and placed a kiss on the tip of her nose. Drowning in her warm gaze, he added, "But I know you love me for other reasons, too."

"You're such a teddy bear, darling, My teddy bear—big and gruff. But underneath," she continued, sliding her hand against his chest, "you've got a heart of gold. I know you care what happens to Colt. And I can see you're worried about him, though there's nothing you can do about it personally. Maybe my plan won't work fully, but Abbie's lonely and so is Colt. Why not bring two lonely people together? Maybe the Five Days of Christmas celebration will help them."

Catching her sparkling gaze, Morgan placed his hand over his wife's as she pressed against his white silk shirt and red tie. "Okay, I'll give him a call. But no promises, all right?"

When the phone rang, Colt Hamlin nearly leaped out of the chair he was sitting in. A bottle of whiskey, one third of the contents gone from his drinking bout the night before, sat next to the red phone. The phone rang again. Irritated, he snatched it up.

"Yeah?"

"Colt? This is Morgan."

Instantly, Colt sat up. Scowling, he changed his tone. "Sorry, boss. I wasn't expecting any calls," he said contritely.

Morgan accepted his apology for the snarling start to their conversation. "Don't worry about it. Listen, I need your help. I'm plowed under here with work. Laura needs my help in setting up things for our Five Days of Christmas celebration, but I can't make it, Colt. I was wondering if you felt well enough to take my place. All it means is a lot of running around, pulling things together, working behind the scenes."

Colt rubbed his bloodshot eyes. He'd barely slept last night. And drinking whiskey probably hadn't helped. He felt fractured. Raw. "I don't do parties, Morgan."

"I understand. I'm not asking that of you, Colt. I am asking for your time, and maybe some driving here and there. Maybe helping some of the women set up decorations at our home. That's all."

Rubbing his chin, which had a two-day growth of beard on it, Colt said, "Yeah...okay...I can do that." After all, he owed Morgan big-time. Under any other circumstances, Colt would eagerly do anything for his boss. Right now, though, he was hurting so much that he wondered if he could keep himself glued together and focused enough to help anyone at all.

"Great. I'm appreciative. Take the car in the garage beneath the condo where you're staying over to Abbie Clemens's place. Here's the address...."

Colt found a pencil and paper and wrote it down. Philipsburg was a small town—less than 2,500 in population—and was like a second home to him when he came off missions. He knew the layout well.

Hanging up, he sighed. The condo, which was decorated in a Western motif, was silent—and lonely. Getting up stiffly, he padded on bare feet across the thick, dark blue carpet to the bathroom. First, he'd better shower and shave. Otherwise, this woman called Abbie would freak out over his rough appearance.

The heavy knock on Abbie's back door, off the kitchen, made her jump in reaction. It was an aggressive kind of knock, not a friendly one, that was for sure. Slipping off the chair and placing the half-finished pine swag on the table, Abbie hurried to answer it. Would that be Colt Hamlin already? It was nearly 9:00 a.m. Laura had called to say he would be coming by to help. Glancing through the window, which was wreathed in pale pink, Victorian style curtains with a swag of holly with bright red berries across the top, she could see a very tall, large man standing on the porch. Snowflakes twirled lazily from the gray sky behind him.

Abbie's heart beat a little harder as she opened the door. The man standing before her reminded her of an angry grizzly bear, a species that lived in this part of the Rocky Mountains. He stood about six foot one inch tall, and his shoulders were massively broad. His black hair was cut very short, with one rebellious curl dipping over his furrowed brow. He was built like a boxer, she decided as she quickly perused the unhappy set of his face. Everything about Colt Hamlin was square—his build, the shape of his jaw, his broad forehead. His nose looked like it had been broken many times. Her gaze ranged upward to his eyes. Though they were bloodshot, she could see they were a forest-green color, the pupils dark and huge. Intuitively, Abbie sensed that he was very tired and stressed out. Laura had warned her when she'd called that Colt was like a bear with his foot in a trap, and to take him in stride.

"Hi," she greeted him a little breathlessly, and stuck out her hand. "You must be Colt Hamlin? I'm Abbie Clemens. Thanks for dropping by to help me with this stuff. I really appreciate it."

Colt stared down at her proffered hand. He hadn't known what to expect, but it wasn't this. Dressed in an apricot mohair sweater and cobalt-blue corduroy slacks, Abbie Clemens stood about five foot five inches in height, her medium-boned frame probably weighing in at about a hundred and thirty pounds. Her face was plain, but was set off by a riot of curly, carrot-red hair tied back from her heavily freckled, pale face by a pink-orange-and-white scarf. What drew him unexpectedly were her large blue eyes, which were soft and warm, and a wide, smiling mouth that sent a sheet of heat all the way through him to his toes. Her engaging smile was genuine. And the sparkle of welcome in her eyes appeared to be, too.

Jerkily, he lifted his hand and enclosed hers. Such a small, delicate hand covered with copper freckles, compared to his own bear paw. Clearing his throat, he growled, "Yeah, I'm Colt. Morgan Trayhern said you needed some help?"

A stream of tingles flew up Abbie's fingers into her arm as she released Colt's massive hand. For all of his masculine strength, she had to give him credit: he hadn't crushed her fingers. When she saw surprise flare in his narrowed eyes, she wondered why. Self-consciously touching her flyaway hair, which always looked uncombed because it was so curly, she stepped aside. Abbie knew she was not beautiful, not even pretty. She had accepted that her oval face, her straight nose with flared nostrils, and her polka-dotted skin slathered with hundreds of freckles she refused to hide with makeup, did not make her look glamorous.

"Come in," she invited, and gestured to the huge, white oak table where the pine swags lay. "Just take off your coat and have a seat here at the table while I finish off these last two decorations."

Abbie watched with compassion as he self-consciously jammed his hands into the pockets of his jeans and stepped hesitantly through the door. The dark brown leather bomber jacket he wore had obviously seen a lot of wear and tear. The white silk scarf beneath, spotted with melted snowflakes, gave him the look of an aviator. As he shrugged out of the jacket and placed it on the back of an oak chair, she smiled a little nervously.

Colt wore a maroon, fisherman's knit sweater, the wrinkled collar of a white shirt peeking out from beneath it. Everything about him shouted of stress. Laura had warned Abbie that he was suffering from PTSD. She knew what it was because some of the children she taught had suffered from it—especially Jason Trayhern, due to his kidnapping at an earlier age.

Treading gently, Abbie watched as Colt's gaze skittered around her bright pink kitchen, with its Victorian-style curtains. Going over to the sink, she put water into the copper teakettle. "Tea or coffee? You look like you could use one or the other." She kept her voice light and teasing. When his gaze whipped to her, she froze momentarily. He had the eyes of a hunter or predator—always shifting, always moving and restless. Abbie knew he worked for Morgan, but not in what capacity.

"Yeah. Hot tea sounds good." When he saw her jolt, then freeze, he realized he was snarling again. *Damn.* Clearing his throat, he added, "Thanks." It sounded lame.

Grabbing the chair, Colt pulled it out and sat down. The fragrant scent of pine surrounded him. There were at least a dozen thick ropes of woven evergreen branches on the large, rectangular table in front of him. Sniffing again, he said, "What's that smell? Cinnamon rolls?"

Grinning, Abbie put the teakettle on the gas stove and turned it on. "Sure is. Have you had breakfast?" Colt probably weighed around a hundred and eighty pounds, she judged. And his cheeks were hollow. He wasn't eating enough.

Shrugging, he muttered, "I'm not hungry." There was that snarl again, he thought with dismay. Every feeling was visible in her face. That shook him. In his trade, no one showed any expressions or emotions. Colt reminded himself that Abbie was a schoolteacher, not a spy or a mercenary. Her eyes were lustrous and so blue that they reminded him of the deep, breathtaking azure of a wide Montana sky in summertime. As he studied her, he saw her eyes grow tender. It was almost a physical sensation he received as she gave him that gentle, caring look.

"Are you sure? I can whip you up an omelette and some bacon real fast. I don't have to have these swags over to Laura's for an hour."

Rubbing his throat with his long, thick fingers, Colt muttered, "I got a cold comin' on or somethin'...."

"Ohh...well, in that case I'll put a little honey and lemon in your tea to soothe it." Reaching up on tiptoes, she grabbed a jar of honey from the cupboard and placed it on the counter. Her heart bounded as she turned and looked over at Colt. He was watching her with such intensity that Abbie wondered if the zipper on her slacks was open or something. Maybe he hadn't been around a woman for a long, long time.

Unused to such raw male scrutiny, she opened the fridge and pulled out a bottle of reconstituted lemon juice. In her job at the high school, she didn't meet many men who were single. Though Philipsburg was a tourist destination during the summer months, it mainly attracted families seeking an outdoor experience in nature. Abbie felt her skin prickle pleasantly. She was enjoying Colt's frowning inspection, but found it hard to believe he was attracted to her—Miss Plain Jane of Philipsburg, as she wryly referred to herself in moments of acute loneliness.

Taking the recently baked cinnamon rolls out of the oven, where she'd kept them warm, Abbie popped one onto a plate and set it before Colt. "I hear cinnamon rolls are cold-killers."

Looking up at her, he saw a grin playing across her full lips. The twinkle in her eyes gave away the fact that she was teasing him. Warming to her, Colt picked up the fork and knife she'd placed beside the plate. "Yeah?"

"Absolutely."

"Better than vitamin C?" He cut into the warm roll, and the scent made his mouth water. The teakettle began to whistle shrilly and Abbie left his side. Colt felt the sunshine leave with her.

"Absolutely. My kids tell me candy and junk food are the best thing for colds and flu," she said with a laugh as she poured them each a cup of tea. Abbie turned for a moment to look at him. Colt was enjoying the huge cinnamon roll immensely. *Good.* He looked like he needed something positive in his life, even a small thing. Placing a teabag into each cup of hot water, she brought them over to the table and sat down opposite him. Moving a half-made pine swag to one side, she spooned a bit of sugar into her tea. When she lifted her head, she met his hooded gaze. Her heart pounded momentarily. The pupils of his eyes were large and black as he studied her. Now she knew what a bug felt like under a microscope. Being a biology teacher, she would have new compassion for them in her class.

"Cinnamon roll okay?" she asked lightly, holding his frank stare.

Blinking, Colt realized he was staring like a starving wolf. What *was* it about this petite woman with the wild, riotous hair? When she smiled at him, he felt that sunny warmth embrace him. She was so honest and unassuming in an emotional sense that it rocked him. "Oh...the roll. Yeah, its good. After where I just came from, food tastes damn—I mean darn—good." Colt had to remind himself he was back in the real world once more, not undercover, and not with military types where cursing was as much a part of daily life as breathing air.

Abbie's heart expanded with joy. Colt was trying so hard to be nice. "You're really tired, aren't you? Maybe if I made you a fortifying breakfast, you'd get some energy back?"

He shook his head and polished off the rest of the roll. "I just came off a rough mission," he muttered in apology, "and I'm sleep deprived. I'll catch up in the next few days and be okay. Thanks, though…" Taking the cup of tea, he dipped the bag up and down a few times and then put it on a saucer. After adding a spoonful of honey and a bit of lemon juice, he found himself thirstily drinking it down. Abbie was right. Within moments, his sore throat disappeared.

She fingered her cup and chose her words carefully. "When my husband was alive, he worked for Morgan as an operative."

Frowning, Colt lifted his head. He heard carefully concealed pain in Abbie's soft voice. She was frowning, too, her thin red brows bunched as she stared down at her cup of tea.

"I'm sorry…I didn't know…." he began. How stupid of him. He looked at her left hand. There was no wedding band on it. "So…you know what we go through…." He found himself giving an inner sigh of relief because Abbie understood.

She lifted her head and nodded slightly. "Yes, I do."

Shifting the cup in his large hands, Colt murmured, "How long ago?"

"Two years." She gave him a game smile. "Ted was in the Marine Corps. A Recon. He quit and came to work for Morgan. I'm a schoolteacher, and I loved moving here to the Rocky Mountains." Her eyes grew bleak. "I always worried about him when he went on a mission. You know how it is, I suppose?"

"My wife divorced me five years ago because of what I did," Colt told her bluntly. Not that he blamed Christine. He was gone nine months at a time, sometimes longer. No marriage could survive those conditions. The distress in Abbie's eyes touched him unexpectedly. "I know the person left behind worries a lot. It leaves you feeling pretty helpless," he added gruffly.

"It does," she agreed. "But Ted didn't get killed on a mission, if that's what you're thinking." Abbie grimaced. "He died in a car accident during a blizzard. An eighteen-wheeler spun out of control and hit him head-on about ten miles from here."

Shaking his head, Colt said, "Damn, I'm sorry."

Taking in a deep breath, Abbie gave him a sad smile. "Yeah, isn't it a sick joke? All along, I thought Ted might die on a mission. Instead he gets killed this way. Go figure... Well, that was two years ago. Laura says I need to start living again."

Abbie gazed fondly around the small, cozy kitchen. "Laura persuades me every year to help her with the Five Days of Christmas celebration, and I love it. It's helped me a lot over the last couple of years." Running her fingers in a caressing motion across the swag of pine boughs and red and silver ribbons she was weaving among the branches, Abbie added, "Family means everything to me, and I know it does for Morgan and Laura, too. Have you ever attended this celebration? Or were you always on a mission when it happened?"

"I was always on a mission." Colt watched, almost mesmerized by Abbie's continued stroking of the thick green swag. For a crazy moment, he wondered what it would be like if she stroked him the same way. What would it feel like? Good. Damn good. Hungry for a woman's touch, he found himself lost in a haze of heat and desire for her. She was a complete stranger to him, yet somehow she'd gotten under his skin without trying. Stunned, Colt admitted he was tired and stressed out. He also told himself Abbie was guileless and open, unlike many of the women he'd met. So how could she become so much a part of him in such a short space of time? It had to be the PTSD, he warned himself. He was raw and hurting, and her natural warmth and vulnerability had opened up his heavily armored heart because right now he needed to be held, to be cared for and nurtured.

Abbie's lips parted as she saw the heated look in his hooded eyes. Her entire body responded violently to Colt's smoldering glance. She was old enough to know what that look meant. Yet she was shocked by it. In the last two years of grieving for her husband, Abbie had never given one thought to the possibility that another man might be interested in her. After all, she was no raving beauty.

"W-well..." Abbie stammered, breathless with the discovery of his attraction, "they throw a huge five-day party for all the Perseus employees who work here. Any mercs coming in off missions and who are staying at the condos outside of town to rest and recoup are invited, too. This year we have fifty people coming." She gulped and added, "It's fun because the whole family is invited. The children have a great time. Laura plans everything for the kids, and we adults magically turn into children ourselves during the process."

She smiled a little as she watched Colt's perennial scowl begin to ease and disappear. Did she have that much of an affect on him? Before, he'd been so dark and snarly. Maybe he was more cheerful because he had some food in his stomach now, or maybe the hot tea had soothed his sore throat. Or maybe it was *she* who had changed his demeanor.

Her conscience prickled her, reminding her smartly that she was only twenty-eight years old and in her prime as a young woman. Laughing to herself, Abbie realized suddenly that she had changed since he'd arrived, too. She'd been so mired in her grief for so long that hadn't realized how down she had been until just now.

For whatever reason, Colt was making her forget

the past for a moment as he sat in her tiny kitchen, which was warmed with a wood-burning stove. Her rapid pulse suggested something was happening between them, that on some level at least he was drawn to her. Her of all people! She was not beautiful. She did not have a stick-straight model's body, but was all curves. Stymied as to why he was interested in her, Abbie gazed at him in puzzlement. As she sat there, however, it felt very good to be with such a ruggedly handsome man—a man she sensed was drawn to her, too.

"I told Morgan I'd work with you behind the scenes. I'm not going to the actual celebration," he said. Then he saw how crestfallen she looked.

"But," Abbie protested, "it might make you feel better...."

Shrugging, Colt set the empty cup aside. "I'm not good company, Abbie." Her name slipped off his tongue like hot, smooth honey. He liked the intimacy they shared right now; it was unexpected, and healing to his tangled emotions. "I nearly ripped your head off a little while ago at the door. Think what kind of damage I could do at a party." One corner of his thinned mouth hitched upward as he attempted to make a joke out of his present condition. He saw her eyes grow tender. His heart opened even more.

"I understand, Colt. I really do." Without thinking, Abbie reached out and touched his thick, hairy hand, which was resting on the table. "Its okay. You do what you can and don't apologize for the rest."

Her fingertips tingled where she'd grazed his taut, hard flesh. There was such a dangerous quality to him. Yet Abbie felt protected and secure in his presence, not scared. Colt Hamlin, even if he was bleeding emotionally from his last mission, had a big enough heart to reach out to her, human to human. And in Abbie's book, that was something she needed and rarely received.

Picking up the swag, she began to weave the red ribbon through the boughs, which had been bound together with copper wire. "Whatever help you can give me, I'll be grateful for," she whispered. "Right now, you need to take care of you—first."

Colt studied another bough, on his side of the table. He laid it aside and then scooted the chair back and rose. Picking up the empty cups, he walked over to the drain board and set them down. Turning, he gazed back at Abbie as she worked effortlessly with the swag. There was high pink color in her cheeks. She looked beautiful to him, like a red-haired fairy princess, with nature all about her. And she was a biology teacher to boot. Moving back to the table, he sat down. As Abbie lifted her head, he said, "Why don't you show me how to weave this thing?"

"Oh, Colt, you don't have to! I just need some help moving the boxes filled with finished swags to the car."

He gave her a slight, one-cornered smile. Picking up a swag, he rasped, "I want to help you, Abbie.

I'll let you know when I'm ready to cash in my chips and slink back to the condo.''

Brightening, she grinned. ''A glutton for punishment.''

''Maybe…'' But he didn't think so. No, for better or worse, Colt craved Abbie's sunny presence in his dark pit of a life. She made him feel hope when he'd believed he had nothing to hope for ever again.

Chapter 2

December 21—Day 1

Abbie tried to still her fluttering heart as Colt Hamlin drove them expertly through the slushy, snow-covered streets, heading toward Morgan and Laura's huge cedar home outside of town. The snow was thickening, turning the sky a gunmetal-gray color. All around them rose the Rocky Mountains, silent and clothed in white, with dark evergreens at their base. It was a beautiful sight. Glancing distractedly out of the corner of her eye, she saw that Colt was paying strict attention to his driving. The roads had been salted earlier to melt the ice, but they were still messy.

Pushing her fingers through her unruly hair, Abbie said, "Laura said you fly for a living?"

Nodding, Colt glanced at Abbie for a moment, taking in her dark green wool coat, her hands in brown leather gloves, as she sat in the passenger seat of the van. "Yeah, I'm a chopper pilot."

Abbie didn't want to pry, yet her curiosity about this stalwart, silent warrior was eating away at her. They were leaving the town limits and heading down a small dirt road covered with slush. "You know Jason Trayhern, their firstborn son, is at the Naval Academy right now? Well, he wants to be a pilot in the worst way. A Marine Corps fighter pilot." She smiled fondly and settled her hands in her lap. "His grandfather, Chase Trayhern, was a pilot in the Korean War. I guess Jason got the flying genes from him."

"The Navy has set tough standards for jet fighter pilots," Colt warned heavily. "Marines go to naval flight schools to be trained. When I was in the Marine Corps, I went for the same thing." His mouth quirked as he slowed the van down. The road was now enclosed by huge Douglas firs that stood like silent sentinels around them. Colt had been to the Trayhern home before and knew the way. He noted that someone had dumped gravel on the well-traveled dirt road, improving driving conditions. "Only I didn't make the grade, so they gave me helicopter duty instead."

"You were disappointed?"

"Sure I was." He maneuvered the van deftly around a slight curve. "I hope young Trayhern doesn't have his sights set too high. I've seen a lot of guys ruin their lives because they didn't get jet fighters. Sometimes you have to adjust to what life gives you versus what you think life owes you." He grinned tightly and glanced over at Abbie. She was watching him raptly, her wide, trusting eyes luminous. There was something so incredibly gentle and nurturing about her. He found himself wanting to blather on to her about anything and everything that flitted through his mind and lay in his tightly guarded heart.

"Jason is a very troubled young man," Abbie admitted slowly. Her thin, arched brows fell momentarily. "That kidnapping wounded him in a way that Morgan and Laura just can't manage to heal."

"I heard from some of the other mercs coming through the office here that Jason was in trouble in high school. You were his teacher, right?"

"Yes, and Jason was very rebellious. His parents, of course, were hoping he would get A's in everything so he could make a run for the Naval Academy appointment. You know only two people from each state are chosen to go to the academy every year?"

"Yes. It's by Senate appointment, and your grades had better be 4.0 or better."

Opening her hands, Abbie said, "Jason started to rebel in his freshman year of high school. He was angry and he was a loner. He was always getting into fights with the bullies, always standing up for kids who had no one to defend them.''

"Nothing wrong with that. Better than being a bully himself.''

"Yes and no. Jason has a strong protective streak for the underdogs, but you can't go around punching bullies out...which is what he did with great regularity. And in today's schools, any kind of aggression hits a hot button, so he was in a lot of trouble.''

"Did he get suspended?''

"Yes. It really hurt Morgan, who has so many hopes and expectations pinned on his son. You know, the Trayherns have a proud military tradition that goes back two hundred years or more. Every firstborn son goes to a military academy, if possible. And with Morgan being branded a traitor to the U.S. during the closing days of the Vietnam War, and not being able to defend himself for years after that, or clear his name, the public still remembers the stain on the family.''

"That's enough of a dark cloud for any teenage kid to be carrying around,'' Colt muttered, "much less a parent's expectations that he make the Naval Academy. No wonder he's rebellious. I would be, too.''

Sighing, Abbie said, "I love Jason so much. He's like the child I never had....'' She lowered her lashes. "Ted and I wanted kids, but he was sterile. Maybe that's why I love my kids at school so much—I can mother *them,* instead.'' Abbie gave a strained laugh.

Her laugh sounded hollow to Colt, who divided his attention between driving along the serpentine road and absorbing the pain he saw banked in Abbie's turquoise eyes. His heart contracted, and that surprised him. In the last year, he'd deliberately hardened his heart and fought against feeling, because of his assignments over in the Kosovo region. The needless, ongoing killing over there had torn him up no matter how hard he tried to remain immune and disconnected from what he saw. Focusing on her soft, trembling lower lip as she admitted the painful secret to him, Colt took his hand off the steering wheel and reached out.

''I bet you'd be a great mother to any kid.'' His fingers closed momentarily on her shoulder and squeezed gently before he returned his hand to the steering wheel. ''So, did you get hold of Jason and straighten him out?''

Beneath her heavy coat her flesh tingled where Colt had unexpectedly touched her, sending an ache through her breasts and a warm ribbon of heat down through her body. Surprised by his unexpected and tender touch, Abbie absorbed his craggy profile as he drove. ''Yes. Even though I only taught the eleventh grade, I had a biology club for all kids at the high school. Jason has a great interest in anything to do with nature, so I had a parent conference with Morgan and Laura, and presented my ideas to them.

They were relieved, really. They were at their wits'
end about how to handle Jason. Morgan was so afraid
he was going to blow any chance of getting into the
academy. They knew his problems stemmed from the
kidnapping. He'd gone through therapy—the whole
nine yards—to resolve it, but nothing has helped
him.''

Colt's mouth twisted. ''Men have a nasty habit of
stowing all their dark crap very deep inside themselves and then sitting on it.''

Up ahead he saw the huge cedar complex and
slowed down. There were a number of SUVs, vans
and pickups in the gravel parking lot outside the res-
idence, and he swung the van in among them. Snow
was falling thickly, and the gold-and-russet-colored
log home of the Trayherns looked like a Christmas
card, surrounded as it was by evergreens.

''No kidding.'' Abbie laughed. She melted beneath his intense, warm perusal for a moment after
he parked the van. ''I took him under my wing and
gave him special projects. He blossomed, and he was
able to talk to me about things he wouldn't to his
parents.''

Shutting off the engine, Colt sat back and gazed
over at Abbie. She looked more like a wild child than
a prim and proper schoolteacher. And he could see
why Jason would have naturally gravitated to her;
Abbie's warmth, openness and gentle nurturing qual-
ities would draw anyone starved for those things.

Hell, Colt was drawn to her for the same reasons!
"And he settled down after that?"

"Mostly, yes. Oh, Jason had his moments. I mean,
what teenager doesn't? I gave him an outlet and a
reason to funnel all his energies into something he
loved. By the time he graduated, he was carrying 4.0s
and received the appointment."

Colt measured her with a warm look. "So, they
owe you big time."

Abbie released her seat belt and opened the door.
"If it hadn't been for them, I don't think I'd have
survived, when Ted suddenly died two years ago,
Colt. I was so devastated. They helped me pick up
the pieces of my life and put it back together.
No…the Trayherns, as you well know, love, care for
and support their friends as well as those who work
for them."

She saw Colt's dark, straight brows gather before
she slid out of the van, the snow softly falling around
them. Opening the sliding door, he picked up the first
bulky box of pine bough swags. Colt thought about
the devastation he had seen in Abbie's eyes over her
husband's death.

As he trudged alongside her up the walk, when
they reached the front door, which was decorated
with a huge pine wreath covered in pinecones and
gold lamé ribbon, he halted at her shoulder, looking
down at her as she rang the bell.

"For whatever it's worth, Abbie, I'm sorry you

lost your husband. I can see you had a great relationship. Those are the hardest to lose...."

Tucking her lower lip between her teeth, Abbie felt his warmth encircle her. For all his granitelike hardness, Colt was surprising her with his gentle side. "Thanks... He was my best friend, too...." Rallying, she forced a slight smile she didn't feel as she drowned beneath Colt's hooded, smoldering gaze. "That's behind me now. Laura says I have to get on with my life. I have to start living again. That's why I'm going to go to this Christmas celebration. For two years I haven't. Oh, I've helped Laura with the decorating, but I just didn't have the heart to be there. I didn't feel like smiling or laughing...."

The door opened and Laura stood there in jeans, a red angora sweater with a cowl neck, and dark brown oxfords. Her face lit up with joy. Throwing her arms around Abbie, she looked up at Colt. "Merry Christmas! Welcome, Colt. I'm so glad you could make it. Come on in! We've been expecting you!"

Colt tried to remain immune to the festive, cheery atmosphere within the huge, eight-thousand-square-foot cedar home, but it was impossible. Soon he was on a ladder helping to hang the swags. Another merc by the name of Wolf Harding stood on the other ladder as they fastened and hung the pine garlands around the octagon-shaped living room. Christmas music was playing in the background as everyone helped ready the room for the festive kickoff event of the Five Days of Christmas celebration: dancing and a jazz band.

Colt knew everyone there. Maybe it was the fact that he knew the mercs and their wives that made him feel more at ease. The crew was pitching in to help make the living room into one huge dance floor. The butter-yellow leather furniture was moved near the walls, beneath the large windows. Swags graced the top of each window and dipped gracefully between them, really bringing out the Christmas atmosphere.

Colt had one helluva time keeping his mind on hanging swags. He wanted to watch Abbie; he was starved for her in ways that completely threw him off his guard. The wives—Shah Randolph, Sarah Harding and Susannah Killian—sat with Laura and Abbie in the middle of the room on the gleaming hardwood floor, making last-minute plans for the dance tonight. They looked like colorful, animated birds to Colt. More than once he keyed in on their low, conspiratorial whispers, little-girl giggles and outright raucous laughter as, cross-legged, they huddled in a circle.

When Abbie got up, went to the kitchen and brought back a tray of hot chocolate and freshly made chocolate chip cookies for him and Wolf, his heart melted. He got off the ladder along with Wolf and consumed a half dozen of the warm cookies as well as the thick, chocolaty drink piled high with

whipping cream. Wolf grabbed a couple more cookies and went over to talk to the women.

Abbie held the tray in her hand as she stood next
to Colt and surveyed the men's handiwork. "It looks
beautiful, Colt. You guys did it up right."

An unwilling smile tugged at his mouth as he
sipped the hot chocolate. "Thanks. Maybe we were
inspired by the nice job you did making these swags.
They're works of art."

Smiling up at him, Abbie saw that the hardness
that had been in his expression earlier was dissolv-
ing. The fact that Colt knew the other mercs, Sean
Killian, Jake Randolph and Wolf, probably helped.
There was a tight bond, an obvious camaraderie between Perseus mercs. And that same rapport flowed
to their wives and children, she knew. She was getting a firsthand reminder of it, and it felt fortifying
to her newly healed heart.

Abbie was trying to find any excuse to be in Colt's
company, she realized. That surprised her. Men had
not interested her in the least since Ted died—until
now. And the gleam in Laura's eyes when she had
nudged her in the ribs to comment about how happy
Colt looked for the first time since he'd come off his
mission made Abbie assess that observation.

Somehow, she *was* having a positive effect on
Colt, she decided. He'd arrived so uptight and withdrawn. Now she thought she could see a glimmer of
happiness in his glacial gaze. She wasn't sure *what*
was making him happy. Men often blossomed when

around their own kind, and here in this warm, Christ-massy environment, Colt was with three of his co-horts. Men always felt better in a group, especially when there was a bunch of women around. Yet Colt had given her many furtive looks throughout the last few hours as she sat with the women planning the myriad details. And every time he looked at her, Ab-bie felt his laserlike gaze moving over her like an incredibly warm, wonderful blanket. When Colt looked at her, she felt safe…and loved….

Loved? Abbie jolted inwardly at that realization. No. That was impossible. Automatically, she touched her cheek, which was heating up with a blush at that last spontaneous thought. Yet as Colt finished off his hot chocolate and handed her the white mug painted with colorful red-and-green plaid ribbons, and their fingers touched, Abbie saw his eyes darken like the sky before a coming storm. But it wasn't a scary storm…it was a storm of promise, and her heart flut-tered wildly for a second.

"Thanks for feeding the animals," he teased, one corner of his mouth lifting.

Laughing softly, Abbie took the cup. She wanted to remain in contact with him, but decided it wouldn't be wise. "You are hardly animals."

"I think mercs see themselves as animals," Colt murmured philosophically, resting his hands on his hips, because if he didn't, he was going to reach out and touch Abbie's flyaway red hair. He itched to run his fingers across that coppery-gold mass of curls that framed her gentle face. He saw so much in Abbie's eyes: unsureness, joy, fear.... Fear of what? Him? Trying hard not to pressure her with his interest, Colt wondered what was going on.

When he looked up, he saw Laura Trayhern studying him with a maternal smile on her lips. She nodded, as if in approval, and then turned and walked to the kitchen with the rest of her planning team, a knowing look in her eyes. Knowing what? Colt wondered obliquely.

"Uh..." He cast around for the right words. "Are you going to the dance tonight?" Abbie probably had a boyfriend. How could she not have one? She was such a sunny beacon of light to anyone lost in the darkness. Simply being in her presence lifted his depressed spirit unaccountably, and he felt like a thief stealing her sunlight because he was so destitute of any within himself. His time in Kosovo had stolen his soul and left him feeling hopeless and emotionally eviscerated.

Abbie avoided his piercing gaze. "The dance?" Her skin prickled pleasantly beneath his intense inspection. They stood only inches apart. She found herself wanting to turn and move into his strong, supportive arms. Somehow, Abbie knew Colt would open his arms to her, pull her against him and hold her. Simply hold her. There was such a powerful protective energy around him; she automatically sensed he'd be a wonderful father to his children. And a wonderful husband to her. Egads! Where had *that* thought zinged out of? Suddenly panicked, Abbie didn't understand what was going on with her. She was having such an irrational, emotional reaction to Colt.

"Yes, the dance."

Stepping away, a little breathless, Abbie whispered, "Oh, no…I'm not going…."

"Why? You've probably got every single guy in Philipsburg standing in line to take you."

Touching her blazing cheek, Abbie jerked her gaze from his. "No…" She laughed, embarrassed. "The wallflower of Philipsburg? I'm afraid you're wrong, Colt. No, I don't have anyone…." She grimaced, hating to admit it.

"But you said you were going to attend the celebration this year. Why aren't you going to the dance?" Colt found himself stunned that Abbie had no man in her life. Hope soared through him. He suddenly felt like a lobo wolf on the trail of finding someone who could ease his loneliness. Abbie. Beautiful, carefree, childlike Abbie, whose smile was sunshine pouring into his devastated soul.

Turning, Abbie forced herself to move a few feet away from Colt. He was too accessible and was opening up to her in a way she could barely say no to. "Well, uh, I just…it's the past, Colt. I know it's been two years, and Laura says its time to move on, but I don't know…."

He stood there, hearing her pain and indecision.

"If someone asked you to the dance, would you go?" His heart stood still.

Abbie hung her head, her lower lip tucked between her teeth as she considered his question. Was *he* asking her? No, that was impossible. Did she want to go to the dance with Colt? Oh, yes! At the mere thought, her heart responded wildly. Casting him a confused look, Abbie whispered, "I know how plain I am. I don't have a model's body, my hips are wide and I'm slightly overweight."

In that moment, Colt felt the doors of his heart swing wide-open. She was so gut-wrenchingly honest. Stepping up to her, he settled his hands on her slumping shoulders. "You're not overweight. You're just right, Abbie. You have wide hips to carry a baby easily." He moved his fingers gently on her shoulders. "Babe, you aren't plain. I wish you'd quit thinking that about yourself. Any man would be crazy not to appreciate what you bring to his table." His heart thudded with fear, but Colt forced out the words he thought he'd never say to a woman. "Will you come to the dance with me tonight? Can I pick you up at nine?"

He saw the shock cross her face as she lifted hers to meet his eyes. "You...you want to take *me?*"

In that moment, Colt wanted to strangle whoever had ingrained in Abbie the belief that she was plain and overweight. Could it have been her husband? The kids at her school? Her parents? He didn't know, but he wanted to convince her otherwise. Giving her his best, charming smile, he rasped, "Yes, I want to take you to the dance tonight. I'll pick you up at nine. No arguments."

The soft jazz music wafted across the crowded dance floor. Abbie sighed and moved slowly, deliciously, in Colt's arms. There were at least seventy-five people in attendance. The children were laughing and dancing with one another, and with various adults. The Trayhern home rang with happiness. The odors of baked cookies, cinnamon rolls and hot chocolate added to the festive atmosphere. Many people were dressed in red, green, gold or silver, and in Abbie's eyes, they looked like bright Christmas ornaments moving around the dance floor.

She felt Colt's arms tighten momentarily on her waist as he swung her around. How handsome he looked in a white cashmere sweater, burnt-sienna corduroy jacket and black wool slacks. She saw where he'd nicked himself shaving, a small cut along his rock-hard jaw. There was such a merry glint in his normally frosty eyes that she found herself drowning in them like a dry sponge in search of water. How long had it been since a man looked at her like that? Wanted her like that? *Too long,* a little voice whispered inside her heart. Sliding her fingertips along the shoulder of his jacket, she smiled up at him.

"I'm glad you asked me, Colt."

He preened. "Yeah?"

"Yes. Thank you..."

"You look beautiful in that emerald velvet dress you're wearing." And she did. In her hair was an orchid affixed with a bright, apple-green ribbon. The orchid, she had told him earlier, was a cattleya, one of her favorite species. It was a white blossom with a bright green lip and scarlet polka dots along the inside. She had gathered up her curly copper tresses and tamed them into a soft arrangement away from her face. The tiny gold-and-pearl earrings she wore, along with a similar pendant, set off her natural beauty.

"That orchid really makes you look like a wild child," he teased. The music was low and soft. Colt was having one helluva time keeping Abbie at arms length as they danced. He saw many of the mercs and their wives dancing, their bodies melded together. He wanted to meld his to Abbie's, but knew it wouldn't be right.

"Thanks..." Abbie whispered. The look Colt gave her was warm and filled with pride. "Tonight I really feel beautiful. Sort of like Cinderella." And she did.

Colt's smile was deep as he met and held her uplifted gaze. "You know how I see you? Like a red-haired fairy princess—maybe an Irish sprite—dancing from one orchid to another. That's quite a nice little greenhouse you have out back of your cabin. I don't know much about orchids, but walking in there tonight and seeing their beauty...well, I can understand why you love to raise them."

Sighing, she turned and eased a little closer to Colt. How badly Abbie wanted to lean her full weight against him and simply relinquish herself to his strong, caring arms. Colt's tenderness was surprising. She gloried in it. "There's one orchid I particularly love, but it's so expensive I'll never be able to afford it—ever—on my teacher's salary."

"Oh?" He saw her eyes light up with sudden enthusiasm. When she moved slightly closer to him, he picked up on her nonverbal signal and drew her more deeply into his arms. The emerald dress she wore was provocative and yet simple in its elegance. It had a scooped neckline, and from the empire waist, which outlined her small breasts, the skirt flared gracefully down to her ankles. The velvet material felt good beneath his hands. How badly he wanted to explore her more.

"You saw the framed print of the orchid in my living room earlier tonight? The one hanging on the wall behind my couch?"

Colt nodded. "Yeah, the white one with the hot pink and gold markings? I think you called it *Cattleya rex?*"

"That one. Yes." Abbie sighed languorously. "They call that orchid the 'treasure of the Incas.' It's found only in Peru, high up in the jungle near Machu Picchu, an archeological site that has wonderful Incan ruins. I would give my right arm to have one!" She laughed. "You saw how beautiful they are—the white petals of the orchid so huge and then that gorgeous central lip spilling out with those fuschia and gold colors. It reminds me of a Christmas tree, it's so breathtaking!''

Spinning her around, Colt absorbed her joy and excitement. The look in her eyes was something to behold, and it made his heart skitter—with happiness. As the music died away, he stopped and opened his arms reluctantly to allow Abbie to step back. To his surprise, she didn't move very far from him, or let go of his hand.

Morgan and Laura Trayhern walked up to the band podium. As Colt and Abbie turned expectantly, a hush came over the room. Colt saw young Jason Trayhern, dressed in his spit-and-polish, dark blue naval uniform with shiny brass buttons, following his parents rather reluctantly. Colt looked down at Abbie, whose attention was centered on the Trayherns.

"Jason is looking a little stiff and starchy."

"He *hates* being the center of attention. Really, he's very shy underneath it all." Abbie clasped her hands to her breast. "But doesn't he look handsome in his uniform! He's in his second year at the academy. I'm so glad he could get leave and come home! Look how proud Morgan and Laura appear...."

Colt followed his instincts. All around him, couples stood expectantly on the dance floor, their arms wrapped lovingly around one another. Well, he wanted to do the same thing. Mustering the last of his courage and hoping Abbie wouldn't step away from him, he slowly lifted his arm and placed it tentatively around her shoulders.

Instantly, her head jerked up. Her eyes flared as she stared up at him.

Fear shot through him. Colt almost pulled his arm away in that moment of panic as Abbie's guileless expression turned to one of shock. And then something crazy happened, something Colt never expected. Her eyes grew soft and he saw tears in them for just a moment, before she blinked them back. He thought she would step away, but instead she gave him a tremulous smile of uncertainty and took a step *toward* him. Her velvet-covered body met his as she slipped beneath his arm.

Colt couldn't believe his good luck. He had to be dreaming! As Abbie shyly slid her arm around his waist, his heart pounded. The courage it took her was enormous, he realized, as he drowned in her lambent gaze. Tightening his arm around her small shoulders, he smiled down at her. More than anything he wanted to kiss her parted lips.

Colt had to temper his desires. In a corner of his mind, he realized that this was the first time Abbie had had a "date" with a man since her husband's death. She was unsure. Maybe a little frightened. He couldn't blame her, and he wanted to do everything he could to make her feel comfortable. Another thought bolted through his spinning senses: Abbie liked him, or she would not have moved against him or slipped her slender arm around him.

Dizzied by what had just happened, Colt tried to listen as the Trayherns welcomed everyone to the party, then proudly introduced their son. Everyone clapped as Jason moved to the microphone to speak. Colt suspected the young man was uncomfortable, but he assumed a stiff military bearing, thanked them in a confident voice and was even able to smile slightly at his proud parents, who stood off to one side, their faces glowing with pleasure. And then Morgan turned and asked the jazz band to strike up another tune. Colt saw Jason quickly flee the podium, relief on his handsome, square face. How much Jason looked like Morgan! Colt thought. He was a younger version, almost a carbon copy, of his heroic father.

Turning, Colt smiled down at Abbie, who had a wistful look in her eyes. "Ready for another dance or am I tiring you out?"

Laughing, she said, "No, I *love* to dance! I haven't done it in so long." And she melted into his arms. How wonderful it was to slide up against Colt's hard form. With a sigh, she felt his arms go around her, intimate and claiming. This time, her breasts and hips grazed his solid form. "I'll probably be so sore and tired that when tomorrow's skiing venture takes place, I'll be glad to be manning the food shack and not moving around much."

Chuckling, Colt eased back a little to catch her gaze. "Do you need me to help you?" He suddenly found himself not wanting to be alone anymore.

Basking in Abbie's sunlit warmth was somehow healing him.

"Sure, I'd love to have some help. Day two of our celebration includes skiing from noon until five. All the families gather at Brandy Hill, a great little slope just outside of town. All it has are rope tows to the top—nothing fancy. I always man the food booth for them."

"Do you ski?"

Wrinkling her nose, Abbie laughed. "Me? Barely. I fall more than I stand on my feet. How about you?" She was deliriously happy with the fact that Colt wanted to be with her tomorrow. Her heart did somersaults and she could scarcely believe all this was happening.

"Skiing isn't one of my strong points," Colt admitted in a droll tone. "If it's okay with you, I'll help you in the food shack. Keep you company."

She met and held his smoldering look, which sent heat flowing through her. His arms tightened around her briefly. "It's more than okay with me...."

Abbie could barely wait for tomorrow. The magic of Christmas had unexpectedly given her a beautiful gift to her...Colt Hamlin.

Chapter 3

December 22—Day 2

The delighted screeches and shouts of the Perseus children filled the winter air as they ran through the twirling snowflakes toward the rope tow located at the base of Brandy Hill. Colt couldn't help but give Abbie a lopsided grin as they trundled boxes over to the small wooden structure that doubled as a make-shift buffet to feed the hungry families. It was noon, and everyone was starved.

Colt had driven over to Abbie's earlier to load the aluminum urns filled with coffee and hot, cinnamon-laced apple cider. They'd picked up sandwiches and bags of potato chips from the Trayherns as the hungry, excited crew boarded the bus leased for the occasion.

Last night, Colt had mustered up the courage to give Abbie a chaste, swift kiss on her flushed cheek at the door to her cabin after he'd brought her back from the dance. He'd wanted to do more…*much more*, but he didn't want to rush things with Abbie, either. The fact that her eyes grew lustrous after his impromptu kiss had made him feel like he was ten feet tall and walking on air.

Abbie opened the door to the shack. It creaked and groaned in protest. The building was constructed of Douglas fir, the wood grayed with age and from the harsh winters they had in this region of the Rockies. The weather was perfect for the afternoon ski party: the temperature was in the low thirties, and just a bit of snow was falling from a sky that was mostly gray with some spots of blue peeking out. It was a weekday, so the Perseus employees had the normally busy place all to themselves.

Setting the first cardboard box on a table inside the shack, Abbie smiled over at Colt as he brought in a heavier box. How handsome he was! The warmth banked in his eyes thrilled her. He gave her a bashful look, that strong mouth of his hitched in a slight smile for her alone.

Jason Trayhern, now in civilian clothes, jeans, hiking boots, a bright red sweater and a dark blue navy jacket, brought in another box.

"Hey, thanks," Abbie called to the young man.

She saw the dark smudges beneath Jason's eyes. At nineteen, he stood six foot three inches tall, with his father's broad shoulders, wide chest and narrow hips. He was almost a carbon copy of Morgan with a square face, wide-set gray eyes and military short black hair. Abbie could see Laura's influence, however, in Jason's mouth; it wasn't as hard looking as Morgan's. Jason had Laura's sensitivity, too—a sensitivity that had caused him much angst over the years, Abbie suspected.

"You're welcome, Ms. Clemens." Jason stepped aside and helped Colt maneuver the largest, heaviest box onto the table—the one that contained sandwiches for the hungry crew hanging around outside the shack. Jason grinned a little. "I'll go get the apple cider dispenser for you now, ma'am."

"Great. Thanks, Jason. I wouldn't know what to do without your help." Abbie glanced at Colt, who worked at her side to unpack the boxes. She absorbed his nearness. He was dressed in a bomber jacket that had seen better days, an apple-green sweater, jeans that outlined his heavily muscled thighs to perfection, and hiking boots. A white silk scarf set off his outfit.

She smiled up at him as he met and held her glance. "I'm so glad you're helping me, too." Abbie glanced out the counter window, where at least twenty children of varying ages were laughing, playing and running around. The adults were helping them get their skis on so they could use the rope tow, now in operation. "This is a hungry crew we have to feed."

Nodding, Colt smiled at her and continued opening boxes. In the process, his hand accidentally brushed hers. Abbie had taken off her leather gloves to unpack and get everything set up, and so had he. Her flesh was warm. Inviting. How badly he wanted to continue touching her. "Yeah, those little rug rats out there definitely have a starved look on their faces. A bunch of hungry lookin' buzzards, if you ask me."

"Rug rats," Abbie sniffed. "What an awful name to call children."

"A loving military term," Colt assured her in a deep voice. He saw Jason coming with the huge aluminum urn containing the apple cider, and moved to the side door to swing it wide.

"Thanks, Mr. Hamlin," Jason huffed as he struggled with the huge urn.

Colt helped him place it on the counter where people could easily put a paper cup beneath the spigot to pour out a drink of the warm, fragrant cider.

"I'll fetch the hot chocolate now," Jason said, and left quickly.

"That boy is tense," Colt said quietly as he came back to the table to help Abbie spread wrapped sandwiches onto a large platter.

Abbie sighed. "I know. Poor Jase! I feel so sorry for him. He's trying so hard to do what his parents expect of him. See the circles under his eyes? I was talking to Laura earlier this morning, and she told me that Jason and Morgan had a big fight.''

"The kid looks like death warmed over," Colt noted. "It musta been one hell—heck—of a fight." He took the first tray of sandwiches and placed them on the counter. Instantly, ten children rushed forward, their little hands eagerly grasping for the food.

"I guess his grades at the academy aren't good," Abbie murmured, low enough that no one could eavesdrop on their conversation. The last thing she wanted was to embarrass Jason; the youth had enough trouble right now. "He's doing the same thing he did in high school before I got hold of him—goofing off, partying, not being responsible. Another form of rebellion."

"Ouch. Not the place to flunk out of," Colt muttered. He gave her a wink. "Maybe what he needs is another Abbie Clemens at the academy to rescue him and set him straight, like you did here."

Giving Colt a wistful look, Abbie said softly, "My heart just bleeds for Jase. He's a complicated child— I mean, young man.... It's funny, I still think of him as a kid and I shouldn't. He's growing up so fast. They always do in their teenage years." She laughed softly.

The kid had probably not slept much after the argument, Colt guessed, because he had bloodshot eyes, too. Life was hard, Colt knew. And life was gigging Jason right now. Did he have what it took to pull himself up by his own bootstraps? Only Jason

could answer that. Colt took a second tray of sandwiches and set them on the counter to replace the
emptied one. Adults were ambling over now that the
kids had their lunches in hand. The shack was being
mobbed by hungry people, and Colt smiled a little
as he watched the food disappear quickly from that
tray, as well. Turning, he saw Abbie handing him a
third tray piled high with sandwiches.

For the next half hour, they fed the hungry Perseus
group. Jason excused himself and went out on the
slope with his sister, Katy, who was now seventeen
and a beautiful young woman, in Colt's eyes. She
was the spitting image of Laura, except she had her
father's height and stood nearly six feet tall, was me-
dium boned and a super athlete. The twins, Peter and
Kelly, now twelve years old, were holding on to the
rope tow, their skis on, with their older siblings in
front and behind them.

Colt was happy when he and Abbie were finally
left alone. Everyone had gobbled up their lunch and
flown off to the beckoning slopes. The shouts and
laughter of the children was contagious. He saw a
lot of the mercs becoming big kids themselves. Taking one of the rough-hewn stools, Colt brought it
over to where Abbie had just sat down at the table.
Neither of them had eaten yet, and he opened his
turkey sandwich. Cups of steaming apple cider sat
on the table before them.

"Are you going to ski pretty soon?" Colt asked.
He watched her eyes widen—beautiful eyes he could

fall into and lose his soul within. Colt knew that with Abbie, he was safe in a way he'd never experienced before with a woman. Her human touch, her ability to work well with both children and adults, was blatantly apparent. But he was a glutton; he wanted her all to himself.

Colt laughed harshly at himself. He couldn't believe all he was feeling—him, the loner. The guy who had planned to camp out in the condo for the holidays, drink himself into a stupor daily to numb the pain he felt. Somehow, Abbie's sunny smile, her dancing eyes and that heart that was a wide as the blue skies of Montana made him want to be with her, and with people. She was magical. And he wanted her—in all ways. Did she want him, however? Colt realized as never before that the loss of her husband had damaged her emotionally. She was just emerging from a long, dark tunnel of grief. Was she ready for a relationship?

What the hell could *he* bring to her? Give to her? A snarly, irritable, PTSD warrior who found it hard to stay in the mainstream of life and society—what a helluva prize catch he would make....

Picking up her cup of apple cider, Abbie sipped it, then smiled as she set it down on the peeled paint of the tabletop. "Me? Ski? Oh, gosh, Colt, I'm all thumbs and left feet! No, I just serve the food, I don't ski. I'd probably break my neck—or my leg—if I tried." She saw a smile lurking at the corners of his well-shaped mouth. Her heart pounded briefly as Colt gave her an intimate, smoldering look. She'd seen that same look last night as they'd stood on the front porch of her cabin just before he'd kissed her. Oh, it was a small kiss, Abbie chided herself. But it did big-time things to her, making her heart thud in her breast, her pulse leap wildly and a warm, throbbing heat settle deliciously in her lower body. She felt herself coming alive as a woman. Colt's one hesitant kiss last night, his lips caressing her cheek, had made her feel as if she were the mythical Persephone leaving the darkness of Hades and emerging back on the surface of the earth, to appreciate all its colors, textures and grandeur once again. Studying him through her lashes, Abbie wondered if he realized that his look was making her heart and body come alive. Did he? Probably not.

His grin widened. "I'm a so-so skier. But let me take you up later. I'll help you stay upright as we go down the hill, okay?" Colt chastised himself silently. If she skied that badly, he could keep his arms around her, hold her and remain close without anyone thinking anything of it. What a sneaky bastard he was. He didn't have the guts to just tell her how he felt about her. Colt was too frightened that Abbie would get scared and, like the clouds moving across the hill right now, snuffing out the sunlight, would run from him.

Easing off the stool, Abbie shrugged. "I'm a kid at heart. Sure, I'll try it." Her pulse throbbed momentarily as she saw his eyes grow hooded and that smoldering look grow more intense. A thrill moved through her. Abbie found herself feeling joyous in a way she'd never been before. As she puttered about, placing sandwiches wrappers into a plastic trash bag, she tried to sort out the myriad feelings Colt was effortlessly evoking within her. One chaste kiss! Just one, and Abbie felt like a teenager head-over-heels in love!

"You mentioned that your parents are in Florida?" she asked him.

Colt finished off the sandwich and picked up his apple cider. Just watching Abbie move around the shack and tidy it up sent a frisson of longing through him. She was so graceful. He wanted her hands ranging up his body with that same grace. Tearing his mind from that thought, he frowned and answered her question. "Dad's in a nursing home now. My mother died three years ago."

"Oh, I'm sorry." Abbie hesitated, then put the bag in the garbage can next to the table. There wasn't much room in the shack and she absorbed Colt's continued nearness. His brow was furrowed. "Were you going to go and visit your dad over the holidays?"

"No. He has Alzheimer's pretty bad. He doesn't recognize me anymore. He doesn't know where he's at mentally...." Colt's mouth flattened. "Usually I'm on a mission this time of year, but I fly in to see him at other times. He has to have twenty-four-hour nursing care."

Abbie sat down. "I'm so sorry...that must be so

hard, Colt, to not have him recognize you, his son.'' She saw the damage it had done to him; it was clearly written in his features, even though he tried to avoid her gaze. She saw Colt try to shrug it off, but the anguish remained banked in his averted eyes.

Taking a huge risk, Abbie followed her intuition and said softly, ''I understand that you've had some pretty awful missions over in the Kosovo-Bosnia region. I'm sure between your dad's deteriorating condition and the stresses on you over there, you must be exhausted.'' Tired all the way to his soul, Abbie guessed. She held her breath, knowing she had to tread lightly because of the PTSD symptoms he'd accrued after those missions. Abbie didn't know why she was broaching the topic with Colt. It was a subject most men would refuse to speak about, especially with a woman.

Just the tender way Abbie gazed at him made the wall around his heart crack open. He actually felt physical pain and rubbed his chest where his heart lay beneath the sweater he wore. Staring down at the cup of apple cider he held, Colt rasped, ''I thought I knew what hell on earth was, Abbie...but I didn't, not until these past three missions....''

She sat quietly and waited. Why was it so hard for a man to talk out his feelings? Colt's hard face was ravaged with emotions that were eating him alive. Abbie saw the way he worked his mouth into a brutal line to stop the avalanche she sensed behind it. As he moved the cup slowly around and around in his large, scarred hands, she felt her heart breaking for him. More than anything, Abbie wanted to slide her arms around his slumped shoulders and just hold him. That was what he needed right now: to be held. And she wanted to be the woman who did it.

The silence between them was strained and tenuous. Abbie knew from experience that if she sat quietly and let the pressure mount, then more than likely Colt would begin to talk. When he lifted his head, she saw dampness in his eyes. It tore at her.

"Three missions," Colt said gruffly. "Three horrible missions with no positive outcome. I'll tell you something, Abbie, that part of the world is a hellhole. There are no happy endings over there for either side. Not ever." He shook his head and took a quick gulp of the apple cider. Avoiding her look, he growled, "When I got off this last one...well, I was reeling from it. My partner, Carol, quit. She couldn't take it anymore. I don't blame her. It's rough over there...."

Abbie knew that mercs at Perseus worked in man-woman teams. And she knew from talking with Laura that Carol had been Colt's partner for a good five years. Abbie understood the camaraderie, the trust and teamwork that developed under dangerous mission conditions, and she was sure he was devastated by losing Carol, too. "And so you were going to hole up here and try to heal?" she murmured gently. When Colt lifted his head again, the dampness in his eyes was gone. He'd shoved all those raw feelings very deep within himself. His hands, however, gripped the paper cup hard.

He snorted. "I wasn't doing a very good job of it. Me and Jack Daniels…"

She flinched inwardly. He had been slugging down whiskey to numb what he was feeling. Getting up, Abbie followed her heart. She moved quietly and sat beside Colt, placing her fingers around his larger ones as they gripped the cup. She heard him take in a swift breath of air. His head snapped up. Heart pounding, Abbie sat quietly and looked at him, her hands wrapped around his.

"I understand a little of what you're feeling, Colt. When Ted died, I felt like someone had thrown me into a dark hole of hell that I didn't feel I could ever survive." Her mouth pulled upward slightly at the corners, and her voice was tremulous with feeling. "What helped me get through it were people who loved me—my friends…my family from North Dakota. The people I worked with at the high school were supportive, too. Laura Trayhern, bless her, became my strength. She, more than anyone, understood what I was going through, because of her own traumas, losing Morgan to the drug lords…."

Abbie's warmth and tenderness sent a hot sheet of longing through Colt. Easing his hands from hers, he placed the paper cup on the table and then picked up her hands again and held them. Drowning in her blue eyes, which were sparkling with unshed tears, he felt his heart rip wide-open from his brutally suppressed feelings. Abbie was so small and slender next to his bulk and masculine strength, yet he sensed with every fiber of his being that she was the stronger one here, not him. He felt as if a huge fist was jamming into his chest, causing very real pain, and he wanted to scream out in anguish.

Abbie watched as his mouth turned hard, his lips thinned. He avoided her eyes and stared down at their hands. She felt him quiver. Colt was wrestling to fight back the overwhelming emotions he'd stuffed away during those missions.

All her life, Abbie had been led by her heart, her passion, and the voice of intuition within her. That voice whispered to her to kiss him...now....

Lifting her hands from his, she slid her fingertips up the rocky ridge of Colt's jaw and framed his face. Her gesture snapped him out of his suspended state. He lifted his head. His gaze narrowed intently on her, his black pupils dilating. She saw the tears banked in his eyes, and moved closer, till her body grazed his. Closing her eyes, Abbie felt her heart beating like a wild bird suddenly caged. Was she doing the right thing? Would Colt take her efforts the right way? Did he know she wanted to cry for him? To hold him? Lost as she was in the hungry need to make physical contact with him, Abbie knew, somewhere in her spinning mind, that it was right thing, even if she was scared to death.

"Colt...let me help...." she whispered. The line of his mouth softened as she grazed his lips with her own. He groaned, and the sound reverberated through her like the roll of a drum. Feeling bolder, she pressed closer and felt some of his tension dissolve beneath her tender ministrations. Repeatedly, she feathered her mouth across his, begging access, asking silently for him to give her the overwhelming pain he was barely holding at bay.

Then his arms came around her and captured her hard against him. The air rushed out of her lungs as he stood up, dragging her with him, her breasts and hips melding hotly against his own. His mouth opened and his lips crushed hers in a ravenous kiss. Fire erupted through Abbie as his arms wound around her back and he rocked her into his embrace. Automatically, her hands opened, and she found them sliding up around his thick shoulders and neck.

Colt smelled of evergreens and his own unique scent, making her respond to his questing mouth with equal ardor. Running her fingers through his short hair, Abbie moaned a little as his hand ranged down from her shoulder, across her rib cage toward her aching, taut breast. Oh, how she wanted this man! Her heart spun with joy. Her pulse throbbed and her lower body melted against his narrow hips, on fire. She felt his desire for her, and more flames sizzled through her, making her knees go weak with need. Need for Colt.

His mouth was bruising and hungry against hers. Abbie felt him tremble savagely as she allowed him open access, his tongue laving her lower lip. As she pulled him tightly against her, his mouth commanding and needy, Abbie relaxed completely within his powerful embrace. She knew that her surrendering to him had triggered something else within him. Abbie felt it, lost as she was in a swirl of joy, hunger and need. She wanted to take his pain, transmute it in order to release it. Love had a way of doing that—of healing even the worst hemorrhaging wound within a person's heart and soul.

Willingly she offered herself—all of herself—to Colt in this magical moment outside of time. His skin was sandpapery against her softer flesh, his punctuated breath warm and moist against her face. She moved her lips against his mouth, and in that instant became aware of the taste of salt clinging to the corners. For a moment she was confused, and then she realized it was from Colt's tears. Tears of pain. Tears of agony. Tears he'd suffered and carried silently for so long by himself.

The salty tears met and mingled beneath their wet, searching mouths. She shifted her hands to his face, framing it as her tongue moved deep within him. Again he trembled, like a bull being shaken by an earthquake. Abbie held him with her womanly strength, guided by her heart, which told her this was healing him, helping him, and helping her, too. Never in all her life had she shared such a kiss with a man. Not ever. Euphoria enveloped her as she felt the last of Colt's tears ease. Drowsily opening her eyes, she burned beneath his stormy green gaze as he voraciously absorbed her into himself. She was small compared to his power and size. Yet as she caressed his cheek and smiled tremulously up at him, the taste of his tears still on her lips, she understood the healing power of one person's love and what it could do to unlock another's armored heart and soul.

Colt stood there, his senses screamingly alive, his lower body aching with a knot of fire and need. Gently, he eased his grip from around Abbie and set her carefully on her feet. He didn't want to let her go—not yet. *Not ever,* his heart whispered. There was such a thunderstorm of emotions raging through him right now that he found it impossible to find words to tell her. Hell, he couldn't even begin to define them himself. Part was rage and frustration over the missions. Another was grief over the people he'd seen die. And just as insistent were the new emotions exploding in his pounding heart—emotions about Abbie. Sweet, soft, strong Abbie. As he gazed wordlessly down into her lustrous eyes, Colt threaded his fingers through the silky, coppery hair that framed her blushing features.

"You're so sweet, Abbie. You're like a dream I've always had, but was afraid to believe in...."

Chapter 4

December 23—Day 3

Colt had cried—the first tears he'd ever shed over his life-altering missions. In fact, he never cried. The last time he recalled even getting close to it was when his ex-wife had walked out on him. Even more disturbing to him, he realized as he slowly got dressed the next morning, was the fact that he'd cried in Abbie's arms. It had been unexpected, the last thing on his mind.

He wondered now if she thought he was a wimp. Frowning, he shrugged into his bright red flannel shirt and tucked the tails into his jeans. Outside the picture window of the condo, the sky was a bright blue, the sun sparkling off the tops of the snow-covered evergreens that surrounded the small valley. The storm had passed.

"Yeah...right," he muttered, picking up his white silk scarf and, out of habit, throwing it around his neck. He'd worn the scarf while flying as a helicopter pilot, as the silk protected his neck from chafing as he rubbernecked around, while looking for the bad guys.

He was meeting Abbie at 9:00 a.m. to help her move her beautiful cattleya orchids, which were all in bloom in her greenhouse, to Laura and Morgan's home for the upcoming family dinner planned for the third day of Christmas.

Halting in the middle of the room, his leather bomber jacket in hand, he scowled, and his gut clenched. He was feeling such pain, such uncertainty, that he really didn't want to face Abbie, Colt realized. He was afraid. There, he'd admitted it. Afraid of what she might think of him crying during their heated, beautiful, healing kiss there in the shack yesterday. What must she think of him? Did she see him as weak? Probably.

Undecided, Colt slowly shrugged into his bomber jacket and straightened the collar. He'd never cried in front of a woman. Ever. But he had with her. What the hell was going down here? Rubbing his recently shaved jaw, Colt scowled darkly out the window. The world was beautiful here in the middle of winter. He didn't feel beautiful inside. Not at all.

Ruthlessly examining himself, which was not something Colt did often, he realized he had to get a grip on his escaping feelings when he was around Abbie. He didn't want to become a blubbering wuss in front of her again. Cringing over that possibility, Colt sensed that was why he was so damned scared and unsure this morning: Abbie just sort of unconsciously catalyzed his feelings—good and bad. He'd never met a woman who could do that. It was like magic, only it was dark magic and he had no interest in having his own private hell of a Pandora's box spontaneously opened without his permission or knowledge. Hell, he'd been kissing her, and enjoying it like an eagle on wing flying directly into the sun's warmth. Then, out of nowhere, Colt had felt warmth leaking out of the corners of his closed eyes and drifting down his cheeks to where their mouths clung wetly to one another.

At first, he'd been shocked by the taste of salt between their lips. And when he realized what it was, and where it was coming from, he'd torn his mouth from Abbie's and taken a step away from her, as if he'd been burned.

He couldn't bear remembering the hurt look on her face as she'd stood there, her lips wet and parted, her eyes huge with desire and, at the same time, shock over his unexpected action. What else was he to do? Cry some more? Weep his heart out in her slender but strong arms? What if someone had come up to the shack at that time and seen him crying? What would they think? Colt knew something like that would be bound to travel very fast in the tight circle of Perseus families. It was a closed community, and everyone knew everyone else's business. He didn't need it getting back to Morgan that he'd been crying like a hurt little boy in Abbie's arms. If anyone had come up and seen them kissing...well, that was acceptable to Colt. But not being discovered crying.

"Damn," he growled, his voice echoing around the living room as he dropped his hand from his chin. What was he going to do? The fact that he had been so vulnerable in front of her was making him feel like hell. And the fact that he'd abruptly turned on his heel and left Abbie alone in that shack, tore him up even more. He'd walked away. He'd run. Like a coward. He had hitched a ride home with another family and hadn't spoken to Abbie since.

"You're a damned coward," Colt muttered. He'd left her in the lurch; left her to move all the stuff back to her van to transport to Morgan's home. Worse, after that life-giving kiss had seared his broken soul, he'd left her without explanation. She probably thought she'd done something wrong. But he was the one who had.

As he lifted his chin and glared out at the sunny morning, Colt knew he had to go over to Abbie's and talk to her. And if she was pissed off at him and his antics, so be it. He wouldn't blame her for her righteous anger over his immature, knee-jerk actions. The least he owed her was an explanation. And in his anguished heart, Colt hoped Abbie would not only understand, but would allow him back into her life. He was frightened by how easily she touched his emotions and freed them. Colt wanted her in every way, but he didn't want to pay the entry fee.

So where did that leave them? Leave Abbie? She didn't deserve this adolescent behavior of his. No, what he was proposing to do was steal the honey from the hive, but not feed the bees who made it. He was like an interloping bear, all he wanted to do was eat dessert and walk away, sated. Glowering as he moved slowly toward the door, keys to his car in hand, Colt didn't like himself at all. Abbie didn't deserve to be hurt like this. And yet he'd done a spectacular job of it. What would she think when she saw him on her porch? Scream? Curse at him? Tell him to get the hell out of her life? Worse? As Colt shut and locked the condo door, he had no hope that Abbie would allow him back in her life.

Abbie gulped as she opened the door. Colt stood there, hands shoved deeply into the pockets of his bomber jacket. He looked like hell warmed over— his skin pasty, dark shadows beneath his narrowed, bloodshot eyes, and his mouth twisted in a line of pain that sent a shaft of hurt through her heart.

"Come in," she invited softly, stepping aside. On her table were ten carefully wrapped pots of orchids, which she was about to carry out to her car and transport over to Laura's place for the dinner party tonight.

Abbie's heart beat hard in her chest as he gave her an anxious look. Then, with hesitation, Colt moved woodenly through the door. She shut it and looked up at him. The tension swirled between them.

"I guess..." Colt began awkwardly, his voice sounding like sandpaper, "I shouldn't have invited myself over here this morning, Abbie." Shrugging his drooping shoulders, he saw her eyes grow warm with compassion—for him. He couldn't help but absorb her beauty in that moment. She was wearing a plum-colored angora shell with a white cotton blouse beneath it. Her hair was wild and free around her face and shoulders. A pang of longing shot through Colt. How badly he wanted to sift those red-gold strands through his fingers as he had yesterday afternoon. Her hair was so soft, and yet so strong and resilient...like her.

Wrapping her arms against her breasts, she clung to his every word. Feeling horribly vulnerable, she managed to answer in a strained tone, "I'm glad you did, Colt. I don't know what happened yesterday between us. You just left..."

Smarting despite her gentleness toward him, he pulled his hands out of his jacket pockets. "I, uh...damn, this is hard, Abbie." Opening his hands toward her, he muttered, "I'm sorry. It was me yesterday, not you. You did nothing wrong."

"I see...." Abbie's senses took over. She saw

such vulnerability in Colt's face right now. His eyes were wide and pleading, his hands open in supplication. He was hurting so much even now that Abbie could almost taste his salty tears from yesterday. Her first instinct was to open her arms, step forward, throw them around Colt's neck and hold him. Hold him, rock him and let him know that he could find safe harbor with another human being.

The silence strung tautly between them.

"If I'm overstepping my bounds with you, Colt, let me know," Abbie whispered. She unlocked her arms and let them fall to her sides. Colt dropped his hands, too. They stood three feet apart, yet it seemed like the Grand Canyon stretched between them. "I feel you're more embarrassed over crying yesterday than anything else. Is that right?" Abbie searched his furtive gaze. At first Colt wouldn't look at her. He stared down at his boots for a long time, his mouth working. Finally, he lifted his head and tentatively met her eyes.

"I...well, I was...but it was more than that, Abbie." Colt nervously cleared his throat. "Well...men just don't cry. At least, I don't. And I enjoyed the hell out of our kiss." He closed his eyes momentarily and then reopened them, looking up at the rafters, which were hung with swags of fresh pine and red ribbons. "I didn't see it coming. One moment I was kissing you and enjoying every second of it. The next thing I realized, this stuff was running down my face."

Gently, Abbie said, "Do you know what the tears were about?" She thought she knew, but wasn't going to say. Colt had to give voice to his trauma, not her.

Struggling mightily, Colt looked around. His mouth became a slash. Damn, it was happening again! He could feel that fist of pressure tightening around his heart, and he could feel the heated prick of tears at the back of his eyes. Just Abbie's voice was triggering all of this. Colt fought his feelings savagely. It seemed like he stood there an hour instead of just a minute grappling with the knot of emotions and tears that so badly wanted to vomit out of him. Finally, he got a handle on himself. Giving her a narrowed look, he rasped, "Yeah...it's about those missions over in Kosovo."

Abbie nodded, feeling as if she were walking on fragile eggs with Colt. He looked unhappy, his eyes burning with unexpressed emotions. How many times had Abbie seen this in Ted's eyes when he would come home after a traumatic mission? This was no different. Taking a huge risk, she walked up to Colt and placed her hand tentatively on his, which was balled into a tense fist at his side.

"Sometimes I hate our society, Colt. I see the damage it has done to men and women. Little boys are taught that it's not okay to cry, to show their feelings or talk about them. And so you go through life believing that if you do have feelings or tears, everyone will think you're weak and unmanly." She grimaced. "What a crock. If God hadn't given you tear ducts and a heart to feel with, that would be one thing. But he did."

She squeezed his hand. "I wasn't surprised at your tears, Colt. I can feel such pain and suffering around you. I figured it probably had to do with those missions you were on. All I could hope for was that you might trust me enough to let all that darkness spill out of you, let me be a shoulder to cry on…a set of ears to listen without judgment to what you went through and survived. That was all I wanted." Abbie gave him a slight smile and drowned in his stormy looking eyes. "I don't know about you, but when I cry, it feels so good to get it out of my system. I feel much better afterward. And there're so many things we should cry over. I felt honored that you'd share your tears with me, Colt. That kiss…those moments were very special to me. And I hoped they were to you, too…."

Had she said too much? Abbie cringed inwardly, then watched Colt's face in awe. Her words seemed to have had a profound physical effect on him. His brow, once scrunched, was easing. His eyes were losing that hurt and hardness. Most of all, his mouth was losing that tight look of silent, anguished suffering. She felt his fist relax and he enclosed her hand within his.

"I'm scared, Abbie." There. It was out. Colt braced himself. He saw her eyes flare with surprise and then…understanding. Her lips parted and she whispered his name like a prayer.

"Oh, Colt…you don't ever have to be afraid of me…."

Heartened, he rasped, "I figured you'd be royally pissed off at me, running out of there like the coward I was."

Shaking her head, Abbie forced back the tears that wanted to rush into her eyes. "I knew something had happened, Colt. I didn't know *what.* But I knew it wasn't me, either. It was something deep within you…and it had caught you off guard, judging by the look on your face." Taking a huge risk, Abbie leaned upward on tiptoe and placed a warm kiss on his cheek, then eased away from him. She saw pleasure replace his pain for a moment at her bold action. Her heart soared with elation.

"Colt, you were scared. And running from your fear. Well…" Abbie looked fondly around the warm kitchen, where sunlight poured through the Victorian lace curtains over the window above the sink. "I've been running for nearly two years, ever since Ted died. When I realized what I was doing, and that it wasn't healthy for me long-term, I stopped it. I faced the music. I faced the fact he was dead and not ever coming back." She touched her chest, above her heart. "The miracle was that when I did that, I started to heal, Colt." Giving him a look of pride, she said, "You came back here…to face me. You didn't have to—you could have hidden in that condo again. You're a lot braver than you give yourself credit for Colt.''

Realizing her wisdom was based upon the harsh experience of losing someone she loved deeply, he nodded. ''I hear you. I'm not proud of what I did to you, Abbie. I was scared. I still am. Right now, I feel like I'm in a helicopter that's tumbling out of my control.'' Giving her a long, intense look, he drowned in her shimmering blue eyes. ''There's something about you that's triggering all this dark stuff in me. It wants to come out. I'm trying to sit on it, but it's alive, like a monster inside me, eating me up.''

''I know, Colt. I know....'' Abbie wanted to throw her arms around him. She saw his pain so clearly in his eyes. ''I've been through that same gauntlet you're going through right now. My trauma wasn't over missions, but it was about death and loss, and that's something we share in common.''

''The only difference,'' Colt said gruffly, releasing her hand, ''is that you've survived your run through that gauntlet and I'm not sure I can or will...and I don't want to put you in the line of fire, either. You don't deserve to be hurt, Abbie. That's what really bothered me about all this—hurting you. You're innocent.''

Whispering his name, Abbie risked everything and stepped up to him. She placed her hands on his cheeks and looked deeply into his distraught eyes. Right now, Colt was hurting so much that she couldn't stand there and not do something to try and help him. "You're innocent, too, Colt. Bad things happen to good people all the time, I've discovered." Her voice grew husky with unshed tears. "What matters is that you know I'm here for you in whatever way is comfortable for you. Okay? I don't expect anything from you, Colt. Let me be your friend? A shoulder to lean on...maybe cry on if you feel like it? I don't run when things get bad. I've weathered plenty of storms. I feel like I can help you with your storm—if you'll let me?" She held her breath.

Gently, Colt took her hands in his. Her face was open and incredibly trusting. "You're a brave woman, Abbie. The way I feel right now, I don't know anyone who'd make the same offer to me that you have."

"I can stand the heat in the kitchen, Colt. Just try me." Abbie gave him an uneven smile that she didn't feel, because inwardly she was weeping for all the pain and grief he was carrying.

Shrugging back his shoulders, he gave her a warm look. "Okay...you're on, pardner. But if I get out of hand, just tell me. I'll slink back to the condo and nurse my wounds alone. Fair enough?" The last thing Colt wanted to do was hurt Abbie. She was putting herself out for him and he was going to try and keep her out of his line of fire.

"Great," Abbie whispered unsteadily. She eased her hands from his and stepped away. "I think I could use your help in getting my orchid girls over to Morgan and Laura's house. Care to help?'' She forced her voice to become bright and cheery. It was not how she felt, but it was what Colt needed. Right now he was raw and unsure of himself, of the boiling emotions that seethed just below the surface.

She hurried to the table and placed one well-wrapped pot of orchids in his large, steady hands. Hands that she wanted to have touch her, love her and draw her tightly against his hard male body. Swallowing, Abbie tried not to pursue that desire. Right now, Colt was hurting. She was sure sex was the last thing on his mind, judging from the unaccustomed brightness she saw in his eyes as he stood there like an awkward little boy, holding the orchid so carefully in his big, pawlike hands.

Looking at the framed picture on the wall opposite the stove, he asked, ''Is this the orchid in the photo?''

Abbie looked up as she carefully balanced a clay pot in her hands. ''What? Oh, *that* orchid? No, that's another *Cattleya rex,* like the photo in the living room. Remember? I told you about it on the first night we were together?'' She laughed gaily. ''I wish I had one!''

Colt did remember now. All his memories were centered on Abbie and how good she'd looked and felt in his arms when they had danced together. ''So why don't you have it in your collection?''

She smiled wistfully. ''Colt, that particular orchid costs a thousand dollars for just one plant! I can't possibly afford it.'' She gently patted the newspaper wrapped around the orchid she held. ''All these girls cost anywhere between twenty and fifty dollars apiece. I have an orchid budget—where I save my pennies for months on end, and then buy one that I want. No, I'm afraid *Cattleya rex*, my most favorite orchid in the universe, is not one I'll ever own.''

''A thousand dollars?'' Colt frowned. ''They cost that much?''

Abbie grinned and opened the door. ''Some orchid fanciers have specimens that cost upward of ten to fifty thousand dollars each.''

''Wow,'' he muttered, following her out into the bright sunlight.

Hurrying to her heated van, Abbie took her girls and put them in the back in special boxes, where they would be protected during the short trip. She watched as Colt shut the door to keep the orchids warm. The plants could not survive cold temperatures for long. Anything below fifty-five degrees would kill an orchid.

As he walked back with her to retrieve more plants, his shoulder brushing hers as they trudged through the snow, he slanted a glance down at her. ''Knowing the shape I'm in, would you like to go to the dinner with me tonight? Or do you want to put this snarly bear out to pasture so he won't bite you?''

Warmed, she laughed and said, ''I'd love to, Colt.'' Her heart speeded up. The look he gave her was that of a predator hunting its next meal. She absorbed his hungry look and remembered that starved kiss he'd plundered her lips with yesterday. Maybe tonight would be healing to him, as it would be to her....

Colt couldn't keep his eyes off Abbie at the dinner table that evening. The Trayhern house rang with conversation, laughter and the giggling of children. A number of tables, draped with white linen cloths, had been placed in a U shape. Abbie's beautiful, colorful cattleyas were arranged among the silver and gold ribbons that flowed down the center of each table like a glittering creek.

Abbie sat opposite Colt at their table, looking delicious in a fuchsia silk, long-sleeved jacket and slacks. Around her throat she wore a strand of pearls, which she'd told him were a gift from her grandmother, and a set of small pearl earrings. Her eyes reminded him of blue sapphires. The softness of her mouth was permanently branded into his memory, on his lips and within his heart and aching body. She had pulled that wild, curly red hair into a girlish ponytail decorated with a large, pale green cattleya orchid with magenta spots on its lip. She looked exquisitely beautiful.

They sat next to Jake Randolph, his wife, Shah, and their three children, ages three through ten. The children were like squirming puppies, their laughter and giggles filling Colt with an unexpected joy. To Abbie's right sat Wolf Harding and his blond-haired wife, Sarah, plus their two children, both girls. Part of what made this night so special to Colt was the fact that the mercs had all brought their families. The smiles, the joking and teasing among them was lifting his dark spirits.

On Abbie's left sat Jason Trayhern. Although he wasn't wearing his Annapolis uniform, he still looked all spit and polish in his casual clothes, and painfully correct in his bearing. Colt could see the young man idolized Abbie, and he also saw their special relationship, the doorway that she had to him. Abbie held Jason's heart…just as she did Colt's. That was her gift, Colt realized as he ate the beef Wellington. She knew how to create an opening to people like himself who were closed up and hurting. It was instructional for him to watch her work her natural magic on Jason. Within half an hour of sitting down, Jason was cracking jokes and laughing with her, and warming up to everyone else around him.

Abbie was so special. An ache built in Colt, so powerful and pulverizing that he wanted once more to feel Abbie's soft, smiling mouth against his. He wanted to drink in, like the starving mongrel he was, her energy, her sunny disposition, her idealism and hope. On some level, Colt knew Abbie could heal him, just as she was helping to heal Jason of his wounds from the past.

Later, after coffee served with a dessert of fruitcake smothered with a white vanilla sauce, Colt mingled with the other families in the den, where brandy and Kahlúa and coffee topped with thick mounds of whipping cream were being served to the adults. Many of the children had gone down into the basement, where Morgan had set up a number of games for them to play. Abbie remained at Colt's side, and he'd taken the bold step of placing his arm around her waist as they moved among the groups and families. When he'd done that, she'd looked up at him, her cheeks flushed and her eyes sparkling with joy over his move. Colt felt like he was walking on air once more.

When the tinkling of a bell sounded, everyone stopped talking and the room grew hushed.

"Come on, everyone!" Laura called excitedly from the living room. "Time to trim the tree!"

Abbie clapped her hands. "I love decorating the tree!" she confided excitedly to Colt.

He grinned lopsidedly. "You're a child in a woman's body, Abbie." He followed the rest of the merry crowd back to the living room. A number of mercs had helped Laura move the tables out of the center of the room, and they were now against the walls, the dishes and flatwear removed. Abbie's orchids remained, the silver and gold ribbons still on the tables to accent their color and beauty. Boxes of decorations, tinsel and lights had been set out for those who wanted to take part in the decorating.

Laughing liltingly, Abbie hurried ahead of him and went to a box of lights that would have to be strung first. How handsome Colt looked in his black slacks and pale pink shirt. He had shrugged off the charcoal jacket he wore, unbuttoned his cuffs and rolled up the sleeves to his elbows.

"Here," she said breathlessly as she looked over his shoulder at the huge, twenty-foot evergreen, "we need all you tall guys to get up on those ladders and string these lights."

Caught up in her infectious enthusiasm for the tree trimming, Colt took the box from her and headed over to one of three ladders that had been placed around the proud tree standing in the living room. Up on the other ladders were Mike Houston and Morgan. Colt climbed nimbly up as other men positioned themselves below to help. Teamwork. Yes, that was what it was all about. As Colt sat perched on the ladder, he gazed across the cheerful crowd of onlookers. His gaze fell on Abbie, who stood near the back of the gathered crowd with Jason. Her eyes sparkled with such life that Colt found himself taking a deep breath. Happiness threaded through him, strong and clean. It helped wash away the darkness still inhabiting him.

Much later, after the tree had been trimmed and the children had put on the final touches of silver tinsel, Colt stood back with his arm around Abbie's shoulders to view their handiwork.

"What a beautiful tree!" Abbie sighed softly, giving him a warm look. The night had been magical for her...and him. Every hour that passed, Abbie saw Colt easing more and more out of his self-imposed shell. By the end of the evening, he was a different man. She absorbed his laughter, enjoyed his easy play with the kids, his joking with the other mercs. This was a side of Colt she had not known existed and she loved him fiercely for sharing it with her. This was the healthy side of him; the part that had not been wounded by those deadly missions. Abbie's heart still ached for him. Hope bounded through her for Colt, and for the two of them. All night, whenever possible, he'd had his arm around her waist or shoulders. Or he'd reached out to touch her in some small, but meaningful way. She appreciated his reaching out to her, and she knew Colt was entrusting himself to her...especially his raw emotions and his carefully guarded vulnerability. Abbie ached to love him, ached to be one with him and find herself waking up with him on some cold winter morning, warm and well-loved in his powerful arms.

Was she dreaming? Was it folly? How could she fall so hard for someone so quickly? It frightened her in some ways, but in others, being around Colt felt so natural, as if he were a simple extension of herself. Was this the magic of the five days of Christmas that Laura had always talked about? Christmas was such a healing time of year, anyway, to Abbie. For the last two years, she'd spent them alone, remembering the past. Now, this year, she was fully in the present and looking forward to a future—with Colt. Was she foolish? Crazy? Abbie wasn't sure, but she was going to take that risk and pursue whatever it was that they had. There was no guarantee of a happy outcome, she knew. Colt was wounded. And although he was showing her in so many small ways that he liked her, she knew it probably didn't match the power of her own emotions toward him. No, only time would tell, and she trusted herself enough to grant herself that gift.

"Come here," Colt whispered dangerously near her ear.

Abbie grinned and looked up at him as he gently grasped her arm and led her out of the living room, where everyone was singing Christmas carols. "Colt! Where are we going?" She laughed breathlessly as he led her into the den, now empty of people.

Giving her a wicked look, he placed her beneath the copper lamp that hung suspended in the center of the den. "Right here," he said, his smile widening.

Loving his unexpected spontaneity, Abbie looked up. There, suspended beneath the lamp on a bright crimson ribbon, was a huge sprig of mistletoe.

"Uh-oh," she murmured. "I'm in trouble."

"Are you ever, sweetheart. Come here...." Colt stepped up to her, slid his massive arms around her slender form and brought her fully against him. As he leaned down, he saw joy, like gold flecks of sunlight, in her eyes. She lifted her arms and slid them over his shoulders. Her lips parted. Groaning, he leaned down and captured them, a man starving for light instead of darkness.

The tune of "Oh Come All Ye Faithful" floated into the room and surrounded them as Katy Trayhern, an accomplished musician, took to the piano. Abbie moaned softly as Colt's lips grazed hers. How glad she was that he had stolen her away! Had he read her mind? Known that she was desperately hungry and craving another kiss from him? Abbie sighed and fell against him, allowing Colt to take her full weight. With him, she was safe, and she knew it.

Colt quivered as she brazenly met and returned the fire of his aching kiss. Abbie was bold. She set him ablaze with her lips, caressing his with wantonness. Feeling the soft press of her breasts against his chest, he slid his hands downward across her small, strong spine and wide hips—hips roomy enough to carry a baby someday.

In those molten moments, with the Christmas music surrounding them and their bodies melting against one another, Colt could only feel desire, happiness and a deep, aching longing in his soul to make Abbie his forever. As he threaded his fingers through her ponytail and eased her away from him, her eyes were slumberous with desire—for him. Her lips were wet and well kissed. He saw her smile drowsily.

"Wow…" she whispered unsteadily.

With this woman in his arms who he considered more magical than real, a woman who held his heart so tenderly that he didn't know what to do or say, Colt could only stand there, grinning. All he knew was that he was looking forward to the fourth day of

Christmas with Abbie, tomorrow. His life, his heart, his soul were inexplicably tied to her. And although Colt still tasted the fear of his dark, wounded side, for at least this moment he wanted to pretend it wasn't there and that Abbie was all that existed in his miserable life. She was light to his eternal darkness. Light.

Chapter 5

Christmas Eve, December 24

There was no way to gird himself for this Christmas Eve ahead of him. As Colt entered the second floor of the Veterans Hospital, which was located in Anaconda, Montana, his hands full of gifts for those who were bedridden, he was grateful for Abbie's nearness. She would help him get through this visit.

Every year, Morgan and Laura, along with the Perseus employees and spouses, took a bus to Anaconda, Montana, a large city southeast of Philipsburg, to visit the Veterans Hospital. The vets there came from all the U.S. military services. Anyone who had served could take advantage of VA hospitals for wounds gained in combat, or if they had no medical insurance of their own, to receive medical help during their civilian years. Veterans hospitals were spread across the states to care for those who had given so much to their country.

As members of Perseus split up to cover the five floors, Colt and Abbie took the second one, where most of the vets were from the Korean and Vietnam eras. Swallowing hard, he felt his gut tightening with a lot of suppressed emotions as they stepped onto the green-and-white tiled floor. On either side of the huge ward, white-haired men lay in white beds, their faces aged, but their expressions alert and expectant looking. Few of these vets had visitors, and he knew how much they looked forward to anyone who would spend a few minutes with them. Families could be hundreds, even thousands of miles away, so most vets languished alone, without support from loved ones or friends. That's why visits such as this were so important. It helped their morale and let them know that others appreciated their patriotic gift.

Colt carried two huge wicker baskets containing Christmas sacks for each vet. Abbie and the other women of Perseus had tucked many thoughtful and useful items into gaily decorated sacks to give to each patient in the ward. There was a slice of thick fruitcake in a plastic box, vanilla sauce in another, plus plastic flatware and a bright red napkin. A twenty-dollar phone card was included so that a veteran who was bed-bound could call his family over the Christmas holiday, along with a gold envelope that contained a hundred dollars in cash. Most vets earned meager government stipends and lived below the poverty level, so the money would come in handy.

His mouth growing dry as they walked past the swinging doors, Colt spotted a number of orderlies, men and women, dressed in white uniforms. One woman, a registered nurse with short black hair and dancing blue eyes, hurried over to them.

"Hey, were glad you came! The guys here have been waiting for you." She smiled and gestured toward the ward. "The only one you can't give fruit-cake to is down there at the end—Mr. Charles Langford. Charlie's blind and has diabetes, so he can't have sugar products." The nurse looked up at Colt. "Why don't you visit with him, sir? He just got a letter from his son, who's over in Kosovo serving in the army? I don't have time to read it to him. I'm sure he'd like you to do that for him. That's a Christmas gift in itself."

Nodding, Colt said, "Yeah, be happy to." *Liar.* He was scared. *Kosovo.* He glanced over at the old man named Charlie, who was sitting up in bed, clothed in wrinkled blue pajamas that seemed too large for him. *Great.* Talking with a man who had a son in Kosovo was the *last* thing Colt wanted to do, but the nurse had already taken the wicker basket from him and set it on a nearby gurney. Then she gripped Colt by the arm and propelled him down the highly polished aisle to the last bed on the right.

"Hey, Charlie! You've got a visitor...." She looked up at Colt as she steered him to the man's bedside and drew out a chair for him to sit on. "Your name, sir?"

"Colt," he told her uncomfortably as he sat down.

"Charlie, meet Colt." The nurse leaned over and patted the sixty-year-old vet's stooped shoulders.

Charlie gave her a slight smile. He lifted his long, thin arm, his large-knuckled fingers extended outward. "Hey, Colt...where are you, son? Nurse Jones here was promising me that someone would read my boy's letter to me." He gripped the badly wrinkled letter in his other hand. "I'd be mighty appreciative if you could do that."

"Of course," he murmured. Charlie had obviously hung on to that letter like life itself; it was wrinkled and worn from the old vet handling it so much. Colt felt panicked when Nurse Jones hurried away. Turning his full attention to the vet, he saw that Charlie's eyes were a milky, opaque color. He was totally blind, Colt realized. Mouth tightening, he lifted his hand and met Charlie's outstretched one. The old man's fingers wrapped strongly around his.

"Good to meet you, Colt. They said Morgan Trayhern's people were comin' in this morning. We've been pretty excited all week. We don't get many visitors, you know? I've been here for five years now.'' He grimaced. ''This diabetes is killin' me inches at a time.'' He managed a sour smile, trying to make a joke despite the serious nature of his illness.

Squeezing Charlie's hand, Colt released it as if it was a hot poker burning him. He looked up to see Abbie chatting excitedly with vets on the other side of the ward. Each man lit up like a lightbulb beneath her effusive warmth and care. Uneasily, he returned his attention to Charlie. ''I'm sorry to hear that,'' he murmured. When he realized that Charlie had one leg missing up to his knee beneath the mass of blankets, Colt winced. When diabetes was serious, gangrene would set in, and then that part of the body had to be amputated or the person would die. The man's skin was washed out and he was gaunt looking. His hair hung in a semicircle, like a halo, around his bald, shining head. Silvery hairs stuck out like a hen's nest, in need of a combing. Despite the old soldier's medical condition, Colt couldn't resist the smile on his nearly toothless mouth. It was clear the man had been through hell, and yet he was still in good spirits.

''What war did you serve in, sir?'' Colt asked.

Charlie sobered. ''I was in Korea with the marines at the Frozen Chosin.''

''Helluva place.''

''Helluva place,'' Charlie agreed grimly. ''Got my legs shot up there. Nearly froze to death. One of my buddies paid with his life to get me help." His smile dissolved. "I've been in and out of VA hospitals since then. About twenty years ago, I got diabetes. My son, who's serving in the Army M.P.s—military police—over in Kosovo, is real worried about me. My wife, Wanda, died five years ago, and now—" he sighed "—I'm a full-time resident here." He brightened and held up the badly worn white envelope. "This is from Stephen, my son. It would be a heck of a Christmas gift if you could read it to me. I'd be forever grateful. Nurse Jones usually reads his mail to me, but they've had emergencies going on for the last two days and no one has had time to spend with me to read it. Maybe you could?"

He held out the envelope to Colt. His hand was trembling badly.

Colt hesitantly took the crinkled letter. It was still sealed. He saw hope burning in Charlie's heavily lined face. "Sure," he rasped, "I'll do that for you...." And he slowly opened it as if it were going to bite him. He didn't want to know what was inside that envelope. A frisson of fear ran through him.

"I'm so proud of my son," Charlie said. "He's an officer, you know. A captain. A chip off the old block here." He managed a strained laugh. "Well, I wasn't too happy at first that he chose the Army over the Marine Corps. I'd have liked him to have been a marine, but it was his choice." Opening his hands, he added, "I worry atrociously about him. He's up there on the front lines tryin' to keep peace between the Serbs and the Kosovars. The people hate each other over there. And over what? Religion, of all things! Whatever happened to 'love thy neighbor'? Where is tolerance? They're a crazy bunch over there, if you ask me."

His conscience eating at him, Colt felt his mouth drying up. He longed for a glass of water, anything to ease the pain forming like a fist in his chest region as he slowly opened the typed letter. "It's bad over there," he managed to say in a strained tone.

Charlie sat forward, attentive, his face glowing with expectation at having the letter read.

Taking a deep, ragged breath, Colt began to read out loud to him.

"Hi Dad...I hope this reaches you by Christmas. I'm sorry I can't be there. I know Frannie is sending you a box of goodies, so let me know if it arrives in time? She said she was making you some sugar-free cookies that you could eat a little of once a day. Just be sure and clear it with your doc first, okay?"

"Frannie is his wife," Charlie said excitedly. He rubbed his hand together in anticipation. "Ain't got the box yet. Bet it will arrive today...I hope...."

Colt heard the excitement in his voice. There were tears glimmering in Charlie's eyes. Shutting his own eyes tightly, Colt dragged in another breath of air. He felt like he was suffocating. Forcing his eyes open once more, he went on.

"I don't know what to do, Dad. This place is hell on earth. The people hate one another. I never knew what hate was till me and my company came over here. They keep telling us to keep the peace, but Dad, it's worse than any nightmare I could concoct. I survived the Gulf War and felt lucky, but this place is worse...."

Colt hesitated. His voice became choked. Glancing up, he saw Charlie's face go slack and heavy with concern. Colt's heart began to pound in earnest as he forced himself to go on.

"Yesterday, we found the body of a dead Kosovar girl. She'd wandered into a Serb part of town, chasing her little puppy, which had gotten loose. They'd stoned her to death before we could reach her because she was on their property. She was just fourteen, so pretty...what a waste of life."

"My poor son," Charlie whispered. He ran his hands across his face and sniffed. "Oh, my poor boy...how awful. And that little girl... I just can't believe it...I just can't. An innocent child..."

Colt fought his own reaction. The words blurred on the paper. The letter trembled in his hand. Flashes of what he'd seen—the blood, the screams, the terror—avalanched through him. Sweat popped out on his deeply furrowed brow as he sat there trying to get a handle on his escaping emotions. In an effort to avoid feeling, he looked up at old Charlie. The man was sitting there, his hands tightly clasped in his lap, tears streaming down his face.

"Finish it," he told Colt in an unsteady tone. "I need to hear the rest. My son…he's hurting, and I know that hurt. Damn war…"

Colt stood up and sat down on the side of Charlie's bed, his back to the rest of the ward. He didn't want anyone to see his face or the tears glittering dangerously in his own eyes. His hip grazed Charlie's. The old man reached out, found his hand and squeezed it—hard. He continued to hold on to Colt's hand with a clinging grip.

"Please…read the rest?" he quavered.

Shaking his head, Colt forced himself to read the rest of the letter in a low, ragged tone that only Charlie could hear. Colt wasn't sure he could finish it; each word ripped more scar tissue off that bleeding wound within him from his own experiences in Kosovo.

"Dad, I'm sorry to send this letter to you so close to Christmas. You don't need to hear this, but I have to talk to someone about it before it eats me up alive. My men can't see me cry...and I don't ever want to tell Frannie about this. You're my only outlet, and I know you understand because of all that you went through in Korea. I got out of the Humvee and ran over to where the little girl was lying in the middle of that cobblestone street. I hoped she was still alive. Her puppy was sitting next to her, howling. It just tore me up, Dad. I leaned down and felt for a pulse. She was gone. All I could do was pick her up in my arms. She was so pretty. I just stood there with her in my arms, holding her and thinking of our own daughter, Tracey, who is almost the same age. I kept thinking about this poor dead girl's parents and what they would do when they found out she died like this. I wanted to cry so bad, but I knew my men were watching me.

"The street was deserted. The Serbs were hiding inside their homes, but I could feel them watching me...watching us from behind the curtains over the windows. I could feel their hatred and I could feel that they weren't sorry they'd taken this child's life. I mean...my God, she was only fourteen and *innocent*. She had her whole life ahead of her. I took her back to the Humvee and we wrapped her in a blanket. I didn't want to let her go, so I sat in the passen-

ger side and held her in my arms. I didn't want
her to be left alone. I wanted her to know someone cared. Some of the guys started to cry, Dad.
I tried to stay firm and brave for them. I tried
to tell them it was all right, when nothing was,
really. I felt so damned helpless and useless to
them—to myself.

"And then the puppy started toward us. I ordered my sergeant to grab the little guy. He was
about the size of a cantaloupe, and my sergeant
stuffed him inside his parka because it was so
cold. I figured the Serbs would kill him, too,
because he belonged to a Kosovar. I couldn't
save the little girl, but we could save her puppy.
And then we left and went back to H.Q.

"Back at our bivouac of tents, the puppy has
become our mascot of sorts. One of the guys
named him Toto, because the little girl reminded
all of them of Dorothy from Oz. She'd been
wearing a rainbow-colored skirt and a white
blouse. In some ways, the puppy has helped us.
But he reminds me daily of what I saw. All I
can remember is holding her...her face so clean,
so unlined and innocent. I go to sleep seeing
her. I dream about her, and it's driving me
crazy. I don't know what to do. I was hoping
you could help me...let me know what will get
rid of her face in my nightmares.

"I'm sorry to burden you with this. I wish I

could be there with Frannie and Tracey to celebrate Christmas with you, but I can't. Maybe next year, if the army sends me stateside, we can make it. Just know I love you. I wish you were here so we could visit. I always liked the times when we'd sit down and just talk. I know you'd have something to say that could help me through this. Merry Christmas, Dad.

> Your loving son,
> Stephen.''

Colt heard the old man sob. He looked up, and found Charlie blurred before him. The old vet had covered his face with his hand, and was sobbing loudly. Shocked that he would cry so openly in such a public place, Colt sat there frozen for a moment. The words from the letter ripped him apart. He'd seen similar travesties over in Kosovo.

Setting the letter on the bed stand, Colt released Charlie's hand and awkwardly patted the old man's shaking shoulder as he wept unashamedly. Then, driven by something deep within him, Colt opened his arms, drew the thin old man forward and held him while he cried for his son's painful experience. As Charlie laid his head on Colt's shoulder, his weeping grew harsher and deeper. He gripped Colt with his thin arms. Colt closed his eyes and tried to breathe, but it was impossible. The world skidded to a halt for him as he sat there holding a man crying for his son's pain.

Tears jammed into Colt's own eyes. It took everything he had to stop them. Bending his head foreword, he held the old man gently in his embrace and let him weep.

Abbie remained near Colt after they'd left the VA hospital. Their second stop was at the main shelter in Anaconda, St. Mary's Shelter for the Poor, which helped street people and the homeless. Morgan donated a hefty check every holiday in support of the organization's efforts, and the Perseus team always came to help serve the Christmas Eve meal. This was the kind of thing Abbie loved the most—helping those who were not as well off as she was. But now, as she stood behind the counter with Colt, helping him serve the turkey he'd been slicing to those who were standing in line, she saw his face fill with silent suffering.

She knew it had to do with what had happened at the VA hospital. She'd seen Colt holding old Charlie. Even the men on the ward had known that something important and touching was going on between them. Charlie's weeping could be heard throughout the room. The men had remained quiet out of respect. Abbie had watched their faces and saw that before long there wasn't a dry eye in the place. She knew it had to do with the letter, but wisely did not ask

Colt for details, even after they'd finished giving out the gift sacks to each veteran.

As she spooned mashed potatoes and savory gravy onto a young woman's tray, Abbie smiled gently at her. The girl was barely fourteen, her black hair matted and uncombed. As she responded with a slight, wobbly smile of her own, Abbie noticed that her clothes were threadbare. Abbie couldn't help crying inwardly for the child. She saw Colt looking at the girl, too, as if she were a nightmare staring back at him. His eyes seemed bloodshot, his mouth a hard line against the suffering he was holding at bay.

Maybe when he took Abbie back to her log cabin tonight, they might be able to talk. She hoped so, because right now, Colt was looking shell-shocked. Abbie knew that whatever transpired in the VA hospital had stirred up Colt's own PTSD symptoms, and he was wrestling with them by the minute. She could feel his ongoing anguish, his pain. And all she wanted to do was provide a safe harbor tonight.... Could she reach out to him? Would he trust her in his vulnerable, raw state?

"Coffee or tea?" Abbie asked as Colt moved tiredly to her kitchen table and sat down. Outside, it was snowing once again. Darkness had long since fallen, and the temperature with it. The scents of cinnamon and orange peel drifting around the warm kitchen from the saucepan on the stove made her feel a tad better. On the bus ride home, Colt had been silent and withdrawn. He'd barely spoken to anyone. She'd seen the worried looks on Morgan and Laura's faces, too.

Colt sat down and wrapped his hands together on the table. "Whiskey," he said abruptly. "I need some. Do you have any?"

Abbie hesitated. The anguish in his tone was harsh and alive. "No...I'm sorry." He refused to look at her, staring at his hands intently. His mouth was tight and it was obvious he was trying hard to hold back his own raging emotions. Moving quietly around the table, she held out her hand to him. "Come here?"

Colt twisted his head at the sound of her gentle voice. He stared at her outstretched hand as if it would bite him. Yet despite the storm roiling unchecked within his heart and gut, he reached out for that slender, strong hand of hers. Right now, he needed Abbie. Desperately.

"Follow me," she whispered as he eased out of the chair and stood up. Leading Colt to her living room, to the overstuffed couch in front of the fireplace, where a wood fire snapped and crackled, Abbie guided him to sit down. When he did, she moved to his side after easing the shoes off her feet. Snuggling next to his bulk, she placed her arms around him and drew him close. At first he resisted. Then she saw his eyes gleam like silver fire, and he capitulated.

Abbie felt diminutive against Colt, but she sighed softly as he slid his arms around her and laid his head against her neck and shoulder.

"There…" she sighed, kissing his hair. "This is better. Much better…" And it was. Christmas music floated unobtrusively around them. The peaceful crackling of the fire reached their ears. Abbie felt Colt begin to relax. In her heart, she knew he needed to be held. Held and kept safe from all that he had experienced today. Her heart soared with the knowledge that she could at least give him this small gift.

"It was a hard day for you," Abbie began gently, and moved her hand up the sleeve of his apricot-colored sweater. "The gift you gave Charlie…well, that was special. You helped him so much, Colt…." Abbie waited. She knew she was treading on thin ice as she broached the subject of Charlie breaking down and weeping unashamedly in his arms. Yet intuitively Abbie understood that this was where the storm within Colt was centered, and it had to be addressed. By providing an opening, she was giving him the opportunity to talk it out if he would. And Abbie knew he needed to talk. She saw his ravaged emotions in his eyes.

Colt nuzzled against Abbie's soft, slender neck. She smelled of a spicy orchid fragrance and her own special scent as a woman. Her arms were strong and caring around him. He desperately absorbed her form, the sound of her husky voice edged with tears.

"How did you know?" he managed to ask in a cracked voice.

"Know what, darling?"

"This. That I need this. You."

Abbie laughed gently and rocked him in her arms. "We all need this, Colt. We all need to be held safe against a world gone mad at times. This is the gift of Christmas. Knowing that other people can reach out and help you, heal you and hold you. We're a big family at Perseus. Morgan and Laura know the hell that everyone goes through, what you might have seen or experienced on a mission...the awful things.... But they also know what helps to heal you—family, care, love and helping others less fortunate than us."

Nodding, Colt closed his eyes tightly and continued to absorb her soft, tremulous voice. Abbie's lips were so close to his cheek. He could feel her moist breath feathering across his flesh.

Her heart was beating in time with his own, her small breasts pressed against his chest. "Yeah," he began brokenly, "I needed this...."

To hell with it, he thought suddenly. He was going to tell her exactly how he felt. Tightening his grip around her for a moment, he rasped, "I need you, Abbie. You're like a bulwark of strength to me right now. I feel so damned weak. I feel like I'm hurtling out of control...."

She rocked him gently back and forth. Tears

squeezed from her tightly shut eyes. "We all feel like that, Colt. Life doesn't always deal fair hands to everyone."

He knew she was referring to her husband's death. Yet Abbie had survived it and was flourishing. "I wish I had whatever it is you have...." he said gruffly.

"What?" Abbie choked back a sob as she felt Colt reaching out to her.

"You've survived the hell of losing your husband, and yet you're whole and can move on. Me? I'm nailed by what I saw during those missions over in Kosovo. Today...that letter... Damn it, Abbie, Charlie has a son, an Army M.P. over there.... The letter..." Colt couldn't go on. All he could do was hold her tightly and bury his face against her neck. Violently, his feeling surged upward. Tears leaked from his eyes no matter how hard he tried to force them back.

Abbie opened her eyes and saw the streaks glistening down his hard, taut cheek. Opening her hand, she caught them on her fingertips. "Its all right, Colt. Let it out...all of it. I'll just sit here and hold you.... Please...you're safe with me, darling...."

Abbie knew her words were healing to him. She felt a powerful shudder work through Colt. His arms held her like steel bands and the air rushed out of her lungs from his sudden, hard embrace. The first sob worked up and out of his tormented mouth, and then another. Her entire body shook as he buried his head against her and sobbed again. Oh, why did men fight so hard to run away from their feelings? She closed her eyes, rocked him and held him with her womanly strength for a long, long time.

Finally, the storm within Colt passed. It seemed like a miracle to him as he eased away from Abbie at long last. He had no idea what time it was and he didn't care. Feeling cleaner and more steady than he had in weeks, Colt gave her a burning look of silent thanks. Abbie's expression remained tender and caring. Her lips were parted, and he could see the remnants of tears drying on her own flushed cheeks. How beautiful she looked to him. Raising his hand, Colt grazed her tear-stained flesh with his fingers. "You are so incredible, so strong, Abbie...and I feel like a limp dishrag emotionally in comparison." He forced a one-cornered smile.

She caught his hand, kissed the top of it and held it in her lap. "Part of caring for another person is being there for them, Colt. I knew you needed this— to be held...to be listened to. I saw how much you were hurting."

Nodding, he sagged back against the couch, eased his arm around her shoulders and brought Abbie against him. She came without resistance, her hand resting in the center of his chest, over his heart. "Thank you..." he murmured gruffly. Leaning over, he pressed a kiss to her unruly red hair. "You're strong, Abbie. I'm so in awe of you. You're small, yet mighty.''

She laughed a little and closed her eyes, reveling in his tenderness toward her. This is what *she* needed, whether he realized it or not. Now that Colt was unafraid to show his emotions to her, he was completely vulnerable with her, too. It was a Christmas gift she thought she'd never share with another man. Ever. Not even in her wildest dreams had Abbie thought there could be another man with Ted's sensitivity or ability to share with her. But there was: Colt Hamlin. "You're such a gift to me, Colt...in all ways...."

"Yeah," he griped good-naturedly, "a crybaby."

She looked up at him. Although his eyes were bloodshot, his gaze was clear now. No longer did Abbie see the murky storm of emotions that had been there before. "I happen to like men who can cry. Crying doesn't make you weak, it makes you look strong to me, Colt. Look how much crying helped Charlie...."

Lifting his hand, Colt cupped her small face and studied her shining blue eyes. "I wanted to cry with him, Abbie, in the worst way. But I fought it like hell itself. That letter...well, it was enough to rip the hardest-hearted man apart. It did me."

"It helped to heal you," Abbie said gently. "Like cures like sometimes." She turned her cheek and pressed a kiss into his open palm.

"You're healing to me," Colt rasped unsteadily as he guided her face upward for a kiss. "You look at me, and I feel my heart opening. Your laughter makes me feel hope again, Abbie.'' He hesitated before he kissed her parting lips. Drowning in her slumberous blue eyes, he whispered roughly, ''It's you…all of you, the way you are, that's helping me, supporting me in a way I've never experienced before. I can't explain it…. And whatever it is, sweetheart, I want more of it. I want more of you….''

His words fell around her like a warm blanket of love. Abbie leaned forward, her lips grazing the hard set of his mouth. Colt's eyes were alive once more with tears, and she understood how open and raw he was feeling right now. Lifting her arms, she eased them around his neck and deepened her kiss, her lips sliding tenderly across his until his mouth melted and opened to receive all that she could give him with her heart and soul.

As Abbie swirled in a golden haze of light and desire, wrapped in Colt's arms, she knew that somehow, through the fires of his anguish and pain, she was falling in love with this modern-day warrior who'd been so deeply wounded by what he'd seen and experienced. Abbie hadn't expected to be able to love again. She drank headily of his kisses, moving her lips tenderly against his.

Colt finally eased away. He didn't want to, but knew he had to or else. He saw Abbie's brows knit momentarily, saw the question in her eyes as he slid his hands across her shoulders.

''If I don't stop, sweetheart, I'm going to lift you into my arms, carry you off into your bedroom and never let you go.'' He gave her a humorous look.

"And I need your okay to do that, first. It has to be mutual."

Her heart pounding with joy, Abbie caressed his cheek. Colt's eyes were alive with raw, burning desire—for her. "I feel like I'm coming back to life, Colt. I never thought…well, I never thought I'd ever feel again after Ted's death, but I am. Its a miracle…." And it was, Abbie thought as she gazed wonderingly up into his eyes. Just the way his mouth crooked, that confidence and strength in his smile, sent a flash of longing coursing through her.

"You're my miracle," he whispered roughly, not wanting to let her go. "And it's all happening so fast that I'm spinning from it. I really didn't want to help you. Morgan persuaded me, and now I'm glad he did." Brushing his fingers across her unruly hair, he smiled lopsidedly. "I'm scared, Abbie. I need to know how you feel about me…us…if there is an us or not…."

Sighing, Abbie gave him a tender look and snuggled back into his arms, her head in the crook of his shoulder. "There is an us as far as I'm concerned, Colt. And like you, I'm bowled over by our attraction to each other. What you do to me, how you make me feel—it's…wonderful, unexpected."

Was it love? Colt wondered, sinking back against the couch with her in his arms. It had to be, yet he was unwilling to speak those words yet. He was afraid Abbie might run or turn him down. "It is for me, too," he confided in a gravelly tone as he ran his fingers slowly across her upper arm. "This is turning into a Christmas I'll never forget," he murmured, kissing the top of her head.

Abbie opened her eyes and stared off through the living room. She felt the solid, heavy beat of Colt's heart beneath her palm. "Do dreams come true, Colt? Or am I a dyed-in-the-wool romantic who doesn't have a prayer?"

Chuckling, he rasped, "We have a chance, Abbie. Wanting a relationship is the first step."

Her heart thudded. "Do you?"

He felt her grow still in his arms. Fear sizzled through him. He forced the truth out. "Yes." And even more fear shot through him. "Do you?"

Abbie whispered, "Yes...but I'm afraid, Colt. I don't know of *what*, I just am."

"Maybe because things have been happening so fast. Maybe because of your loss of Ted..."

She sat up and eased away just enough to look deeply into his hooded eyes, which still regarded her with desire. "Do we have the time? Are you going back on the merc schedule soon?" Inwardly, Abbie was fearful. Would she lose Colt, too? Oh, she knew Ted had died in a stupid automobile accident, not on a mission. But every time he'd gone on a mission, there was a chance he'd never return. Abbie knew she couldn't put herself through that emotional gauntlet again and survive. Did she have the right to tell Colt that? Anguished, Abbie searched his vulnerable face. Her heart, her body, responded wildly to his look. How badly she wanted to make love to Colt. But to do that, there had to be something of substance, something lasting, between them. She waited painfully for his answer.

Searching her eyes, Colt sensed her trepidation about the possibility of his returning to mission status. "Right now, the way I'm stoved up from the last one, I'm not going back on the roster, Abbie. I have to leave after Christmas to go visit my dad in Florida, to make sure he's okay and see if he needs anything. Then—" he shrugged, "—I was going to come back here in hopes that we could pick up where we left off."

Relief flooded through her. Wetting her lips, Abbie whispered, "Yes…I'd like that, Colt. I really would…."

His grin was boyish. "Yeah?"

She giggled a little. "Oh, yes."

He touched an errant curl near her cheek and twisted it gently around his index finger. "I gotta get going now…got some stuff that needs taking care of…."

Abbie tried to hide her disappointment. She wanted Colt to stay, but lacked the courage to ask him. Okay…"

"Tomorrow we have brunch over at the Trayherns, and then the kids get to open up their Christmas presents. May I escort you?"

Sometimes he was so achingly formal. Abbie gave him a tender smile and grazed his stubbled cheek, which felt like sandpaper beneath her sensitive fingers. "Of course you can. It's my favorite day, Colt.

The kids—'' she laughed excitedly ''—oh, the kids love it! Morgan and Laura buy everyone a gift, including the adults. They're such generous people—almost to a fault. But the children just go crazy. I love to watch them digging for their own gift in the pile under the Christmas tree.''

Colt absorbed the shining quality in Abbie's eyes. ''You were made to be a mother,'' he told her quietly. And she was. The unexpected thought that he could give her the greatest gift of love—a baby—filled him with a sense of power that set his heart pounding. There was no question that he was falling helplessly in love with this sunny woman with red hair and an incredibly giving heart.

''I'll see you tomorrow morning,'' he promised with a growl. There was something very, very special he had to do first....

Chapter 6

December 25, Christmas Day

Abbie sat on one end of the couch with Colt's arm around her shoulders as they waited for Morgan and Laura to begin passing out the gifts from beneath the huge, sparkling Christmas tree. Sighing happily, Abbie felt a contentment that she'd never thought she'd feel again. With snowflakes twirling lazily outside the huge picture windows of the Trayherns' massive living room, Christmas was as beautiful as a picture postcard.

It had snowed all night, so the evergreens surrounding the cedar home, the rounded hills embracing it and the massive Rocky Mountains in the distance all had a new layer of glistening powdered sugar. The sky was a leaden gray and hung low, promising more snow throughout the day. That was all right with Abbie.

Her heart, her thoughts, were centered on Colt, and she was enjoying his nearness. She hadn't slept much last night because her feelings churned from giddy joy to abject terror. Colt's ability to shed his hard warrior mask and be incredibly human with her had forced her to look at what she really wanted out of life.

Giving Colt a tender look, she watched one corner of his mouth crook in a grin as he met and held her gaze. Abbie felt him squeeze her shoulders gently. All around them, the volume of noise was rising as the children sat in a semicircle around the tree, squirming eagerly as they waited for the gifts to be handed out. The adults had cameras or videocams ready to record the exciting event.

"You think these kids are going to make it?" Colt asked her, his lips near her ear.

Abbie giggled. "They look like they're going to burst with excitement, don't they?" The littlest children, beaming with barely contained anticipation, had scooted up to within inches of where Morgan and Laura stood in front of the tree. The older children sat back with more decorum and patience. It was the littlest tykes, the ones who believed fervently in the spirit of Santa Claus, who kept crowding right up to the gift givers' feet.

"Yeah, they do. It's nice to see that kind of innocence," Colt replied, gazing down at Abbie. She looked beautiful this morning. He had learned that she loved velvet, and today she wore a violet-colored velvet turtleneck along with some very sensual looking black satin jeans that were driving him crazy. A spray of white Dendrobium orchids with red lips, which hailed from Australia, was fastened expertly into her gleaming, curly hair, which she'd tamed and clipped up at the back of her head. The resulting cascade of curls shone gold and copper in the light of the chandeliers above them.

Abbie absorbed his words and saw the happiness in his eyes. Colt looked so handsome this morning. He wore a white cowboy shirt with pearl snaps, a tan-colored corduroy sport coat, dark brown slacks and his black cowboy boots. She had the maddening urge to tame that slight, rebellious curl that dipped over his brow back into place, but she stopped herself. When she was around Colt, Abbie found herself wanting to touch him all the time. From the moment they'd arrived this morning for brunch, Colt had kept his arm either around her waist or around her shoulders, and it had raised some eyebrows. Abbie had seen many of Colt's friends nod and smile at them, as if approving of their newfound closeness. Especially Laura, who practically beamed like the rising sun.

"May I have your attention for just a second?" Morgan called out in his deep baritone voice. He held up his hands, a grin on his face. Dressed in a bright red sweater, comfortable Levi's and cowboy boots, he looked down at his wife.

Laura laughed. Gazing down fondly at the eager three-, four- and five-year-olds gathered anxiously around their feet, she said, "You'd better hurry, darling, or these kids are going to overwhelm your position, tactically speaking." Today Laura had chosen a gold lamé long-sleeved top with a glittering red-green-and-white scarf around her neck. Since satin jeans were the rage, she wore a pair of wine-colored ones with her sensible black loafers. Smiling down at the excited, squirming children, she said, "Better hurry, Morgan, they're going to overrun us any moment now!"

Everyone laughed.

Morgan chuckled and gave the children at his feet a warm look. Off to his right was his son, once again in his dark blue uniform with shining brass buttons down the front.

"Well, I guess if I don't want to get swarmed, I'll make my thirty-minute speech very, very short."

There was a collective groan from the crowd. No one wanted a long speech at this point, particularly the antsy, eager children.

"How about a two-minute speech?" he asked, grinning.

Everyone clapped and cheered.

Laughing, Morgan slid his arm around his wife and drew her near. "Everyone, we're glad you were here to celebrate Christmas with us.'' He gave Laura a look of love and pride. "This was her idea, not mine, but over the years I've come to see that it's a great one."

Again there were claps and cheers.

Laura laughed. "We want to thank all the hard workers behind the scenes who helped bring this off. You know who you are. And we hope that you have a wonderful Christmas Day. Morgan? Should we start handing out the presents?"

The children leaped to their feet, screeching and clapping loudly. The adults broke into laughter.

Morgan raised his thick, black eyebrows. "I think we'd better, Laura, or they're going to charge us."

Abbie watched as Laura and Morgan went to the massive tree and began pulling out the bright, colorfully wrapped presents. She knew that Laura had gone to great lengths to contact the mothers to find out what each child would like to have for Christmas. Because Perseus was top-heavy with money, the Trayherns spared no expense on the many charities they funded around the globe, nor did they stint on holiday gifts for the kids.

Colt sat there, Abbie beneath his arm, her warm body leaning against him while he watched the children's faces light up with anticipation as the gifts were quickly distributed. Giving her a glance, Colt saw that her cheeks were suffused with pink. Her hands clasped on her knees, she was raptly watching the children, a soft smile playing across her lips.

How badly he wanted her. All of her. Colt had
done a lot of thinking last night, and he'd had a long
talk with Morgan earlier this morning before everyone had come to brunch. Would Abbie approve of
his new plan?

He noticed that when they'd strolled into the living
room earlier, before everyone settled around the
U-shaped table for brunch, she'd spotted the three-
foot-tall, gold-foil-wrapped gift with a huge, bright
red ribbon on top, at the rear of the Christmas tree.
She'd commented that some lucky little kid was going to get a really big gift. Colt had smiled and said
nothing. Little did she know that gift was for her!

Although the Trayherns gave everyone a present,
parents included, no one else was exchanging gifts
at this party. However, Laura had enthusiastically en-
dorsed Colt's idea that he give his gift to Abbie after
all the others had been distributed. His heart hammered briefly with anxiety. Would Abbie like it?
Would she see the symbolism behind it? Realize
what he hoped for them? Or would she be horribly
embarrassed? Angry at him? Colt wasn't sure. However, when he'd talked to Laura about it, she'd been
over-the-moon enthusiastic. Her blatant approval had
convinced Colt to go ahead with his wild plan. Now,
if only Abbie would approve of what he'd done....

Morgan stood amid the torn Christmas paper,
bows and ribbon. Laura stood with him, a satisfied
expression on her face. The children were already

raptly playing with their new toys, lost in their own happy world.

"Morgan, dear…"

"Yes?" He smiled down at her and then lifted his chin and held up his hands. Everyone began to quiet except the little ones.

"I think…" Laura said dramatically, "that there's one gift still left under our Christmas tree. Did you not hand it out for a reason, dear? Hmm?"

Grinning mischievously, Morgan gave his wife a teasing look. "You can really ham it up, can't you?"

Everyone tittered at their obvious dramatics.

"I'm not the one who is gulping down Krispy Kreme doughnuts, darling. The only ham around here is standing next to me…."

The crowd erupted with laughter and giggling.

Morgan frowned good-naturedly and patted his waistline. "Well, it's true I've got a little more 'ham' than I should…." He chuckled. Waving his hand toward his audience, he said, "We have a very special occasion for a very special person. Colt? Would you like to come up and tell us more?"

Abbie looked up at him as his name was called. She saw trepidation in his expression as he looked down at her. Giving her a slight smile, he stood up. What was going on? Morgan and Laura were beaming at him like proud parents.

The crowd quieted as Colt carefully wove his way through the scattered gift wrap, children and toys. Sitting up, Abbie saw Laura smiling widely at her from across the room. Something was going to happen, she sensed. Colt went to the back of the tree to carefully pick up the gold-wrapped gift with the huge red bow. As he brought it forward and held it in his hands, the Trayherns moved off to one side, arm in arm, waiting expectantly for him to speak.

The room grew very quiet.

Colt looked around. He nervously cleared his throat. "I want to thank Morgan and Laura for letting me do this," he said, nodding in their direction. Colt's heart hammered with anxiety. He saw the quizzical look on Abbie's face. She didn't have a clue; that was good. Managing a boyish, shy smile, Colt said, "I'm not much good at speeches. In fact, standing up here is like getting put in front of a firing squad."

Everyone tittered.

Swaying from one foot to the other, Colt held Abbie's gaze. Swallowing hard, he forced himself to speak. "Sometimes life has a funny, quirky way of handing out gifts that we never expect to receive. Five days ago, I met Abbie. I was just going to help her behind the scenes here, and that was all. But she has a way of making a person feel good about himself, making him feel that he's a part of her world and life." Colt saw Abbie's expression grow soft.

"And with the Trayherns' approval—" he lifted the package "—I wanted to give Abbie something that comes from my heart to hers. I've seen her give so much to everyone else that I felt this special gift was deserved. Abbie? You want to come up and open it? Please?'' He held his breath as she sat there with a stunned look on her face.

And then she stood.

Everyone cheered loudly, calling her name and urging her to go up there.

Winding her way among the children, toys and scattered gift wrap that littered the room from one end to another, Abbie came forward amid the clapping.

Her cheeks had high color as she approached. Colt handed her the gift and then pulled up a chair so that she could sit down and open it in front of everyone.

"Colt?" she whispered. "What is this all about?"

His mouth stretched in a smile. "It's for you, Abbie. Go ahead and open it. Don't tip it, though. It has to stay upright. Okay?"

Abbie sat and smiled at the crowd. "I don't know what this is all about," she said with a laugh.

"She will!" Laura called out gaily.

Laughter circled the room.

With trembling fingers, Abbie carefully removed the exquisite wrap and ribbon, keeping the box upright on her lap. Colt was at her side, his expression one of pride and, if she wasn't mistaken, of love— for her. Heart pounding as she set the box on the floor next to the chair to open the top, she felt Colt's large hand on her shoulder.

As Abbie opened it, she gasped. She jerked her head up and twisted to look up at Colt, who was grinning unevenly. His eyes were alive with warmth and anxiety.

"Colt!" she gasped. "You didn't!"

He became terribly bashful and avoided her widening eyes. "It's for you, Abbie...."

Disbelievingly, Abbie quickly pulled the huge, vibrant orchid out of the box. It had been swathed in bubble wrap to protect it. Colt knelt down on one knee next to her and held the clay pot while she removed the packing material from around the lush bloom.

"Oh!" Abbie whispered as Colt held the exotic plant toward her. "It's a *Cattleya rex!* Oh!" She reached out with trembling fingers to touch one of the six stunning blossoms.

Everyone clapped and cheered.

Abbie was speechless. Colt smiled up at her as he placed the pot in her hands. He saw the tears swimming in her eyes.

"How..." she began brokenly as she looked down at the healthy green plant in her hands.

Feeling good at her reaction, Colt leaned forward and kissed her on her flaming cheek. The crowd erupted with lusty cheers.

"I called up an orchid warehouse in California. The guy had one plant and I had him ship it here overnight." He gazed into her wide blue eyes, which sparkled with gold in their depths. He saw how happy the gift made Abbie, and his heart swelled with pride and joy. Colt knew now that he'd made the right decision to get the orchid.

Tears slipped down Abbie's cheeks as she stood and held up the gorgeous white blooms, with their yellow and fuschia lips, for all to see. After the applause and whistles subsided, she said, "What you don't know is how rare and expensive this particular orchid is. It's called the Christmas orchid." She gave Colt, who was now standing self-consciously at her side, his hands clasped in front of him, a tender look. "And this guy…well, I'm stunned at his gift. It costs so much…and I've always dreamed of owning one someday." She smiled brokenly. "Of course, on a teacher's salary, that would never happen."

Everyone laughed.

Colt placed his arm around her. "What Abbie doesn't know is that, to me, she's like this orchid— rare and special. I found out orchids can live to be over fifty years old." Giving her a fond look, he rasped, "And this is my way of hoping that what we have will last as long…or even longer. But like an orchid, friendship takes a lot of care, feeding and watering. I'm willing to do that if she is…."

"Colt, this is such a surprise…the orchid is so beautiful," Abbie sighed as she looked at it one more time. It sat in the center of her kitchen table as she and Colt enjoyed a cup of eggnog in the late afternoon. Her hands around the bright red ceramic cup,

Abbie gave him a smile and shook her head. "I'm
still in shock. This orchid cost you a lot of money."

Shrugging, he said, "What's money, Abbie? Look
at the Trayherns. They're worth multimillions. They
give a lot of it away." He gazed at one of the huge
blossoms, nearly the size of his fist, and then held
her teary gaze. "I wanted in some way to tell you
how much you've come to mean to me. When you
told me that it was your favorite orchid, and that
you'd never be able to have one...well, I wanted to
make that dream come true for you. It was the least
I could do for all you've done for me."

Abbie gave him a wry look. "All the care, watering and feeding?" she teased gently. Her heart
opened as he flashed her that shy, boyish look again.
How easily touched Colt was.

"Yeah...you could say that, Abbie. I feel like you
rescued my soul from a dark, dark place." He pushed
his empty cup aside and turned to her. "It's you.
Your heart. Your love..." And he grazed her hair
with his hand. Her gaze turned lambent with desire—
for him.

"I'm so afraid, Colt," Abbie whispered unsteadily, her scalp tingling deliciously at his touch.

"I know you are. And I think I know why...."

She could barely hold Colt's gaze as he quickly
wiped her tears away with his thumbs. When he
placed his hand on her shoulder, she sniffed. "I'm
such a coward, Colt. I—I lost one man...and I'm
afraid to lose you, too. You're a merc...."

"I understand," he told her in a deep, quiet tone. Sliding his other hand over hers, which was clenched in her lap, he whispered, "Abbie, I've made some decisions. And you need to hear them." He bowed his head for a moment, worked his mouth and then looked up at her shining blue eyes, which were soft with invitation. He felt her love, her need of him in every fiber of his being. How badly he wanted to return that love, but some things had to be said first. And depending upon how Abbie received the news, Colt knew they'd either move forward with their relationship or it would dissolve. Never in his whole life had he felt as frightened as he did now, because he realized that he loved her with a burning fierceness that would never die.

Abbie sat very still as she watched Colt wrestle with unspoken emotions. His hand curling protectively around her shoulders made her feel a bit better. "W-what do you want to say?"

"That I'm scared to death, Abbie. Scared of how you might take what I say...what I feel...." He shook his craggy head. "Well, here goes. Life's a risk, anyway. Right now, I'm putting my heart in your hands...." He took a deep breath. "Five days ago, when you crashed into my life, I never thought it possible to fall in love with someone so quickly. You just kind of walked in with your sunshine smile and that wide-open heart of yours, Abbie, and took me by storm."

Colt grazed her hair and forced a lopsided smile.

Her expression was tender and it gave him the courage to go on. "That's what I feel for you—love. And respect. And I want to keep exploring what I've discovered about us. I know we need time to continue to get to know one another, and I'm more than willing to give us that if you are. This morning, I went over and talked to Morgan. I told him I wanted a desk job here, at the main headquarters of Perseus. I want off the merc mission list for good."

"I—I see...." Abbie gulped. She clung to Colt's gaze, absorbed his hesitant, grazing touches. Hope warred with fear in his eyes. "You wouldn't miss being on missions?" Abbie knew that Ted had lived for that kind of life and would never have left it even if she'd begged him to. Searching Colt's serious expression, she waited.

"Abbie, no matter what you say, what you decide, I'm not going back in the field. I'm done with that part of my life." His mouth quirked. "My last missions over in Kosovo showed me that." Shaking his head, Colt murmured, "No, I want to settle down. You've shown me what I've been longing for deep inside, but it was something I was afraid to even dream about."

"What was that?" Her voice was off-key.

"A family." He shrugged heavily. "Kids... Just being a part of the last five days, celebrating Christmas, has made me want to settle down and have a family. I think I can be a good father, or at least I'll try to be." Lifting his head, Colt smiled gently at

Abbie. "And I know I've found the woman I want as my life partner, who will be the best mother to our children I could ever find."

Shaken, Abbie closed her eyes. She pressed her hand against her eyes, tears spilling down her face. "Oh, Colt…"

"Come here," he urged in a husky voice, and he pulled her chair out and took her in his arms. "I love you, Abbie. Will you give me a chance to prove to you my love is real?"

Slipping into his embrace, Abbie whispered, "Yes…yes, I will, Colt…" After embracing him fervently, she eased away, took his hand in hers and said, "Follow me?"

Wordlessly, he followed her though the living room, past the snapping, crackling fire that warmed the cabin, to her bedroom. Christmas music played softly in the background. The room featured old Victorian lace, a brass bed, a plum-colored velvet quilt that looked very old and well-loved, and dainty white curtains framing the window.

Turning, Abbie looked up at him, her hands resting on his massive chest. "I don't know how it happened either, darling. I love you…." There, the words were out. The truth hung suspended between them as she saw his green eyes flare with surprise, and then burn with joy. Abbie saw all the tension bleed out of Colt with her softly spoken vow. She began to unsnap each pearl button on his cowboy shirt, one by one. "Like you, I was scared at how powerfully I was drawn to you. And over the last five days I knew...I knew in my heart, Colt, that you were the man I wanted in my life...." Her hands stilled as she met and held his burning gaze. "I know we haven't had the time to really be together...and I want that with you."

Abbie eased the shirt off his massive shoulders, revealing his darkly haired chest. He helped her by placing the shirt over a chair near the wall. As his fingers brushed the hem of her sweater, she whispered, "Now that you're not going to be out in the field anymore, I know we'll have that time...." She smiled tremulously up at him. "Love me? I want to lie with you, love you and be a part of you...."

Her words cascaded like molten heat over Colt. Nodding wordlessly, he eased the sweater off Abbie. She wore an ivory silk camisole beneath it, but no bra. Colt removed the spray of orchids from her hair and unclipped her unruly hair. It fell in silky abandon around her shoulders like a living waterfall.

"Come here...." he rasped as he pulled her onto the bed.

Time slowed until each moment was a thing of beauty to Abbie. As they continued to undress one another, then lay naked and warm on the velvet coverlet, she saw a predatory look come to Colt's eyes. Moving into his arms, her slender form pressed against his hard masculine body, she closed her eyes and lifted her head. Colt's mouth closed over hers with such hunger that a bolt of jagged heat flashed through her. Abbie's lower body exploded with need of him.

She inhaled the sweet pine scent that clung to Colt, and tasted the strength and cajoling power of his mouth as he rocked her lips open. Sliding her hands up his muscled arms to his bunched shoulders, Abbie felt herself being eased onto her back. His fingers trailing fire, he cupped her breast with a gentle but possessive grip. A sigh, a moan of need, escaped her parted, well-kissed lips. As she arched upward, so that her hips met his, his lips settled on one hardened peak. Abbie gave a little cry as he began to suckle strongly.

Her world exploded. Behind her closed eyes, fireworks shimmered in vivid color, sending sparks through her being. Never had Abbie felt so cherished as in this moment. Every touch of Colt's hand as he slid it down her rib cage, across her hip to her thighs, told her how much he loved her. A fierce ache sprang to life as he stroked her moistness, a ragged sigh escaped her. She tried to please Colt in return, but he seemed bent on pleasuring her completely, instead. Abbie felt like a prisoner, captured within his arms, surrounded by his massive body. All she could do was surrender to the white-hot pleasure now throbbing up through her as he continued to stroke her in slow, delicious exploration. How badly she wanted him!

As if sensing that, Colt moved carefully on top of her. Abbie opened her eyes as she felt his knee settle heavily between her thighs. The glint of a hunter who had captured his quarry burned in his eyes as he held her gaze. She smiled tremulously and eased her arms around his damp neck. Without speaking, she moved her hips upward and drew him deeply into herself, and the action freed her soul to fly on wings of joy.

Colt's world shattered. A groan ripped from him as her slender legs wrapped strongly around his and brought him fully into her hot, liquid depths. His mind exploded. No longer did he think; he could only feel. The spicy fragrance of Abbie reached his flared nostrils, her little cries of pleasure rippling through him like fiery caresses. He gripped her hard in his arms, never wanting to let her go. As she arched provocatively, her hips melding with his, he thrust into her. Somewhere in the haze and fire of his being, he knew they were making love without any protection. Yet his heart whispered that even if Abbie became pregnant from their coupling, it was something they both wanted. Above all, Colt wanted to give Abbie the child she'd always wanted, but had been denied.

Time throbbed to a halt as he brought her into heated rhythm with himself. They fit together like two lost puzzle pieces. Each brush of her lips upon his, each movement of her hands, ranging teasingly across his damp, tense body, told him of her love for him. Their primal need for one another culminated rapidly, and within seconds, Colt felt her tense in his arms. He could feel the fiery liquid of her body surround him, and he surged forward, hoping to prolong her pleasure. And then he felt a massive explosion occur, and all he could do was cling to her, their heads resting against one another.

Golden seconds spun between them in the aftermath. Abbie was breathing in gasps as Colt continued to hold her. Slowly, very slowly, she felt him ease out of her, then gather up the velvet quilt and pull it over them. Sighing happily, she lay her head in the crook of his shoulder, her arm around his rib cage. Her breasts were pressed against his heart, which was pounding in unison with hers. Smiling softly, she nuzzled against him and felt his lips caress her temple and then her hair.

"I love you," she whispered unsteadily.

"I know you do," Colt rasped. Leaning down, he watched her open lustrous blue eyes that glowed with gold in their depths. Abbie was happy.

His heart soared. Colt had desperately wanted to please her, to give her joy to replace the tragedy and loss of the last two years of her life. "I love you, sweetheart. And I want to spend the rest of my life showing you how much you mean to me."

Abbie closed her eyes as Colt caressed her cheek, her neck and shoulder beneath the coverlet. "You're such a gift to me, darling."

He chuckled indulgently. "I hope I'll be like that orchid of yours out there on the table—around for a long, long time."

Laughing softly, Abbie opened her eyes and

drowned in his forest-green ones. How young Colt looked now, with the stress of the days before erased. In some part of her fluttering, joyful heart, she sensed it was because he was no longer going out on missions that could rip him apart inwardly. Everyone had a limit to the amount of trauma they could endure. She knew Colt had reached his. And because he had, he was looking for a new life—a better one…with her.

"And like that orchid, my beloved, you are strong, enduring, and so easy on my eyes…." she whispered.

Colt ran his hand across her slender yet strong, womanly body. "Can you put up with me? Or when I get irritable and cranky, are you going to put me in your greenhouse to cool my heels?"

Giving him a wicked, teasing look, Abbie teethed his earlobe gently. "Not a chance! We'll talk it out. Communication is the key."

Laughing freely, Colt dodged her lips, his ear tingling. "You're going to teach me how to talk to you, Abbie. I admit I'm not good at it…." His smile slipped as he leaned down and captured her soft mouth in a kiss. Eventually, he eased back and whispered, "And I want to learn, because I want to make you happy…forever…."

* * * * *

Look for

WOMAN OF INNOCENCE
(Special Edition #1442)

*as Lindsay McKenna begins a brand-new
series featuring Morgan and his team:*
Morgan's Mercenaries: Destiny's Women.
Available in January 2002!

TWINS UNDER THE TREE
Stella Bagwell

To my editor, Mary-Theresa Hussey,
who just happens to be a Christmas angel all year long.
Thank you for appreciating the Murdocks as much as I do.

Dear Reader,

Down through the years I've had the pleasure of writing several books revolving around Christmas and love. After all, the two just naturally go together. Romantic sparks are bound to fly whether you're sharing eggnog in front of a cozy fire, stealing a kiss under the mistletoe or dancing cheek-to-cheek to "White Christmas."

Each of us has our own different meaning of this special holiday and how to celebrate it. But beneath the baking, caroling, shopping and visits from Santa, I believe most of us agree that Christmas is all about giving to those we love. Not just gifts wrapped in bright paper, but the true, unselfish giving of ourselves.

In "Twins under the Tree," Oren Lassiter is a man alone, fearful to give or receive gifts, especially the kind that come from the heart. I hope you enjoy reading how the magic of Christmas soon works its way and convinces this hero that a family of his own is a gift too precious to refuse.

Happy holidays and love to you all,

Chapter 1

Several times throughout the day, Mary Jo came close to turning the car around and heading back home to Aztec. A three-hundred-fifty-mile trip for a woman who was in her seventh month of pregnancy wasn't easy. Her back was aching and her ankles were fat from her being confined behind the steering wheel for nearly six hours of driving.

Even though it was only the first part of December and the babies weren't due for another eight weeks, Mary Jo's doctor had advised her not to travel. And if she simply had to, she should ride with her feet up while someone else did the driving.

Well, this was something far too important to be handled with a phone call, Mary Jo reasoned with herself. And there was no one else to do the driving for her. There was no one else to do anything for her, including paying the bills and buying the groceries. Missing a couple days' work at the diner to make this trip was going to run her short this week, but there was little she could do about it.

Last night she'd made up her mind that this trip to Hondo was important to her unborn twins, even herself. But now that she'd turned her car onto Bar M land, she was plagued with serious doubts.

What was she going to do, just walk up to the front door and announce who she was? And expect them to believe her? Or even care? They were going to think she was crazy.

As she drove deeper into the ranch, her nerves stretched so tight they seemed to hum like electrical wires on overload. This whole thing was wrong, she kept thinking. Her showing up on the Bar M would only cause the Murdocks trouble, or God forbid, heartache. She didn't want that for anyone.

With grim resolution, she stepped harder on the accelerator. As soon as she found a wide spot in the road, she was going to turn around and forget she'd ever heard of the Murdock family.

"Yip, yip, ho! Get along, cattle!"

Oren Lassiter slapped a coiled lariat against the heavy leather of his chaps, creating a popping noise loud enough to make the small herd of cattle trot down the graveled dirt road.

"A quarter of a mile and we'll have them, boss."

A cowboy to his right spoke up. "Did anyone remember to open the gate?"

"It's open, Lucky. Just make sure that little wiry heifer up at the front doesn't turn back on you."

Oren had barely gotten the words out when a car rounded the curve up ahead of them at a speed too fast to avoid running straight into the herd of Black Angus.

"Hit the ditch!" Oren shouted to the other two cowhands.

The startled cattle began to run and the three men spurred their horses out of the car's path, which by now was skidding sideways and heading straight toward a grove of pines. Red dust and gravel spewed high into the air, momentarily turning the visibility to zero.

"Watch the herd!" Oren yelled. Then, digging his heels into the sides of his mount, he rode through the cattle and the blinding red haze.

Thankfully, the car had come to a dead halt in a shallow ditch before it had reached the sturdy pine trunks, he discovered. A quick glance assured him there weren't any cattle down on the road, but the driver of the car might not have been so lucky.

Sliding from the saddle with lightning speed, he hurried to the driver's door. Through the window he could see the shape of a woman's head slumped over the wheel.

Adrenaline pumped through him as he jerked open the door. "Lady! Are you all right?"

She lifted her head and stared at him blankly. Her hands continued to grip the steering wheel with white knuckles.

"I—I think so," she said. "What—what happened?"

She sounded dazed and Oren wasn't surprised. The whole incident had happened in the amount of time it took to blink an eye.

"You were driving too fast to stop. You nearly ran head-on into the herd of cattle we're driving down the road."

Her forehead wrinkled with confusion as she touched a hand to her temple. "Was I? Normally I don't drive fast."

She peered beyond the thick male shoulder partially blocking her view. Black cattle were running in every direction, bawling and kicking up clouds of red dust. She caught a glimpse of another cowhand trying to round them up and quiet them down.

Her eyes flew back to the man leaning over her. He had the brownest eyes she'd ever seen, the rich color of polished coffee beans. His skin was brown, too, with leathery crinkles at the corners of his eyes and lines bracketing his chiseled lips. Most of his hair was hidden beneath his gray hat, but what she could see was somewhere between dark brown and black. Equally dark brows were drawn together, forming an angry-looking line across his forehead. He smelled of sagebrush, horses and cold wind, a combination that was as mesmerizing as his tough features.

"Well, you were driving fast this time," he said in a deep, hoarse voice. "Did you hit your head? Is anything hurt?"

Easing back against the seat, she forced her gaze away from him, then with a glance down at herself, shook her head. "I think I'm okay. I'm just not sure…where am I?"

Glancing up, Mary Jo noticed his gaze was riveted on her belly. Since there was only about an inch or two of space between it and the steering wheel, he was no doubt thinking she was the most pregnant woman he'd ever laid eyes on.

"You're going to have a baby," he said, stating the obvious.

Mary Jo frowned more at herself than at his inane comment. She wasn't feeling exactly right in the head. What had happened? She didn't believe she'd hit her head, but at the moment her thinking was so fuzzy.

"No. I'm going to have two babies," she corrected, then held her hand up to him. "Could you help me out? I think—I'm about to be sick."

"Good Lord!" he muttered with a horrified look. "Maybe you'd better not move."

Annoyed with him now, she said, "Oh, for crying out loud, help me out of here! You don't have to watch!"

A big, tough skinned hand was suddenly thrust in

front of her. She latched on to it and was relieved when his strength did all the work of lifting her out of the car.

"Can you stand?" he asked, while his other hand planted itself in the middle of her back. "Look, lady, I don't want you falling."

Her head was swimming and beads of perspiration had popped out on her forehead and upper lip. Funny, it had been cool when she'd eaten lunch. But where had that been? Where was she now?

"I'm...I won't fall," she tried to reassure him as her stomach began to roil with nausea. Quickly, before she lost the sandwich she'd eaten earlier right on this man's boots, she pulled away from him and hurried to the rear of the car.

A few steps away, Oren turned his back and waited for the woman to gather herself together. At the same time, Lucky pulled his horse to a stop on the road.

"Is everything okay, boss?" he called. "Need some help?"

"No. You and Red take the cattle on," Oren told him. "I'll handle things here."

The sorrel Oren had been riding was grazing nearby. He fetched the horse and tethered him to a small mesquite tree. By the time he finished the task, he noticed the woman had returned to the side of the car.

Now that Oren could take a more leisurely look, he realized she was much younger than he'd first thought. At least five or six years younger than his thirty-one. Long, strawberry-blond hair hung straight to the middle of her back and her skin was as white as a yucca blossom. She was pretty, too.

A damned important fact there, Lassiter. He silently cursed himself. The only thing that *should* be on his mind at the moment was the best way to deal with this whole incident. Accidents on the Bar M, even if there didn't appear to be any damages, had to be regarded seriously.

Not more than six weeks ago another young woman had trespassed onto Bar M land, then tried to extort money from the Murdocks because her horse had gotten tangled in a piece of barbed wire and permanently injured an ankle. The woman had sworn she'd gotten lost while out riding, but later it was learned she'd deliberately staged the incident. Not to say this woman was the same conniving sort, Oren thought. But he'd be negligent if he wasn't concerned for his employers' welfare, along with the health of this young woman.

Stepping to within a couple of feet from her, Oren asked, "Feeling better, ma'am?"

She nodded. "I'm sorry—I guess the shock of nearly hitting those cows must have upset my stomach."

His gaze dropped from her pale face to the mound of stomach pushing at the plum-colored sweater and faded jeans she was wearing. He didn't know much about pregnant women, but it was clearly evident she

had quite a load to tote around, especially for someone who appeared to be on the small side. The top
of her head scarcely reached the height of his shoulder.

"I think we'd both feel better if I drove you to
Ruidoso and had a doctor check you out. Or is there
someone close I could call for you? Your husband?"

"I'm not married," she answered. Then, with a
perplexed shake of her head, she added, "And I
don't know anyone around here. At least, I don't
think I do."

Concerned by the odd look in her eyes, Oren
stepped closer. "What's your name, ma'am?" he
asked, continuing to study the puzzled expression on
her face.

Cornflower-blue eyes lifted to meet his. "Mary Jo
Bailey."

He breathed an inward sigh of relief. At least the
woman knew her name.

"Uh...you're not from around here?"

The frown on her face deepened. "I'm—not sure.
Where am I, anyway?"

Dear God, was this for real? Oren wondered. He
had more than two hundred head of cattle to move
before dark. The last thing he needed to be doing
was standing around on the side of the road with a
pregnant, disoriented woman.

Trying to hide his agitation, he said, "You're on
the Bar M Ranch, Mary Jo. Is that where you were
going?"

Mary Jo thought long and hard, but her mind was stuck in a whirling blank circle.

Making a helpless, palms-up gesture, she looked at him. "I don't know," she said simply. Then in a voice tinged with fear, she repeated, "I don't know!"

Seeing the blood was draining out of her face, he placed a reassuring hand on her shoulder. "Don't panic. That will only make things worse. Just breathe deeply and try to relax. Do you remember where you live?"

Even though the closeness of the big cowboy unnerved Mary Jo, the answer came to her effortlessly. With a tiny smile of relief, she nodded. "Yes. I live just a few miles out of Aztec."

A flag of warning was suddenly waving at Oren. The Murdocks hadn't mentioned company coming for a visit. Plus this woman was awfully pregnant to be traveling alone, so far from home.

Careful to keep his skeptical notions to himself, he said, "That's good. Now do you remember when you left Aztec?"

She touched fingers to the middle of her forehead. Oren couldn't help but notice the slight tremble of her hand. Something was truly wrong with the woman, or she was a damn good actress, he decided.

Aghast, she exclaimed, "No! I—can't think. It could have been days ago!"

Squeezing her shoulder, he said, "You'll figure it

all out. Just go back to the last thing you do remember and start from there.''

Mary Jo strained to retrace her earlier movements in the day, but she had no recollection of getting in the car or driving anywhere. Nothing would come to her mind, except the impression that she'd been nervous and excited about something. Whatever it was must have prompted her to go somewhere, but where? And why was she here on this ranch with a man she'd never seen before in her life?

"I'm totally blank. The last thing I remember clearly is that I was leaving the diner where I work to go home. That was seven o'clock—last night." She flattened a palm against her forehead as if the pressure of her hand could summon up the answers she needed to give this man and herself. "I have this feeling that maybe...I turned around and was heading back home. Am I very far from Aztec? Maybe I could call someone there to come after me?"

Something definitely wasn't ringing true here, Oren decided. He could feel it all the way to his bones. "You're probably close to four hundred miles from Aztec. I hope your family is ready for a long drive."

Her pink lips popped open to form a shocked O. "Four hundred miles! Surely you're joking!"

Oren didn't know what to think. She apparently remembered some things, but was conveniently blank when it came to why she was here on the Bar M. His ex-wife, Heather, had done the same thing when she'd been trying to hide the truth from him. Maybe it wasn't fair of him to compare her to his ex, but he'd be a fool to ignore the similarities.

"Look, lady, I don't have time to play games," he said, trying to keep a tight rein on what little patience he had left. "You need to get out of this cold wind and I need to get back to work."

His curtness stiffened Mary Jo's spine. She might be a little woozy headed about where she was going, but she wasn't about to let this man talk down to her.

"My name isn't 'lady.' It's Mary Jo," she reminded him flatly. "And I can see I'm keeping you from your work."

Glancing down the road, she noticed two men were pushing the large herd of black cattle around the bend and out of sight. Belatedly, she wondered if one of them would have been more help to her than this crusty cowboy.

"If you'll just point me toward the main highway," she added, "I'll be on my way."

Those brown eyes that had first caught her attention now narrowed and transformed his face to an even tougher image than before. "Sorry, I don't think I can allow you to do that, Ms. Bailey."

Uneasy now, she continued to stare at him, her mouth open, her eyes wide. "Are you crazy, mister?"

The grim line of his lips twisted to a mocking slant. "The name is Oren Lassiter. I'm the foreman of the Bar M Ranch."

Tilting her chin to a fairly defensive angle, she met his gaze head-on. "Well, Mr. Oren Lassiter, I suppose I owe you an apology for—as you said—driving too fast around that curve, but other than that misdeed, I don't see that I've hurt you or your cattle. I'm not injured and my car doesn't seem to be, either. So you don't have a right or a reason to keep me here!"

She turned to climb back into the car. Oren's hand immediately snared her upper arm.

She snapped her head around to glower at him. "Take your hand off me!"

His rigid expression never wavered. "I just told you I'm not letting you leave. Not until we go up to the big house and make sure this matter is settled between you and the owners of this ranch."

Try as she might to focus on his brown eyes, for some strange reason his face was fading in and out of her vision. "What...do you mean?" she asked weakly.

"It means that since you can't explain to me why you're here on the Bar M Ranch, maybe Chloe and Wyatt will have more luck getting it out of you."

She frowned at the masculine features wavering in front of her. *Chloe and Wyatt. Who was he talking about and why did her legs feel so strange?*

"Well, are you ready to explain?" Oren prodded. "Or do we have to do this the hard way?"

Mary Jo tried to speak, but everything around her began to tilt wildly. A rushing noise exploded in her ears. Too late, she felt herself pitching forward and grabbing for the front of his jacket.

"What the hell!"

Her deadweight fell directly against the middle of Oren's chest, then began a quick downward slide. Somehow he managed to grab a hold beneath her arms, preventing her from falling completely to the ground. But it took a little more maneuvering to lift her off her feet. When he finally had her braced in the cradle of his arms, her head rolled lifelessly, then plopped against his chest.

At the sight of her quiet, pale face, Oren groaned with disbelief. "I guess this means we do it the hard way."

"Oren, there isn't any reason for us to be suspicious of this young woman. The sheriff in Aztec verified that the information she gave you was true."

The female voice was low, insistent and full of empathy. Drawn to it, Mary Jo struggled to open her eyes and see the person it belonged to.

"Okay, Chloe, I'll admit she didn't lie about her name or where she lives, but what was she doing here on the Bar M?" Oren countered.

"She probably got lost and then the near wreck scared the wits out of her."

"I don't mind telling you, Chloe, I have an uneasy feeling about her."

That man again, Mary Jo thought fuzzily. Did he have to pester her even in her dreams?

The woman called Chloe laughed softly. "You have your doubts about all women, Oren. I'd be worried if you felt good about this one."

His reply was a snort.

Mary Jo tried to speak, but the words came out as a groan instead. Immediately, a hand touched her shoulder, and Mary Jo willed her eyes to open. A beautiful woman with deep auburn hair and an anxious expression was hovering over her.

"Hello," she said warmly. "How do you feel?"

Blinking, Mary Jo slowly became aware that she was lying on a bed made of polished pine. Standing at the carved footboard was the man with the brown eyes. Except for a pair of worn leather bat-wing chaps, he was dressed entirely in dark blue denim. His gray hat rode low on his forehead, partially shading his features. Yet Mary Jo could see enough of his face to tell he was still regarding her with misgivings.

With her gaze still locked on Oren Lassiter, she answered the woman. "I'm much better, thank you."

"I'm Chloe Murdock Sanders," she introduced herself, "and this is the Bar M's foreman, Oren Lassiter. He carried you up here to the house after your little mishap."

Yes. Her near miss with the cows, Mary Jo thought. She'd wanted to leave the ranch, but the man standing at her feet wouldn't let her. In fact, he'd been downright rude.

"Did I...faint or something?" Mary Jo asked.

"You've been out for a few minutes," Chloe explained, then to Oren she said, "Go tell Ivy she's awake. I imagine she's on the telephone in the study."

Mary Jo watched the tall, lean cowboy leave the room before she glanced up at the woman. "Is this your house?"

Smiling, Chloe nodded. "Yes. You're on the Bar M Ranch. My husband, Wyatt, and I live here alone—that is when we don't have grandbabies, relatives or friends visiting," she added with an affectionate chuckle.

Mary Jo started to rise, but the woman once again laid a hand on her shoulder. "Don't try to get up just yet. My daughter is a doctor. She's going to check you out—just to make sure nothing is wrong with you or your babies."

Before Mary Jo could assure Chloe she didn't need a doctor, a slender young woman with copper-colored hair strode into the room, carrying a black medical bag. Directly behind her, the foreman stood in the door, his arms folded against his chest, his face stoic.

Mary Jo tried to dismiss him as she looked up at the woman looping a stethoscope around her neck.

"Mary Jo, this is my daughter, Ivy. She'll take good care of you," Chloe promised, then headed to the door, where she grabbed Oren's arm in a motherly fashion. "Let's go, Oren."

He didn't argue with Chloe, but tossed one more

probing look at Mary Jo, then shut the door behind him.

A pent-up breath rushed out of Mary Jo. "I'm afraid I've annoyed your foreman."

Ivy laughed. "Don't let that bother you. Oren doesn't take to women very well."

It was on the tip of Mary Jo's tongue to ask why, but she pushed the question aside. Once she left this ranch she'd never see the man again. It didn't matter why he'd taken an instant dislike to her.

As Ivy began to wrap a blood pressure cuff around her arm, Mary Jo said, "There's no need for you to go to all this trouble, Ivy. I'm really feeling fine now."

"Let me be the judge of that," Ivy responded gently. "Oren tells me you're carrying twins, is that right?"

Mary Jo was surprised the foreman had remembered about her babies. Maybe he wasn't made entirely of steel. "Yes. They're due in about eight weeks."

Ivy's smile held a fond glow. "Twins are special. Believe me, I know. I have a twin brother and sister, Adam and Anna. So we need to make sure yours are okay after this little fainting spell. Okay?"

Put so kindly, Mary Jo could hardly refuse, and she wondered how she'd managed to run into such caring people. It just wasn't her usual luck.

More than a half hour later, Oren was adding a log of piñon to the flames in the fireplace when Ivy entered the living room of the ranch house. He waited for Chloe to ask the question that was on both their minds.

"How is she?"

Joining her mother on the couch, Ivy said, "Physically she seems perfectly normal, and the babies sound very healthy. But she's still a little confused and can't remember why she was driving on Bar M property or what her intentions were when she left Aztec. I've called Victoria Ketchum, her doctor there. Victoria explained she'd warned Mary Jo not to travel. But for some reason the woman ignored her doctor's advice."

"Did this Victoria Ketchum have any idea what Mary Jo's plans were?" Chloe asked her daughter.

"No. But she did enlighten me a little. Apparently Mary Jo has been under a lot of emotional strain the past few months. Her mother passed away recently and then the father of her babies walked out on her. Victoria doesn't know the story behind that, but it's probably safe to say the ordeal has been traumatic for Mary Jo."

"Does she have any other family or a job? She might need to contact someone."

"From what Victoria says, Mary Jo has no other family. She works as a waitress in a diner there in Aztec. She's been taking college correspondence classes, too. The other doctor and I both believe the stress she's been under, coupled with the tiring drive, got to her.''

Chloe shook her head with sympathy. "The poor little thing. No family. And such heartache. It's no wonder she's so distressed and confused.''

Ivy gave her mother's knee a reassuring pat. "I'm having her come into the clinic tomorrow morning for a more thorough examination just as a precautionary measure. For the remainder of this evening and tonight, I've ordered her to rest.''

"I think that's a good idea," Chloe agreed, then turned to Oren. "Tell Lucky he's to take over in the morning, Oren, so that you can drive Mary Jo to the clinic.''

Oren couldn't believe what he was hearing. Throwing up both hands, he protested loudly, "No way. You're much better suited for that job, Chloe.''

"Sorry," Chloe informed him. "I've got to catch a plane early in the morning to meet Wyatt in Houston.''

This news put a frown on Oren's face. "Well, there're plenty of other hands around the ranch who'd be more than willing to drive Ms. Bailey into Ruidoso. Especially one of the hands on the fence-building crew.''

Chloe looked at him with obvious disappointment. Which, under any other circumstances, would have made Oren feel awful. He didn't like to let his boss down. She'd not only given him the best job he'd ever had, she'd become like a second mother to him.

Still, though he wasn't exactly sure why, the need to avoid Mary Jo Bailey was more important to him than making Chloe Sanders proud.

"Why, Oren, do you honestly think I'd put a vulnerable young woman like Mary Jo in a vehicle with one of those rough cowboys?"

"*You* hired those rough cowboys. Surely they can't all be bad."

She grimaced. "That's right. I hired them to build fence and buckaroo, not see after a young lady."

That Chloe automatically considered Mary Jo a sweet, innocent young lady didn't surprise Oren. She had a soft heart. Especially where strays were concerned. The fact that she'd taken Oren under her wing without knowing one thing about him proved that much.

"You didn't hire me for that particular job, either," he reminded her.

"No," Chloe agreed, unaffected by his bluntness. "But after four years of being here on the Bar M, you ought to know that as foreman you have to be ready for anything. I'm appointing you as the man for this job."

Seeing there was no getting out of the chore, Oren turned a look of reluctant resignation on Ivy. "When do I need to have her at the clinic?"

"By nine. And Oren," Ivy added pointedly, "try to be easy with her."

His brows lifted innocently. "Why wouldn't I be?"

Ivy studied him. "She thinks you don't trust her."

He didn't. For the rest of his life, he would never trust another woman. Not completely.

Picking up a sheepskin jacket from a nearby armchair, he thrust his arms into the sleeves. "Whether I believe Ms. Bailey is genuine or not makes little difference," he said. Then, tugging the brim of his hat down on his forehead, he headed toward the door. "Now if you two ladies will excuse me, I've got real work to do."

Chapter 2

The next morning Mary Jo was watching at the window for Oren Lassiter when he drove up in a white pickup truck with the Bar M brand emblazoned on the side of the cab.

Leaving the house, she walked as briskly as she could down a short path of flagstones that led out to a graveled parking area. The morning sun was hovering with pink splendor over the mountains to the east, but there was little warmth to be felt from the weak rays spilling across the yard. December in New Mexico was rarely ever mild, especially in the higher elevations.

Not a comfortable time to be carrying twins, Mary Jo thought as she tightened a red plaid muffler around her neck. But then her pregnancy had been as much of a surprise to her as it had been to the father, the only difference being she'd viewed it as a pleasant shock.

Shoving that grim thought aside, she looked up to see Oren was standing outside the truck. Once again he was dressed all in denim, only this morning he was minus the chaps and spurs. Yet even without those tough outer trappings, he looked as formidable as she remembered.

The idea had her drawing in a bracing breath, then slowly releasing it before she finally came to a stop a few feet away from the man.

"Good morning, Mr. Lassiter."

He returned her greeting with a slight incline of his head. "Ready to go?" he asked.

"Yes. I want to get this over with just as quickly as you do."

She headed around to the passenger side of the truck and opened the door. She was on the verge of climbing in when a gloved hand suddenly gripped her elbow and his low voice sounded close to her ear.

"It's a high step up into the cab. You'd better let me help you."

Like yesterday, when he'd assisted her out of the car, he did all the work for her, lifting her effortlessly up and into the truck. The gentlemanly gesture was an odd contrast to his negative opinion of her. But then, he was probably that sort of man, Mary Jo thought. Not hesitant about speaking his mind, yet carcful to remember his manners.

While she made sure the belt was buckled safely below her tummy, he joined her in the cab and quickly headed them away from the ranch yard and down a red dirt road.

Off to the right, smoke was spiraling up from a chimney in what appeared to be a bunkhouse. Next to the building, in a round corral, a young cowboy tossed a lariat at a spotted yearling. The huge backward loop missed the young horse's neck by a small margin, and the animal trotted away with his head and tail high, as though laughing at his momentary escape.

"The Bar M is a beautiful ranch," she mused aloud, her gaze focused on the unfolding scenery. "And very prosperous, it appears. I've never seen so many barns and outbuildings, or cowboys and live-stock."

Oren grunted. "The Bar M is more than prosper-ous. It's probably the richest ranch in the southern half of New Mexico."

She turned her head slightly to look at him. The faint, sardonic twist to his lips said he figured she'd already known that fact and was merely acting ig-norant for greedy or malevolent reasons.

Damn the man, anyway, she silently cursed. What Oren Lassiter thought or didn't think of her was moot. If he had a problem with women that was his own fault. One that he would just have to get over without her help.

"If I knew anything about the Bar M before, I don't now. My memory still has some black holes in it. But I'm trying not to let it worry me. Ivy says it will jolt right back in place soon—at a moment I won't even be expecting it to."

Ivy was like her mother, Oren thought. Too damn trusting. But then maybe he was judging Mary Jo with a narrow vision. Just because he'd had some dealings with deceitful women in his past didn't mean Mary Jo was the same sort. Still, he'd learned the hard way that it paid to be careful.

"I've never heard of this kind of memory loss," he said frankly. "Just forgetting certain things."

"Neither have I," Mary Jo agreed, "but Ivy explained it sometimes happens. When a person gets overly frightened or under too much stress. I'm…trying my best to believe her. Otherwise—I could only think—there's something wrong with my mind."

The little worried catch he heard in her voice almost convinced him she was being totally honest. But without proof, he wouldn't take the chance of allowing her to make a fool of him or the Murdocks.

"I seriously doubt there's anything wrong with your mind, Ms. Bailey. I'm sure we'll all soon know why you came all the way down here from Aztec."

His tone of voice was smooth, too smooth for Mary Jo to discern whether he was being flip or sincere. In either case, she got the impression he wanted her away from the ranch as quickly as possible.

If anything, Mary Jo should have been angry with him, but to her dismay all she could feel was the pain of rejection. *Don't be a ninny, Mary Jo. For one reason or another, you're going to meet people in this world who don't like you. It just so happens that Oren Lassiter is one of those people.*

The cab was rapidly growing warm. Rather than ask him to adjust the heater, she unwrapped the wool scarf from her neck, then unbuckled the seat belt long enough to shrug out of the coat.

"I'm really sorry you were elected to drive me into Ruidoso this morning," she said. "I'm sure you had plenty of other things to do."

He shrugged. "I do. But I'll manage."

Mary Jo sighed inwardly. This whole thing was like a nightmare. She didn't know why she was here or what she'd been planning. Now she had a long drive back to Aztec to get home, one that she didn't feel quite up to making. On top of that she was being forced to endure Oren Lassiter's cool company.

From the corner of her eye, she peeped at him once again. She'd seen a lot of cowboys, oil field workers, businessmen and lawmen come through the diner back in Aztec. Men of all ages, shapes and sizes had talked and flirted with her, but never had one garnered her attention like Oren Lassiter. Everything about the man, from his brown skin and brown eyes to his tall, lean frame, was commanding. Even his brooding silence intrigued her, and with each mile that passed Mary Jo found herself wondering about him more and more.

"How long have you worked for the Bar M?" she asked after a long stretch of silence.

"Four years."

Mary Jo waited and hoped he would elaborate. When he didn't, she tried again. "Are you from around these parts?"

He grimaced. "I've always lived in New Mexico. But not necessarily in Lincoln County."

She wanted to ask him what had brought him to this part of the state, but she felt the question would be particularly forward. Especially since she didn't have a clue as to why she was here herself.

"Do you, uh, have a family, Mr. Lassiter?"

The frown on his face deepened. "No wife or kids, if that's what you're asking."

His blunt answer told her much more than the fact that he wasn't married.

He had no desire to share anything about himself with her.

Cursing herself for feeling hurt by his distant attitude, Mary Jo turned her attention on the passing landscape.

They were now traveling a state highway that snaked a path through a narrow valley bordered by tall mountains dotted with cacti, sagebrush, mesquite and pine. To their immediate left was river bottom land, much of which was planted in orchards. The trees were bare now, but Mary Jo could easily imagine how lush and green it all must look when the fruit was ripening. Interspersed among the orchards were small ranches, which appeared to be raising horses rather than cattle.

Under different circumstances, getting the opportunity to see new places and faces she'd never seen before would have thrilled Mary Jo. Up until now, the only long-distance journeys she'd taken were through books. But even without her memory intact, she knew she'd not come all this way to southern New Mexico just for a sightseeing tour. In her condition it wouldn't make sense. Plus there was the expense; she could barely afford to buy gas to drive back and forth to work, much less four hundred miles.

Across the seat from her, Oren was trying his best to forget he had a passenger. But the tactic wasn't working. He couldn't dismiss the woman seated a few inches away from him any more than he could ignore the danger of the oncoming traffic.

In the years since his divorce, Oren's notice of women had been pretty much limited to necessary glances. And even before that bitter experience, he'd certainly never taken an interest in a woman in Mary Jo's condition. He'd never realized a woman as pregnant as her could look pretty, or, God help him, so downright sexy. Everything about her appeared lush and glowing and fertile.

Shiny, red-gold hair slithered like silk against her

shoulders and the mounds of her breasts. Her skin was smooth and dewy, with just a hint of pale golden freckles scattered across the bridge of her nose.

At the moment she was looking away from him, but he didn't need a second glance to remind him that her eyes were as blue as the New Mexico sky after a rain and fringed with lashes so long they created little crescent shadows against her cheeks. A pair of full, dusky pink lips expressed her thoughts and feelings with each little movement they made. And not for the first time since he'd met her yesterday, Oren wondered how those lips would look if he were to plant a kiss on them.

Giving himself a hard, mental shake, he asked, "When are your babies due?"

The unexpected sound of his voice caused Mary Jo to turn a curious gaze on him. Did he really want to know, or was he just breaking the silence to be polite? she wondered.

"The latter part of February."

He kept his eyes riveted to the highway. "So what are you going to do then? I mean, after you give birth."

Unconsciously, her hand moved in a protective gesture against her swollen stomach. "Aztec has always been home. I'll continue to work at the diner there, and eventually, I hope to get started on a writing career."

Skeptical, he said, "I'd think writing was an iffy

choice of careers. Do you have any background for such a job?''

She wondered why he thought it okay for him to question her, but not the other way around. Yet she didn't risk asking him. The man was talking. Right now that was enough for Mary Jo.

Her chin unconsciously tilted upward. "I have a degree in English and I'm taking a couple of psychology classes now.''

She certainly hadn't been idle these past few years. Oren would have to give her credit for that much. "Have you sold anything that you've written?"

Her features suddenly softened and her eyes glowed with pride. "Three short stories to different magazines. One paid me five hundred dollars. My mother was thrilled and now—well, I'm just glad she was still alive then to see my check and the story in print.''

"Have you sold anything lately?"

Sensing his underlying question, she studied his rugged profile. "No. I haven't tried. I've been working on the psychology classes," she said, then added, "Look, I'm not a ninny. I understand it takes years to make any sort of living at writing. That's why I work at the diner. The salary is small, but it's steady.''

"And what about the babies?" he persisted. "Who's going to care for them while you're at work?"

"I have a couple of friends who run a day-care

service. They've promised to care for the babies at half the regular fee. But I don't want to take advantage of their generosity for very long. The task of taking care of two infants won't be easy. It's a cinch I'll have to put off furthering my education for a while and budget as closely as I can. But that will be a small price to pay for having a family of my own.''

She seemed determined. Oren would grant her that much.

''Don't you have any other family that could help you? What about your father?''

Mary Jo's head swung back and forth. ''No family. My mother was an orphan raised in foster homes. I never knew my father. He died before I was born.''

Of all the people Oren was acquainted with, it was impossible to think of one who didn't have some sort of family. It was hard to imagine this young woman alone and on her own without anyone to support her. And yet, on this count, he believed Mary Jo. Something in the way she'd shaken her head and the way her eyes had suddenly become shadowed told Oren she was speaking the truth about having no family.

The notion sent his thoughts hurtling back to his ex-wife. Though Heather's parents hadn't been exactly rich, they had surrounded their daughter with love and spoiled her with far too much attention and things. Try as he might, he couldn't imagine Heather being in Mary Jo's position. For one thing, his ex-wife had made damn sure she never got pregnant. At least, not with his children. And for another, he was pretty certain Heather didn't have the inner strength to make it through any sort of crisis without a circle of people to carry the major part of the load for her.

More curious now than he wanted to be, he glanced over at Mary Jo. "Have you always lived around Aztec?"

She nodded. "I was born in Raton, but Mother moved to Aztec shortly afterward. I've lived there all my life." She smoothed her hair back behind her ear while continuing to study his profile beneath the brim of his Stetson. "I know that you or someone in the Murdock family talked to Sheriff Perez in Aztec yesterday."

She probably believed the call had been made only for the Murdocks' protection, Oren figured. But frankly, he'd made the call for her sake, too. He'd been hoping the sheriff would know of some kin willing to come after her, or at the very least explain her presence here. But as it turned out, the sheriff had confirmed what she'd just now implied. She was a woman completely alone.

"I talked to Sheriff Perez," he conceded.

"I'm sure he told you that my mother and I were so unimportant we were hardly worth mentioning, just two more numbers in the county population."

Oren was trying to decipher the meaning of that when she let out a little groan and shook her head.

Pressing a hand against a red cheek, she said, "I'm

sorry. I shouldn't have said that. I don't know why I did. I'm not normally this way at all. I guess my…''

Her pause stretched into silence, and as she shifted on the seat, Oren could feel her embarrassment. Yet he wasn't exactly sure why she was so flustered over her own remark.

"Go on," he urged.

Shaking her head again, she gazed out the windshield rather than at him. "I'm ashamed of myself. I said that like—like I had a chip on my shoulder or something. And that's not true. I have much to be thankful for."

She had no family or husband, she lived on financial ground that was obviously very shaky, and she had two babies coming soon. Yet she considered herself blessed. Either she was crazy or he didn't know the first thing about life.

"Actually, Sheriff Perez didn't say anything of the sort," Oren stated. "He said he didn't really know you or your mother personally."

"That's true," Mary Jo agreed. "I don't suppose I ever talked to the man. He doesn't frequent the diner like Jess or the other deputies."

Oren glanced at her sharply. "Are you talking about Jess Hastings, the undersheriff?"

Surprised, she looked at him. "Yes. Do you know him?"

For one brief second something like jealously flashed through Oren. Jess was recently widowed and good-looking to boot. Maybe he had eyes for Mary Jo or she for him.

Well hell, Oren, what would be wrong with that? You don't want any woman. Much less a pregnant one.

"I'm acquainted with the man. He's made a few visits to the ranch to purchase horses," Oren said, answering Mary Jo's question. "I was told he's currently out of town on some sort of training conference and won't be back for two or three weeks."

That was just her luck, Mary Jo thought. Jess could have explained to this man that she was an honest, decent citizen of Aztec. But then, why should she have to prove anything to Oren Lassiter? she asked herself. Other than driving her car into the ditch, she'd done nothing wrong.

"Oh well, the fact that we have a mutual friend doesn't matter now," she said quietly. "I'll be leaving this afternoon, anyway."

One brow arched sardonically. "You think so?"

Mary Jo frowned at him. "I may not remember why I came here, Mr. Lassiter, but I do know for certain that I have to go home. I can't stay away from my job." She turned her gaze on the highway stretching in front of them. "Is it very much farther to Ruidoso?"

"We're almost there," he answered.

Thank goodness, she thought. She wanted this medical checkup over and done with so she could go home to Aztec and try to forget she'd ever met this man.

An hour and a half later, Mary Jo walked out of the clinic to find Oren waiting in his truck. His head was resting against the back of the truck seat, the brim of his hat tilted down over his eyes. The restful pose was deceptive, however. The moment she drew near, he was out of the vehicle and rounding the cab to help her make the climb up to her seat.

"I'm sorry you've had such a long wait," she apologized as she settled herself on the bench seat. "I didn't know Ivy was going to give me such a thorough going over."

The pale, drained looked on her face filled Oren with concern for her and the babies. But he hid it well and held the question back that was uppermost in his mind, until he was behind the wheel and heading the truck onto the main highway.

"So what's Ivy's verdict?" he asked.

Mary Jo shrugged and tried to not allow her disappointment to show. She desperately wanted to go home. But the health of her babies was the most important thing. "I'm fine. The babies are fine. But Ivy says I can't make the trip back home just yet. She says I need a few days rest first."

Oren hadn't needed a doctor to tell him this woman was in desperate need of rest. He could see that for himself. And it made him want to shout at her for putting the health of her babies and herself in danger. Didn't she have any sense? What had possessed her to make such a journey? he wondered. What could possibly be more important to her than her children?

Watch it, Oren. You're sounding like a man who cares, and you have no intention of ever doing that again.

"What about your memory?"

Grimly, she shook her head. "Ivy says there isn't anything medically wrong with my head. She believes the blank spots will eventually return. But she says there's also an outside chance that I might never remember all of what happened yesterday."

Oren tried to tell himself Mary Jo's partial loss of memory wasn't anything to be suspicious about, but it all seemed too pat to him. Heather had taught him that women were good at conveniently forgetting the important things. Like what she'd done with the money in their checking account, where she'd been for half the night, and the major one, the vow to love her husband until death did them part.

Catching the sound of Mary Jo's heavy sigh, he asked, "What's the matter? Were you hoping she would find something more concrete, something you could use in a lawsuit?"

Her head whipped back around, and Oren could feel her eyes boring into the side of his face. The idea that she was looking at him so intently, even in anger, disturbed him.

"That's sickening!" she muttered.

"Maybe so, but things like that do happen. And I think you should know I have no intention of allowing anyone to take advantage of my good-hearted friends."

Mary Jo's blue gaze slid up and down his sinewy frame. Instinct told her he was a man who would throw off lots of hot sparks in a woman's bed, but outside it, he appeared to be a chunk of unfeeling ice.

"I guess you think anybody that gives an ounce of kindness toward another human being is a fool."

"It's not the kindness that makes a person a fool, Ms. Bailey. It's the trusting that goes along with it."

Her head swung back and forth with disgust. "You know, I really don't know how you sleep at night. If you think a woman who's soon to give birth looks dangerous, this world must be a terrifying place to you. I'll bet you keep a loaded gun or a guard dog by your bed."

No one, not even his hard-nosed father, had ever accused him of being afraid. That this woman saw him in such a light irritated the hell out of him.

"I manage to sleep alone just fine," he drawled. "How about yourself?"

Her nostrils flared with outrage. "Look, Mr. Lassiter, I'll be the first person to admit I need money in the worst kind of way. I have two babies coming soon, no husband and a job that doesn't supply medical insurance. I'm looking at years just to pay back the doctor and medical care, along with student loans for my education. Not to mention the fact that I have to feed and clothe my babies, and pay utilities along with other expenses. Yes, Mr. Lassiter, if anyone needs a big bulk of cash handed to them, it's me. But I don't work that way. What little money I do have, I've worked for honestly.''

He'd angered her, and after Ivy had warned him to go easy. What in the hell was the matter with him? Oren wondered with self-disgust. He wasn't a man who went around badgering women or accusing them of being con artists. So why was he getting so bent out of shape over this one little woman carrying two tiny babies?

He glanced at her. ''You have to admit you arrived on the ranch under unusual circumstances,'' he said.

''*Weird* would be a better word for it.''

Because she was being so agreeable, he felt an even deeper need to justify his suspicions. Which was foolish on his part. It didn't matter if Mary Jo Bailey thought he was a number one bastard. He knew he was. Besides, it wasn't like they were soon to be neighbors or even friends.

''Just because you're about to become a mother doesn't necessarily mean you're an innocent angel. And the Murdocks are very rich.''

To his surprise she let out a cynical laugh. ''In this condition I could hardly pose as an innocent. And in case you didn't know, rich people live in northern New Mexico, too. Don't you think it would have been much easier for me to have preyed on them rather than drive all the way down here?"

Before he could answer, she shook her head. "Don't bother with a reply. I can see your mind is already made up about me."

"I haven't made up anything yet. Have you?" he goaded.

The pickup braked to a halt and she looked around to see they had arrived back at the ranch house.

Greatly relieved, she levered the truck door open with intentions of sliding to the ground before he could stop her, but belatedly remembered her seat belt was still fastened.

Groaning with frustration, she fumbled with the latch until a big brown hand brushed her fingers out of the way.

"Here, let me do it, before you break something," he said gruffly.

Mary Jo drew in a swift breath as he leaned closer. Beneath the thin material of her jersey top, she felt his fingers inadvertently brush against her belly as he worked to release the square latch on the belt. It was a strangely bittersweet sensation. Since the babies had extended her waistline, no man had touched her there, or anywhere else, for that matter.

"Thank you," she murmured. Heat quickly filled her cheeks and she deliberately avoided his eyes as she reached for her coat and handbag. "Uh—you don't have to help me out. I can make it on my own."

"Independent little thing, aren't you?" he said, his quiet voice threaded with humor. Then just as quickly, his hand closed around her arm and his tone sharpened. "Stay put. I don't want you falling."

An angry lump of pain suddenly knotted her throat. He wasn't worried about her falling and hurting herself or her babies. No, he was thinking of the Murdocks now. He didn't want her to have any excuse to sue them. As though she'd driven four hundred miles to do that, she thought bitterly.

You don't know why you've driven four hundred miles, Mary Jo. Or why you're even on this ranch.

Mary Jo was trying to shake away those troublesome thoughts when she realized Oren was standing outside her door, one hand reaching up for her. Suddenly she didn't know which fascinated her more, the sight of his callused fingers waiting to close around hers or the tough angles and planes of his face, shadowed by the brim of his hat.

Angry at herself for such foolish, maudlin thoughts, she reached for his hand and did her best to ignore the sweet sensation of his other hand closing around the side of her waist, the gentle, caring way he steadied her on her feet once she reached the ground.

He's only looking out for the owners of this ranch, she quickly reminded herself. He didn't give a damn about her, and she needed to remember that. She also needed to let him know right here and now that she wasn't about to be fooled again by him or any man.

Straightening her shoulders, she said, "Look, Mr. Lassiter, I'm deeply grateful to you for taking me to the clinic. I realize it was the last thing you wanted to do. But as far as I'm concerned your job with me is finished. So why don't you go be a foreman and stick to your business of cows and horses."

He studied her for long moments as though he'd been expecting such an outburst, but was disappointed in her just the same. "The name is Oren. And seeing that you're going to be staying here a little longer, you might as well use it. As for my job, you might be interested to know my job includes a few more duties than just cows and horses. Furthermore, as long as you're on this ranch you'll be my business. And believe me, Mary Jo, I'm going to be watching your every move."

Chapter 3

Later that evening Mary Jo was in her room when a light tapping on the door slowly penetrated her dreams.

Groggily, she rose up on one elbow and pushed her tangled hair away from her face. "Come in," she called, her voice husky from hours of deep sleep.

The door swung open and Mary Jo was instantly shocked to see Oren step into the room. After their sharp parting words this morning, she'd neither seen nor heard from the man. And though he'd promised to keep an eye on her, she'd not expected him to do it literally.

"You've been asleep," he said.

Even though she was fully clothed, she had to fight the urge to reach down and draw the light quilt covering her legs all the way up to her chin. The man had a gaze that could pierce a piece of steel, she thought. And sear a woman like herself.

She nodded, then looked at him with faint alarm. He wouldn't be here in her room without a reason. "Is something wrong?"

"No."

She let out a long breath as she wondered what he was going to say or do next. Other than the twins' father, she wasn't used to a man seeing her in bed. The fact that this was Oren Lassiter's second time didn't make her feel any better about the situation.

"What time is it?" she asked.

"A quarter of seven."

Amazed, she jerked her head toward the window to see that night had fallen. Like a shot she was sitting on the side of the bed, reaching for her shoes.

"Oh my, I can't believe I've slept so long—nearly all afternoon!"

Quickly, she pushed herself to her feet, then immediately reached out blindly as she swayed one way and then the other. Before her hand could make contact with the bedpost, Oren was at her side, his arm sliding around the back of her waist.

"Whoa, girl, I think you need to take a little more time before you get up like that."

For a moment Mary Jo forgot that she was supposed to dislike the man, and leaned her head against his shoulder. He was as hard as a rock, and the faint scents of horses, juniper and sagebrush clung to his clothes, created an alluring odor she was already starting to associate with him.

"I—I'm sorry. Just give me a minute."

"Maybe you should lie back down," he suggested.

His voice was deep and soft. Nothing like it had been this morning. The gentle sound enveloped her, along with the heat of his arm pressing against her flesh.

"No. It'll pass. I just got up too quickly." She bent her head as she waited for the blood to return. In the meantime, she felt Oren's fingers smoothing the tangled hair against her back. It was an oddly tender gesture, she thought, for a man who held her in such low regard.

Disturbed by the notion and her own reaction to the man, she managed to push herself away from him. "I'm okay now," she said. Then, daring herself to meet his gaze, she asked, "Did you need to see me about something?"

"Just checking on you. I thought you might be ready for a little supper."

Obviously, she wasn't aware that he'd stopped in earlier and found her sound asleep. Oren wasn't going to tell her, either. The last thing he wanted her to think was that he might be personally concerned for her. Even if she was simply lost and confused, he didn't need her getting the wrong idea about his actions.

"Actually, I'm starved," she said, heading toward the door.

He followed closely behind her. "I brought you a plate from the bunkhouse. The cook who does all the meals for the ranch hands is excellent."

Mary Jo was glad she was walking ahead of him down the hallway, otherwise he would have seen the shock on her face. "Oh. You shouldn't have bothered. Chloe showed me where everything is in the kitchen. The pantry and the refrigerator are stuffed with food."

"I didn't think you'd feel like preparing anything tonight."

They had reached the swinging bat-wing doors to the kitchen. Pausing, Mary Jo looked up at him. "Are you trying to be nice to me? Or is this some of Ivy's medicinal orders?"

To her surprise, a dull flush spread along his jawline.

"Ivy doesn't give me orders."

Maybe he wasn't a devil, after all, Mary Jo thought. Unable to prevent a smile from teasing the corners of her lips, she said, "Well, in that case, thank you. It was very thoughtful of you."

Sheepishly, he motioned for her to enter the kitchen. "The food is on the table. It should still be warm."

Inside an insulated foam container, Mary Jo found a meal of *carne guisada,* pinto beans, coleslaw and several flour tortillas. She poured herself a glass of milk to go with it, then quickly dipped into the stewed beef.

"Mmm. This is delicious. Much better than a can of soup or a cold sandwich."

"I'm glad you like it."

Mary Jo glanced up to see him sliding into a chair opposite her. The fact that he wasn't immediately leaving surprised her almost as much as his bringing the meal to her.

"I actually believe you mean that," she said.

"I'm not bad, Mary Jo. At least, not all the time," he added with a wry grin.

She figured he was a man who could either be very bad or very good, and whichever way he chose to be, women found him irresistible. And if she wasn't careful, she would become one among many.

Trying not to let that grin of his get to her, she asked, "Do you stay in the bunkhouse with the other men?"

Oren enjoyed the way she seemed to be savoring every bite of food, as though eating was a sensual pleasure rather than an act of nourishment. Her face was still flushed from sleep and her hair slightly tangled. Beneath the glow of the lamp hanging over the table it appeared more red than blond, a pale copper color that warmed her cheeks. The neckline of her blouse had slipped to one side, exposing a rectangle of milk-white skin along her throat. Oren figured her skin would no doubt be as soft as her hair had felt as it slid beneath his fingers.

Shifting on the seat, he made himself look elsewhere before he finally answered her question. "I
live on up the mountain from here. In the honeymoon
house. It's where all the past foremen on the Bar M
have resided. Before I worked here, Miguel Ramirez
lived in the house. He was the foreman then. But he
married Chloe's daughter Anna, and after a time they
moved out and onto a little ranch of their own."

Intrigued by the information, Mary Jo glanced at
him between bites. "Why is it called the honeymoon
house?"

Oren shrugged. "It's a long story that goes all the
way back to Tomas Murdock, the guy who first built
this ranch. Back then, he erected a little secluded
getaway cabin for him and his wife. Later, Chloe's
husband had a house built in its place."

"Tomas must have been a romantic man."

Oren's short laugh was a bit sardonic. "I don't
know about romantic, but from what I hear he was
a bit of a ladies' man. The fact that the twins, Adam
and Anna, were fathered by him pretty much proves
that notion."

Not able to follow his meaning completely, Mary
Jo frowned. She hadn't met the twins, but Ivy had
spoken of them as her brother and sister. "The twins
were fathered by Chloe's dad? I don't get it."

"Old man Murdock had an affair, which resulted
in the twins being born. Not long afterward, Tom
passed away and then the mother—her name was
Belinda—she died, too. She was a sister to Wyatt,

so that made the twins his niece and nephew and Chloe's half brother and sister. After they married they adopted the babies and raised them as their own.''

Mary Jo continued to eat as she sorted through the short history lesson of the Murdock family. The fact that the patriarch was fast and loose with women didn't surprise her all that much. She'd already learned firsthand that married men often forgot their vows about clinging only unto their wives. The thing that did surprise her, however, was that Chloe and her husband must not have held any ill feelings against him for his transgressions. Otherwise, they wouldn't have taken his illegitimate children in and raised them as their own.

"Do the twins know about the circumstances of their birth?" she asked.

Oren nodded. "Sure. The Murdocks have always been candid about the whole thing.''

"Chloe and her husband must be openhearted, loving people,'' she murmured, then glanced up to see his eyes were studying her closely, as if he was still trying to size up her motives for being here. Since this morning Mary Jo had lost some of the anger she felt at his suspicious attitude. She'd kept thinking about Ivy's comment. *Oren doesn't take to women.* She wanted to know why. Moreover, why did anything about the man matter to her?

"The Murdocks are special people,'' he agreed. "Including Chloe's full sisters, Rose and Justine.''

The talk of family had Mary Jo suddenly feeling very melancholy, and she turned her gaze on the darkened windows rather than him. "I really don't know what I'm going to tell my twins when they get big enough to want to know about their father. I don't want them to know he rejected them. But I...I don't want to lie to them, either. I'm hoping by the time they reach that age, I'll know the right thing to say. And maybe by then, if I'm really lucky, I'll have a man in my life who will be proud to be their daddy."

His expression keen, Oren leaned forward in his chair and rested his forearms against the edge of the table. "These babies are very important to you, aren't they?"

With solemn blue eyes, she studied his face. "More than anything. You probably don't understand that because you have family somewhere. But in my case, these twins I'm carrying are the only family I have. And that means more to me than anything. Even money."

Yes, he had family, Oren thought. A mother, a dad and two sisters. Each of them split up by miles and bad memories. Once upon a time he'd dreamed of having all that Mary Jo hoped to have. A wife and kids and a chance to build a better home life than the one he'd grown up in. But those dreams had belonged to a young, naive man who'd believed in love and happy ever afters. Down through the years that young man had disappeared. So had his dreams.

Along the way, he'd learned that being happy and loved was something given only to a privileged few. Like Chloe and Wyatt. Not someone like him. And probably not a woman like Mary Jo, either.

The sad thought weighed heavily on his shoulders and he decided it was time to leave.

Pushing away from the table, he rose to his feet. "I understand more than you think, Mary Jo."

She could see that his expression was closed, as though his mind had already moved on and there was no use asking him to go back and explain what he meant.

"Are you leaving?"

Tugging the brim of his hat lower on his forehead, he said, "I'll go build up the fire in the living room for you. Then I'd better be heading home. I have a lot of work planned for the boys tomorrow."

He left the kitchen, and Mary Jo realized she'd eaten all she could hold. She cleaned away her spot at the table, then walked out to the living room. Oren was coming through the front door, a load of firewood stacked in his arms.

He dropped the small pieces of logs into a wooden box near one end of the rock hearth, then threw a couple on the bank of glowing embers. After a few jabs with the poker, flames began to crackle and lick at the dry piñon.

Satisfied with the fire, he turned to see Mary Jo taking a seat on the couch. Once again he was struck by how beautiful she was and also how needy. A part of him wanted to go to her and press her hand between his. He wanted to reassure her that everything would eventually be all right, that her babies would be healthy, that she'd be able to provide for them and that someday some man would come along and love all three of them more than his own life.

What in hell was coming over him? he wondered. He wasn't even sure he trusted this woman. This deep urge he was feeling to console and protect her didn't make any sense. Damn it, he was getting downright soppy. If he wasn't careful he'd wind up looking like a jackass.

Placing the poker back in its holder, Oren stepped off the hearth and walked over to where she sat. The moment his gaze connected with hers, he had to fight the urge to get closer.

"I talked to Chloe earlier this evening," he told her. "She wants me to make sure you stay here until Ivy says you can travel."

Like the glow of a candle flame being pinched between two fingers, Oren watched her eyes go flat. For some reason, he'd disappointed her, and that made him feel like hell.

"Oh," she said in a small voice. "Do you know when Chloe will be coming back?"

Not soon enough to suit him, Oren thought. He'd already had too much connection to this woman. She was making him think things, do things that he hadn't done in years. Even the cook had raised an

eyebrow when Oren had ordered the extra meal for
Mary Jo.

"She's not exactly sure yet," Oren said. "In a day
or two, I'd guess. She and Wyatt often have to en-
tertain his oil cronies. Why?"

Shrugging, Mary Jo glanced away from him as
though she were having trouble meeting his gaze. "I
wanted to see her before I left for home. To thank
her for putting me up like this. She didn't have to
do it."

He studied her profile. "So you're thinking you'll
be heading back to Aztec soon? You don't even
know why you're here."

Shaking her head with regret, she said, "I may not
ever find out what brought me to this area. But I do
know that I can't continue to stay here. I have to get
back to my job."

The woman wasn't in any condition to work, Oren
thought. Not at a job that required her to be on her
feet, like waitressing in a diner.

"I can understand that you need to get back
home," he told her. "But I don't think you're in any
shape to be working."

Her short laugh was a mix of disbelief and exasperation. "I'm not frail, Oren. Just because my memory is a little haywire doesn't make me an invalid."

His gaze slipped from her head to her toes. In spite
of her bulging stomach, she looked slender and delicate to him. If she was his wife, carrying his babies,
he'd want her pampered and cared for. Nothing

would matter but the health and well-being of her and the two little lives inside her.

But you're not her husband, Oren. You're not ever going to be anybody's husband.

Annoyed that he could even be thinking such things, he frowned and said in a voice sharper than he intended, "You were swaying on your feet earlier when you got out of bed."

"That was nothing," she said with a dismissive wave of her hand. "I just got up too quickly. Besides, I don't have any choice in the matter. Presently, I have no other income. I have to work until the babies get here."

Oren didn't know what disgusted him more, the fact that she'd gotten herself into such a plight in the first place or the blind, obstinate way she was approaching the problem at hand.

"You must be a little fool! If you were—"

The remainder of what he'd been going to say was cut off as she shot to her feet and confronted him with blazing blue eyes. "You've got this idea that because you're the foreman on this ranch that gives you the right to make me your business. And maybe it does. But outside of this place—that's where me and you end, buster. What I do when I get back home is no concern of yours!"

She was standing so close Oren could see the fine pores of her milk-white skin, the faint pink color seeping to the surface of her cheeks and the telltale quiver of her bottom lip. The urge to shake some sense into her was instantly replaced with a longing so powerful he couldn't stop himself from reaching out and pulling her into his arms.

Shock had shaped her mouth into a perfect O for kissing, and Oren didn't waste the opportunity. Dipping her head back against his arm, he quickly covered her lips with his.

For an instant, Mary Jo was so stunned she couldn't respond or retaliate in any form. Held within the circle of his arms, her body was stiff, her mind boggled with tumbling questions. How could this man be kissing her? He disliked her. He'd made a habit of insulting her. But oh my—suddenly it didn't matter how or why any of it was happening. His lips were no longer just possessing hers. They were tasting, teasing, coaxing her to open up to him.

What little resistance she had crumbled away like sand against a raging surf. Every muscle in her body was being invaded by a glowing, delicious heat. Limply, she sank against him. Her lips parted and her arms slid upward until they were circling his neck.

Her eager response elicited a moan deep within his throat. His hands clasped her closer as they roamed against her back. His fingers snared strands of silken hair and twined them tightly within his grip.

Years had passed since Oren had kissed a woman or held one in his arms. He'd believed his need for the opposite sex had died. But the burgeoning fire in his loins told him he'd been wrong. Like a hot jolt of whiskey, Mary Jo's soft, rounded body was reminding him he was a man and she was the only thing that could ease his craving.

It was her need for air that finally forced her to break the contact of their lips. And even then the embrace went on as he nuzzled a hot, wicked trail of nibbles and bites down the side of her neck.

In the back of Mary Jo's mind, she knew she should end this thing that was happening between them. All that could come of it was trouble. But she'd never felt so wanted or been so drunk with need. If this was his way of punishing her, he could gladly go on doing it forever.

Behind them, the fireplace crackled louder, and somewhere outside a car motor idled to a stop, a door slammed, followed by one man calling to another. The sounds somehow managed to infiltrate Oren's muddled senses. Slowly, reluctantly, he lifted his head.

As he looked down at her flushed face and drowsy eyes, Oren knew he should say something. At least try to explain his behavior. But there was no explanation. Other than the fact that he wanted her. And still did.

Mary Jo was appalled at herself. She didn't even know this man, yet she'd been kissing him as though he was her soul mate. What must he be thinking? That she was fast and loose? Maybe this whole thing was a test, she thought sickly. Just to prove she was wanton, along with being a gold digger.

Quickly, before he could see her distress, she turned her back to him and pressed the tips of her fingers against her swollen lips.

After sucking in several deep breaths, she said, "We shouldn't have done any of that, you know."

That she was reiterating what he already knew didn't make him feel any better about himself or do anything to ease the ache of longing that still had him tied in knots.

"You're right," he said thickly.

"Why did you then?" she asked in a low, trembling voice.

"I could ask the same question of you."

She let out a heavy sigh. He was right, of course. She'd been just as much a participant as he'd been. There was nothing she could say. At least not anything that would make sense.

Seeing she intended to remain silent, he asked in a frustrated tone, "What do you want from me, Mary Jo, an apology?"

"No. I—" She broke off as she realized the aftershock of their brief lovemaking had left her trembling. "I just want you to leave me alone." She whirled around, her expression wounded as she stared up at him. "Maybe you have the idea a woman in my situation doesn't have any pride. But I—"

His hands were suddenly gripping her shoulders. Anguish twisted his features. "Look, Mary Jo, I don't know what you're thinking, but I don't go around coming on to women. It was just—aw hell, I don't know—you were close and so beautiful. I just wanted to kiss you and when I did—well, it got out of hand.''

The sincerity in his voice made her chin drop. With her head bent, she shook her head in disbelief. ''There's not a man alive who would think I'm beautiful like this,'' she mumbled.

Suddenly he knew what was bothering her. It wasn't exactly what he'd done that she was troubled about. It was why.

''You're wrong, Mary Jo.'' To further prove his point, he settled his hand gently on her stomach. ''This doesn't make you any less beautiful. Only more.''

Her eyes full of misgivings, she studied his face. ''You're just trying to make me feel better now.''

A faint smile flickered at the corners of his lips. ''I've never touched a pregnant woman before. I always wondered what it would be like—if a person could actually feel the baby.''

The gentle reverence in his voice affected Mary Jo as much or more than his hot kisses. He might not consider her to be grade A stock, but he obviously respected the little lives growing inside her.

Placing her hand over his, she moved it farther down, on the side of her stomach. ''In my case you can feel two. And one of them must be doing somersaults at the moment. Feel that?''

Oren felt a small, round bulge beneath his palm,

then a slow rolling movement. The sensation was thrilling and humbling at the same time. That he was sharing it with Mary Jo rather than a wife or lover seemed odd, but right somehow.

"Yeah," he murmured, then smiled at her fully. "I see what you mean."

The sparkle suddenly returned to her blue eyes, and the sight of it pleased Oren far more than it should have. He was getting too close to this woman, he thought with a sudden rush of unease. Far too close for his own good.

Dropping his hand, he quickly stepped back from her and tugged the brim of his hat back down on forehead. "I've got to go. Are you going to be okay now?"

No, Mary Jo thought. Now that he'd touched her, kissed her, she would never be the same. But she couldn't tell him that. To him she was just a momentary diversion. Nothing more.

"Sure," she said with forced steadiness. "I'll be fine. Good night, Oren."

"Good night," he replied.

Mary Jo waited for him to move past her. When he continued to linger, only inches away from her, she got the impression he wanted to kiss her again.

Her eyes flickered up to his in silent question. For a few tense moments, his gaze searched her face, then finally he walked around her and across the room.

Limp and trembling, Mary Jo watched the door close behind him.

Chapter 4

The next two days passed slowly for Mary Jo. By the end of her third day on the ranch, the only thing she was certain about was that she had to leave the Bar M as soon as possible. As Ivy had prescribed, she'd been resting, and physically she felt much stronger. But emotionally she was a wreck.

With Chloe and her husband out of town and Ivy working and living in Ruidoso, Mary Jo continued to have the run of the ranch house all to herself. Yet as huge as the place was, she couldn't hide from or avoid Oren Lassiter. He'd been checking on her twice daily—once in the morning and then in the evenings. Each night he'd brought her a meal from the bunkhouse and stayed until she finished it. During those visits he'd not touched her in any way or even behaved as though he wanted to. Mary Jo figured he'd mentally sobered up since that first night when he'd kissed her. No doubt he'd cut himself up pretty good for letting himself sink to her level. Obviously he was determined not to repeat the sin. Yet when he sat at the kitchen table with her, kissing him, touching him, remembering the way it had felt to be held in his arms was all she could think about.

Mary Jo wasn't naive or dumb. Since Jeremy had opened her eyes with his trick on her heart, she'd wisened up to men's ways. She realized Oren would never be interested in her romantically. Yet even when he was out of the house, she was wondering about him, waiting for the time he would return. She was being foolish. Her preoccupation with the man couldn't be good for her mental health. She couldn't expect her brain to remember anything when it was filled with Oren Lassiter.

Several times throughout the past two days, she'd considered carrying her things out to her car and driving away. But even in her worst moments of desperation, something told her that Oren would know if she tried to leave the ranch. No doubt he'd stop her before she could get to the main highway. And he'd figure she was running away because she was guilty of something. He would never understand that she was running away from him.

Slowly, Mary Jo became aware of footsteps in another part of the house. A glance at her wristwatch said it was too early for Oren to be coming by with her supper. She tossed the book she'd been trying to read to one side of the bed and stuck her feet into her loafers.

Halfway down the hallway toward the kitchen, she met Chloe. The sight of the older woman filled Mary Jo with an immense sense of relief.

"Oh Chloe, you're home."

"There you are!" she exclaimed with a warm smile, then reached to give her a tight, welcoming hug. "How are you feeling?"

For a moment Mary Jo was overcome with emotion. Not even people she'd known for a long time made a fuss over her like this. She was so touched that tears stung her eyes.

"I'm fine," she answered huskily.

Chloe released her, then took her by the shoulder. "Let's go to the kitchen. I could use a pot of fresh coffee. That stuff they had on the plane was awful."

While Chloe put the coffee makings together, she related all that she and her husband, Wyatt, had been doing while they were in Houston.

"Did he come back with you?" Mary Jo asked. If her husband was back home, Chloe would probably be only too glad for Mary Jo to get out of her hair.

"Yes, thank goodness." She laughed sheepishly as she took down two cups from the cabinet. "Isn't it awful? We've been married for nearly twenty-seven years and we still can't bear to be away from each other."

A tiny pang of envy sliced through Mary Jo. The

other woman's face glowed with a love that was still young and burning bright. Mary Jo couldn't imagine having someone love her like that. Even for just a day, much less for years.

"I think it's wonderful," she murmured.

Seeming to sense Mary Jo's melancholy, Chloe waved her hand in a dismissive way. "That's enough about what I've been doing. Tell me what's been happening with you?"

For the past three days Mary Jo had been waiting impatiently for this moment. But now that it was here she was reluctant to speak out. This woman had shown her such genuine kindness. The last thing Mary Jo wanted was for Chloe to think she was ungrateful. "Well—uh, I need to talk to you about going home. Back to Aztec."

Chloe didn't say anything until she'd poured two cups full of coffee and carried them over to where Mary Jo sat at the table.

"Now what is this about going home?" she asked. "Has Ivy given you permission to travel?"

Mary Jo shook her head. "But I've got to get home, Chloe. I have to get back to my job."

Chloe sighed. "You're not thinking, honey. Ivy and your doctor back home both believe you shouldn't be traveling four hundred miles or working on your feet."

Oren had said the same thing, rather vehemently in fact. What neither of them understood was that Mary Jo lived from one paycheck to the next. It took every penny she made just to keep the utilities going and food on the table.

"Chloe, don't misunderstand me, I'm very grateful for all your help and concern. But...I can't survive without my job. I have bills—"

Reaching over, Chloe caught Mary Jo's fidgeting fingers in a warm, reassuring grip. "Don't worry about your bills or anything like that now, Mary Jo. They'll all be taken care of."

Mary Jo's eyes widened with alarm. "But how—"

With a shake of her head, Chloe said, "That doesn't matter. Much later, after your twins are older and you're back on your feet financially, then you can think about paying us back. If that's what you'd like to do. But Lord knows I'd rather you consider our help as a gift to you." She leveled a benevolent look on Mary Jo. "In the meantime, to make you feel better, I'll let you help me get caught up on my bookkeeping. It's personal stuff, not anything to do with the ranch's records. What do you think?"

Oh dear heaven, Mary Jo silently groaned. She couldn't take money from these people. Even if it was going to pay her bills. If she allowed that to happen, Oren would be right about her. He'd really believe she'd come here to fake an accident or something in order to get financial help. But how was she going to stop it, when Chloe seemed so adamant?

"Sure, I'd be glad to help you. But—"

"Good," Chloe interrupted, before Mary Jo could voice any more of a protest. "Now that we have that all settled, we can talk about Christmas,'' she said happily.

Mary Jo knew when she was whipped, so she gave up gracefully and allowed Chloe to turn their conversation toward Christmas. But in reality she was even more distressed than ever. When Oren heard she would be staying on the Bar M for a somewhat indefinite time to come, he wasn't going to like it. Not even a little.

A week later, Oren was in the weaning pen when he noticed Chloe's dark cherry Lincoln pull to a stop at the back of the ranch house. After a few moments, three women got out, all of them with arms piled high with packages.

From the look of things, Chloe and her older sister, Justine, had been out Christmas shopping, and they'd taken Mary Jo with them. The sound of bawling calves and the grunts and swears from the men working nearby drowned out all other sound, but he could tell the three women were laughing.

Mary Jo was wearing a midnight-blue coat, and her long, strawberry-blond hair hung like a bright scarf against her back. Even with the coat on, the bulge of her waistline was unmistakable.

Like unwelcome visitors, the memories of warm skin, soft lips and silky hair entered Oren's thoughts and plagued him. He couldn't stop thinking about holding her, kissing her, pressing his hand against the movements of her belly.

More than a week had passed since that night, yet the whole episode was so fresh in his memory it still had the power to quicken his breath and curl his fingers into fists. Even so, he'd been trying to forget, trying to tell himself that none of it had meant anything. But it had. And that scared him a hell of a lot.

Oren didn't know what to do about the Bar M's visitor from Aztec. From what he could see, the Murdocks were drawing her into their family and beginning to care about her in a personal way. Especially Chloe and her sisters, Justine and Rose. Hell, even Wyatt seemed to treat her as an adopted daughter about to spring a pair of twin grandbabies on him.

But whether the Murdocks wanted to take her under their protective, and very wealthy wings was their own business. The thing that was troubling Oren the most was his own feelings toward the woman. He couldn't let himself care about her, then later learn she'd been deceiving the lot of them. It would crush him. No, before that happened, he had to find out what the real Mary Jo Bailey was all about. And in order to do that, he was going to have to get close to her. Maybe too close for his own good.

Less than an hour later, Mary Jo was in the living room, wrapping packages in bright, festive paper, when she sensed another person had entered the room. She lifted her head and her heart skipped a curious beat. Oren was watching her from the doorway. His expression was guarded until he realized she had spotted him, then his features suddenly turned wry and sheepish as though he almost wanted to apologize for something. Which didn't make sense, since she'd hardly seen him this past week.

"Hello," he said.

Her pulse skittered into overdrive.

"Hello," she replied.

He inclined his head toward the boxes and papers littering the long, polished pine coffee table. "I see you're busy."

She followed the direction of his gaze to the simple gifts Chloe had purchased earlier today during their shopping excursion. "Chloe's taking these things to a small party for the children at her church. I offered to wrap them for her."

Stepping into the room, he walked over to where she sat. "I thought you might be wrapping gifts to send back to your acquaintances in Aztec."

His comment put an amused frown on her face. "I wish I could afford to buy gifts for a few friends. Unfortunately, cards will have to do." She paused, then chuckled. "I keep promising my boss at the diner that I'll buy him a Stetson for Christmas some-day—when I write a bestseller. He says by then he'll be so old he'll be in the nursing home and won't have any need for a Stetson. It's a running joke between us."

A self-conscious smile tilted her lips as she looked up at him. "What about you?" she asked. "Have you already done all your Christmas shopping?"

He shook his head. "Since my family is scattered, I don't do much for the holidays."

Her smile changed to a teasing one. "Don't tell me Santa doesn't come to see you."

Clutching his gray hat with both hands, he eased down on the cushion next to her. She noticed his hair was slightly damp and curling at the back of his neck, his jaws freshly shaved and scented with spicy aftershave. A hunter-green corduroy shirt covered his broad shoulders, and his bullhide boots were clean of manure. He must be going out somewhere, she thought, then immediately wondered if he were on his way to see a woman. She didn't like the idea. Which was ridiculous. She didn't have any claims on the man. And he was human, with a man's needs. Sweet mercy, that kiss he'd given her had more than proved that, she thought.

"I'm not usually good enough to make it onto Santa's list," he said.

Her heart still refused to settle down to a normal pace, and she supposed it was because she'd missed his company this past week. Most every evening he stopped by the house to give Chloe a roundup of the day's happenings on the ranch, but during those times he hadn't singled her out and Mary Jo hadn't made a point of speaking to him. She'd already been having a hard enough time trying to get the man out of her mind without creating more memories to linger over.

"Oh."

Oren noticed there was a faint blush on her cheeks, as though it embarrassed her to picture him being naughty. The image was not one he'd connect with a cunning woman out to cheat someone. In fact, there were times he got the impression that she was almost virginal. Which didn't make sense, since she'd obviously had a relationship with a man. Yet he was certain that Mary Jo wasn't a seasoned lover. The shocked reaction she'd displayed over their kiss had proved as much to him.

"Don't look so grim," he said. "I usually wind up getting a gift or two in spite of my behavior."

Mary Jo stared at him, amazed that he actually might be teasing. Every time she'd seen the man so far he'd been as serious as a judge. And a hanging judge, at that.

"Uh—did you want to see me for some reason?" she ventured, while thinking he'd probably stopped by the ranch to have a word with Chloe and Wyatt. Still, something had sent him out here to the living room to see her. A foolish part of her wanted to believe it was because he'd missed her. Because, like her, he couldn't get the kiss they'd shared out of his thoughts.

He rubbed the heels of his palms against his thighs as though he were itching either to get up or to grab her. Mary Jo wasn't sure which one she wanted him to do the most.

"I thought if you weren't too tired, you might like

to drive up to my place and eat supper. Chloe says you haven't had your evening meal yet."

Mary Jo couldn't help it. She was suddenly melting like a piece of warm, gooey chocolate. "You really want *me* to have a meal with you? At your house?"

The awe in her voice made Oren feel like a complete heel. Even though he'd expressed his doubts about her motives for coming to the ranch, he'd never intended to make her feel inferior to him in any way.

"That's what I'm asking."

For appearances sake, she should have at least made a show of considering his invitation. But she was just so darned pleased that he was finally being friendly, she didn't want to spoil the moment.

A bright smile spread across her face. "Then I would very much like to go. Thank you for asking."

Her eagerness squashed his self-image even more. For the past few days he'd made a point of ignoring her. And before that he'd said some pretty crude things to her. That she was still willing and eager to spend time with him filled him with a strange mixture of feelings. The most of which was elation.

Rising to his feet, he clapped his hat on his head. "I'm sure you'll want to get a coat. It's gotten windy outside and much colder."

He reached to help her up, and with another smile, she placed her soft little hand in his. "I'll be right back," she promised.

As Oren watched her leave the room, he felt an unfamiliar sensation in his chest. Then, slowly, like a man coming out of a dream, it dawned on him that his heart was thudding with happy excitement.

Aw hell, Lassiter, quit being a sap. She's just a woman. You can find all of them you want over at Roswell or down at Ruidoso.

But not like Mary Jo, he thought. Never like Mary Jo.

Chapter 5

Minutes later the two of them were in Oren's truck, traveling south and up into the mountains. Even though it was dark, Mary Jo could make out the tall pines and twisted juniper lining the road. In the headlight beams, a few snowflakes were beginning to appear.

About the time she thought the road was becoming too steep to climb, it leveled off and she could see they were on a small shelf of a mountain. To their left, a low, rambling house was nestled snugly against a cliff of sheer rock.

"This place is beautiful," Mary Jo exclaimed once Oren had parked and was helping her into the house. "I'm sure it's even more so in daylight."

"It's very quiet and secluded. I like that about it."

She wanted to ask him if he got lonely living up here all by himself, but the one time she'd questioned him about having a family, he'd cut her short. If she tried again, she might start their supper off on a bad note and that was the last thing she wanted.

Inside the house, Oren took her coat, then led her through a spacious living room with varnished pine floors and comfortable furniture that invited a person to sit and admire the view beyond one wall of plate glass.

In the kitchen Mary Jo's attention was first caught by the rows of shiny pine cabinets, then the white appliances, which were all older deluxe models—the sort that were meant to last a lifetime. Across the room, a small round table was situated near a sliding patio door. Two places were already set. A sign that he considered her easy, no doubt. Which really didn't matter to Mary Jo. She was easy to persuade when genuine friendship was being offered to her.

With his hand still attached to her upper arm, Oren led her over to the table. "I hope you like green enchiladas," he said as he helped her into one of the wooden chairs. "I asked the cook not to smother them with hot sauce, just in case the heat bothered you."

Warmed by his thoughtfulness, she smiled at him. "I'm sure they'll be delicious. But I was hoping I was going to be eating some of your cooking."

He chuckled as he carried a tray ladened with several dishes over to the table. "Oh no you wouldn't. I can fry eggs and bacon or make soup and peanut butter sandwiches, but that's about it. I'm not a kitchen kind of guy."

"A man born to the saddle. Is that the way it is?"

Placing the meal before her, he answered, "Yeah. That's pretty much how it is. I came from a long line of ranchers. My dad had me riding before I could hardly hold the reins."

Heartened by this personal disclosure, she studied his face as he took a seat across from. "Does he still ranch for a living?" she asked.

Like a cloud blocking out the sun, his eyelids drooped. His jaw tightened ever so slightly. "Yeah."

The one word told two things. Oren and his father weren't close enough to ranch together. And he had no intention of saying more about the matter.

Motioning toward the glass of milk he'd served her, he said, "I took it for granted you'd want milk to drink. On account of the babies. But I have other things if you'd like something else."

Unconsciously, she laid a protective hand on her stomach. "No, I'll stick with the milk. And when they get older, maybe I can ward off a bunch of trips to the dentist."

Oren encouraged her to fill her plate. While she busied herself, he allowed himself the pleasure of a leisurely look. Tonight she was wearing a pale pink sweater with big shiny buttons down the front. Her thick hair was pulled into a loose knot atop her head and fastened with tortoiseshell combs. Her cheeks were washed with a rose color, while the rest of her skin had an iridescent glow, like the tiny pearls fastened in the lobes of her ears. As his eyes drank their fill, he was thinking he'd never tasted skin so soft, so honey sweet. The thought of having her in bed beside him, of being able to touch her at will, was far too much for a celibate man to be thinking about.

Clearing his throat, he reached for his fork. "How have you been feeling?"

Her smile was joined by a twinkle in her blue eyes. "I've never been so rested. Chloe and her sisters have pampered me silly." The smile quickly fell from her face. "But I—if you're wondering if I've remembered anything—the answer is no. I made some calls to Aztec and talked with all the people I'm closest to. But none of them had any clues to what I was doing. From what they all tell me, my plans were to be out of town on business for a couple of days."

"You didn't tell them why or what kind of business?"

A worried frown tugged at her brow. "No. I guess I wanted to keep that part of it private. But I can't imagine what sort of business I'd have down in this part of the state. At that time I didn't know anyone in this area. Not before I met all of you here at the

Bar M.'' She started to fork a bite of the cheesy enchilada into her mouth, then paused to glance at him. "Actually, I'm glad you've given me this chance to talk to you, Oren. I'm sure you've been wondering—well—I just wanted to assure you that I've been trying to leave and go back home. But Chloe won't hear of it and Ivy isn't helping matters. She keeps insisting I shouldn't travel.''

"Chloe does have a persuasive way about her.''

Mary Jo released a long breath. "I realize all this looks bad on my part, like I'm just hanging around for a free ride. But I don't want to seem ungrateful to the Murdocks.''

Desperation edged her voice and the almost stricken look on her face said she half expected him to lash out at her for not jumping in the car and heading home in spite of their protests. She seemed so guileless, so completely innocent and vulnerable that Oren found himself wanting to believe her more than anything he'd ever wanted in his life.

"What would you like to do, Mary Jo?''

His softly spoken question caught her off guard. During her stay here on the ranch, she'd been considering everyone else's concerns and feelings. Not hers. A part of her realized it was imperative that she should say goodbye to these people and get on with her life.

But leaving the ranch would mean never seeing Oren again. She looked down at her plate, afraid he would see something in her eyes that she wasn't quite ready to admit, even to herself.

"I'd be lying if I said I didn't like it here on the Bar M," she answered. "How could I not? I didn't know real people lived in such comfort. And everyone is so good to me. But, this isn't my home and I need to get back to reality."

Yeah, Oren thought, maybe he needed a big dose of reality to get over this strange pull Mary Jo seemed to have on him. The reality being that she was soon to become a mother. She needed a husband and a father to her babies. He couldn't play those roles. He'd already tried being a husband and had failed at it miserably. As for being a father, he'd never been one. And he wasn't at all sure he had the makings to be one.

Yet this talk about her going home wasn't making Oren nearly as happy as he'd expected it to, and he quickly decided it was time to back off the subject so that they could both enjoy their meal.

To Mary Jo's surprise, Oren even had dessert to go with after-dinner coffee. Out of politeness she allowed him to cut her just a sliver of the Italian cream cake. They carried the treat out to the couch in the living room.

Mesquite crackled in the fireplace, and beyond the partially pulled drapes, snowflakes were beginning to pile up along the windowsill and on a nearby juniper branch. Mary Jo could hear the faint howling of the wind in the pines, but other than that, the room was quiet. The lack of sound made her even more aware of Oren sitting only inches away.

Even when he wasn't talking, his presence was a tangible thing. He was a physically strong man with a mind to match. He was the sort of man who would shelter and cherish a woman. If he loved her. But Mary Jo wasn't at all sure Oren was the loving kind. At least, not with his heart.

At the moment, he'd finished his cake and coffee and was placing the empty dishes on the floor to one side of his boots. When he straightened back up and turned on the cushion toward her, Mary Jo's heart took off like a shot.

"You, uh, don't have a Christmas tree," she said, making a point of glancing around the room.

He shook his head. "It's only me that lives here. Why bother?"

She shot him a censuring look. "For the spirit and the magic of it all. Santa doesn't like to visit houses without trees. He doesn't have anything to put the gifts under."

Oren let loose with one of his rare chuckles. "Like I told you, Mary Jo. I'm bad. Santa skips over me."

She slanted him a glance from the corner of her eye. "Maybe you could change."

They both knew she was talking about more than just putting up a tree at Christmastime. For a moment her suggestion had him envisioning what it might be like to have her as his wife, to see the twins playing on the floor among scattered boxes and Christmas wrappings. There would be laughter and squeals of excitement. Baked goods would scent the kitchen and decorations would brighten the rooms. The house would be alive and happy, and so would he. More alive than he'd ever been. But that was just a rose-colored dream. And he didn't have dreams anymore.

"Too late for that. I'm an old dog. Too old to change."

Mary Jo laughed, partly because his answer was ludicrous and partly to ease the sexual tension that had been building around them ever since they'd sat down on the couch.

"Just how old are you, Oren?"

"Thirty-one."

She smiled. "That's crotchety, all right."

"And how old are you?"

"Twenty-six, going on twenty-seven." She glanced at him. "And I know what you're probably thinking. That I should already be fixed in a career. But...well, about the time I graduated high school, my mother became disabled. I had already made plans to go to San Juan College at Farmington, but she needed a lot of care and we couldn't afford a nurse. So I canceled my plans and stayed home to look after her."

Suddenly Oren was studying her with new eyes. Any young woman who would sacrifice her own plans to help out a parent couldn't be selfish or greedy. No more than she could be capable of hatching up a con job. The realization filled him with such relief it was all he could do to keep from snatching her up in his arms and holding her close to his heart.

"You said you had a degree in English. What happened? Did your mother's health improve enough for you attend college later?"

With a tinge of sadness shadowing her face, she said, "No. Mother never got better. Only worse. But fortunately, there's a long-distance college right in Aztec. You know, one of those institutions where you take your classes at home. It was a slow process, but I finally graduated."

Thoughtfully, he said, "So you've always lived at home."

Mary Jo nodded. "Mother always felt guilty about that. You see, she wanted me to move to a city and work for a big newspaper. But I never could have left her. Not with her needing me like she did. Besides, I never wanted to work in journalism. I want to write fiction," she said, then smiled earnestly. "That way I can always make up my own endings. And trust me, I'll always make them happy ones."

Slowly, Oren was beginning to understand why she'd seemed like a sheltered innocent. So far her whole young life had been spent in a small town, taking care of an ailing parent. And being done wrong by some man, he thought grimly. It was amazing that she still believed in happy endings.

"It sounds like you haven't had much time for your personal life these past few years," Oren said. "That must have been tough."

With a slight grimace, Mary Jo shrugged one slender shoulder. "Sometimes it was," she agreed. "I didn't have much of a social life. But that never bothered me. I've never been the sort to party with friends. But I..." Her gaze slipped away from his face. "By the time I was twenty-five I could count the dates I'd had on one hand. After a while I began to think I'd never get the chance to have a husband or children. I guess that's why...when I met the twins' father I didn't use good judgment."

"Do you still have contact with him?" he asked.

"No," she said firmly. "Nor will I have in the future."

Oren discreetly studied her face. Her features were tight, her lips pressed together. He wondered if her grim thoughts were directed at herself or the man who'd gotten her pregnant, then walked out on her.

"So he doesn't want to be their father? Even on a part-time basis?"

Her eyes turned toward Oren and for a moment he caught a glimpse of raw pain, overlaid with bitter acceptance. Some selfish man had hurt this woman in the deepest possible way. Oren wanted to track him down and break his neck.

"No."

Solemnly, Oren dragged a thumb and forefinger over his newly shaved jaws. "I don't know what it's like to father a child. But I'm dead certain of one thing—I couldn't turn my back on it. I like to think most any man couldn't."

Warmed by his remark, she decided it wouldn't hurt to talk to him about her mistake. Tonight, for the first time since she'd met him, things felt different between them, as though he'd decided he liked her, after all.

"Yes, but you're not like Jeremy," she said with a sigh of regret. "He was a flat-out phony. I just wished I'd been wiser, but..." Her gaze moved to her lap, where she'd laced her fingers tightly together. "Mother was dying at the time I met him and I guess I needed some human connection in the worst kind of way. I didn't stop to question his motives. I just knew I was twenty-six years old and life had been passing me right on by. I grabbed at the happiness he promised me."

"How did you meet him?"

"At the diner. He was a stranger in town. Part of a construction crew that was building a nearby highway. At first I snubbed him. I figured he was a drifter. But after a while he convinced me that he'd been looking for a place to settle down and his interest in me was sincere." She released a little scoffing laugh. "Boy, I was a real little fool."

The fact that she was still beating herself up for making a mistake bothered Oren a great deal. He knew firsthand what a black hole that could make in a person's spirit.

Reaching over, he took her hand and squeezed it.

"How did you find out he wasn't what he first appeared to be?"

She drew in a quivery breath, then let it out slowly. "When I told him I was pregnant. I believed he'd want to get married right away. He'd often talked about us getting married and moving to some little house in Santa Fe. That's where writers were supposed to live, he'd told me. But all of that was just a part of his con. It turned out Jeremy already had a wife in Colorado. He'd only been stringing me along. Using me for entertainment until the road job was finished."

Oren found himself wanting to draw her into his arms, to hold her tight and somehow ease the pain and humiliation he heard in her voice. No doubt the man had taken her virginity, along with the dreams in her heart.

"Sounds like a real ace of a guy."

In a low, strained voice, she said, "At that time I was in the very early stages of pregnancy. I think Jeremy had the idea I'd get an abortion. But after he understood that wasn't an option with me, he told me to do whatever I wanted. Just as long as I understood he wanted no part of being a father."

She visibly shuddered, and Oren unwittingly slid his hand up and down her forearm in a soothing gesture. "What happened after that? You kicked him out—or he left?"

She remained silent for a long time, her head bowed, her fingers clamped together on her lap. Oren could only imagine how crushed she'd been. And maybe she still was. Maybe she still loved the bastard. The notion tore a hole right through him.

"I...pulled myself together and tried to think of the best thing to do for my children's future. Eventually, I had a lawyer draw up papers releasing Jeremy of all rights and responsibilities to the babies. He was only too happy to sign them."

Oren's fingers paused in their movement against her arm. "But that means you signed away any financial help you might have gotten from him."

Mary Jo nodded. "That's true. But it's worth it to me. To have the security of knowing he can never intervene in my children's lives. For any reason." Her head lifted and moisture gleamed in her eyes as she looked at him. "He's not the sort I'd want around the twins. That's why I'm not sure what I'll do when they start asking about their father. The truth is too ugly."

Oren couldn't help himself. He moved across the small space of cushion that separated their bodies and pulled her against him. With a tiny sigh, she laid her head on his shoulder, and his fingers slid down her long silky hair with slow, hypnotic movements.

"I wish you'd never been hurt like this," Oren whispered. "But I'm glad he's out of your life."

Lifting her head, Mary Jo searched his face for long, silent moments, then she smiled. A sweet, pleased smile that pierced right through the middle of his chest.

"Thank you, Oren," she said softly.

His brows lifted ever so slightly. "For what?"

Shifting slightly away from him, she framed his face with both hands. To Oren it was a simple gesture that somehow felt as intimate as a kiss.

"For deciding to be my friend. It's the best Christmas present I've ever been given."

Groaning partly out of protest and partly from need, he set her away from him and quickly rose from the couch. After walking to the middle of the room, he glanced over his shoulder at her. Irritation twisted his lips, while a look of warning glinted in his brown eyes.

"Don't get confused about me, honey. I'm not a man who cares a whole damn lot about people. And I've never had a woman for a friend."

To his amazement, she laughed softly. "Then I guess I'm your first."

She was a first all right, Oren thought. The first woman who'd ever created such a tangled web of emotions in him. She took away the gray in his world and made everything look alive and wonderful. She made him believe he was a man worthy of a woman's love, a family of his own. Yet at the same time just looking at her scared him. Because he was beginning to want her. More than anything he'd ever wanted in his life.

With that sobering thought in mind, he walked back to the couch and reached down for her hand. "Come on. I'd better take you home before the snow gets any heavier."

She rose to her feet, but made no move to step away from him. Instead, she continued to cling to his hand, and he was prompted to look down at her. Which was a mistake on Oren's part. The instant his eyes connected with hers his mind shut down to everything but the invitation glimmering in the blue depths and the provocative tilt to her pink lips.

"What's wrong?" she asked. "Are you afraid for us to be alone like this?"

Her taunt caused his breath to quicken, his body to grow taut. Resisting her was no longer an option for Oren. His hands lifted to her face, and with tantalizing slowness, he kissed her lips, tested the smoothness of her cheeks beneath the pads of his fingers. He could taste sweetness and warmth. And a connection that urged him to hold on and never let go.

Mindless to everything but the heady taste of his kiss, Mary Jo slid her arms around his neck and pressed herself against the hard length of his body. Instantly, his hands deserted her face and flattened at the back of her waist. When they urged her even closer, heat encased her from head to toe. She opened her mouth, then whimpered with pleasure at the immediate invasion of his tongue.

The sound fueled Oren's already heated senses, and without breaking the contact of their hungry mouths, he lowered her down on the couch until her back was resting against the cushions.

Kneeling on the floor, he bent over her as he continued to kiss her. At the same time his hands slid under the hem of her sweater and worked their way up to her breasts, which he quickly discovered were covered in lace. He kneaded their fullness with his fingers until he was craving to touch the soft skin, to feel her budded nipple in his mouth.

Impatiently, he tugged the fastening of her bra loose, after which he pushed it and her sweater aside. Then, tearing his lips from hers, he stared down at her. The sight of her breast, so creamy and pink, was enough to turn his breathing short and raspy.

"Mary Jo!"

Her name was little more than a groan as he bent his head and tasted the smooth, satiny skin.

Her hands were suddenly on his head, her fingers sliding through his hair, urging him to take more. The moment his teeth gently closed around the rigid nipple, she made a guttural sound of pleasure that echoed the desire whipping through his body.

"Oren! Oh, Oren, make love to me!"

Somehow, her passionate plea was enough to snap him back to reality, and with a great groan he managed to lift his head. Slowly, the image of her face swam into focus, and he could see that her lips were swollen from his kisses, her eyes half closed and drowsy with desire. She wanted him. Maybe as much as he wanted her, and that made it even harder to hang on to his common sense.

"You were right all along, Mary Jo," he whispered huskily. "I am afraid to be with you like this. And you should be, too."

She opened her mouth to say something, but Oren didn't give her a chance. At this moment his resistance was so weak that her just crooking her finger would be enough to break it. He couldn't let that happen. For either of their sakes.

Quickly, he went to fetch her coat. Back in the living room, he helped her into the garment, going so far as to fasten the row of buttons down the front.

When he reached the last one at her throat, his hands lingered. Mary Jo bent her head slightly and pressed a kiss against his fingers.

"Thank you for the lovely evening, Oren."

Like warm rain, tender emotions washed over him, then right behind came the cold sense that he was losing control. He was falling for her. Totally. Helplessly. To regain some of his footing, he wanted to tell her that what they'd shared tonight was nothing, that none of it would happen again. Not the conversation, the looks, the touches. Nothing.

But Oren couldn't force a word past his throat. In the end, the only thing he could do was lead her outside to the truck and drive her back to the ranch house.

Chapter 6

"Maybe this is a big mistake," Mary Jo said as she added a coil of shiny Christmas garlands to the basket of ornaments sitting on the kitchen table. "Oren might not appreciate this idea at all. I think I should forget the whole thing."

"Don't be silly, Mary Jo. You've already gotten the tree, and there're enough ornaments in that box of leftovers to decorate several trees. Why let it go to waste?"

Mary Jo glanced over at Chloe, who was standing at the kitchen cabinet decorating sugar cookies with red and green frosting. Beside her, Rose, the middle redheaded Murdock sister, was shaking her head.

"Mary Jo, quit fretting," Rose urged. "This is going to be a great surprise for Oren. I think it's wonderful that you thought of it."

Mary Jo groaned with misgivings. "I must have been a little drunk. Are you sure that eggnog we drank before we went to town wasn't doctored with something?"

This time both women laughed—something Mary Jo noticed the Murdock sisters did frequently, and the sound never failed to lift her spirits. All three of them were quite beautiful and intelligent women with much about them to be admired. They'd drawn Mary Jo into the bosoms of their families, and she felt a closeness to them that went beyond friendship.

Given the short time she'd known them, it was a connection she didn't understand. Yet it was something she cherished. Once she left here, she knew she would take back sentimental snapshots in her mind of each woman and the love this family had shown her.

"You like Oren very much, don't you?" Rose asked gently.

Mary Jo nodded, then her gaze dropped to the basket of ornaments. "I guess it's...foolish of me. He's not looking for a woman. Especially like me—with a ready-made family on the way."

Chloe laughed, and Rose instantly scolded, "Hush, Chloe! That's not funny to Mary Jo."

Stepping away from the cabinet, Chloe joined Mary Jo at the table. "Forgive me, Mary Jo, I was only laughing because I think you're so off base it's ridiculous. If Oren really wanted a woman, he wouldn't let two little babies stop him."

Maybe not, Mary Jo thought, as the memory of two nights ago, when they'd shared supper, burned its way through her mind. There was no doubt that he'd wanted her physically. She'd felt it in his kisses and the urgent touch of his hands. But he'd stopped short of taking her to his bed, and since that night she'd been asking herself why. Was his past still haunting him? she wondered. Or did he still not trust her completely? Her heart had to know.

"If that's the case, you can't back out on giving him the tree, Mary Jo," Rose insisted. "Hurry and get those ornaments sorted. While he's still out working with the hands, I'll take you up to the honeymoon house and help you get the tree into the living room and in a holder. After that, you'll be on your own."

Mary Jo's eyes widened. "He might come in and be so angry he won't give me a ride back down here to the ranch house!"

Chloe chuckled slyly. "Maybe you won't *want* a ride back down here."

Mary Jo was hanging the last of the ornaments on the blue spruce when she saw the lights of Oren's pickup flicker across the picture window. Moments later, there was the sound of the front door being opened and closed, then boots hitting the pine floor, spurs jingling a rhythm as he crossed the small foyer.

Her heart was hammering with anticipation as she turned just in time to see him entering the living room. Bat-wing chaps, the leather scarred from years of use, covered his long legs. A waist-length canvas jacket lined with sheepskin was buttoned up to his neck, while a battered black Stetson rode low on his forehead. White flakes dotted the brim and the top of his broad shoulders, telling her snow was falling again.

Slowly, he removed his gloves as he walked toward her. Mary Jo studied his face, hoping to find a flicker of pleasure as his gaze traveled from her to the tree. Instead, all she could detect was disbelief.

"I wondered who was in my house," he said in a low voice. "You never entered my mind."

She flashed him a nervous smile. Suddenly it was crucial that he be pleased. Deep inside her, she realized that if he rejected the Christmas tree, he would be rejecting her. And she couldn't bear that.

"I hope you don't mind. I promise I haven't been snooping. Just decorating," she said in a rush.

With his gaze still locked with hers, his big brown fingers began to unbutton his jacket. "Who helped you get the tree up here?"

"Rose. She tugged it into the house and put it in the holder. She didn't want me to lift or strain." Mary Jo flashed him a smile as she gestured toward the nearly decorated tree. "I've been doing all the fun part."

"Hmm. Rose," he murmured thoughtfully. "Who would have guessed. This is more like Chloe's style."

"Well, please don't be angry with her for helping me. She's so gentle and sweet."

He smiled then, and suddenly Mary Jo knew it was all okay. He was happy and that was enough to make her heart soar.

"Yeah," he replied. "Sorta like someone else I know."

He tossed the jacket toward the couch, then bent at the waist and twisted his torso so that he could reach the snaps on the back of the chaps.

Seeing the difficult strain he was in, Mary Jo quickly stepped behind him and pushed his hands out of the way. "Here, let me do that for you," she told him.

To have her so close again and doing such a personal task for him made Oren's voice take on an odd raspy note as he spoke. "It isn't necessary. I get in and out of these things all the time."

Ignoring his protest, she proceeded to unclip the fasteners placed at intervals along the back of each leg. "I can do it much faster. Besides, your fingers are probably cold and stiff."

There was nothing cold about him, Oren thought, as he stood facing forward while she knelt and went through the motions of undressing him from the chaps.

To get his mind off the soft brushes of her fingers against his jeans, he did his best to focus on the tree. It was at least six feet tall and twinkling with tiny lights. Silver garlands were scalloped around the branches, while ornaments of all shapes and colors dangled among the fragrant needles.

"Do you like it?"

The softly spoken question brought his head around. She was standing beside him now, a glow in her eyes as she studied the tree.

"Yes. It's very pretty," he said, and was surprised at how much he truly meant it. This tree was nothing like the ones Heather had set up during their married years. She'd always insisted on the artificial kind to avoid the pungent scent of evergreen and the mess of falling needles. All the decorations had been color coordinated, placed at perfect intervals among the branches, and once the job was finished she'd ordered a hands-off policy to anyone who got near the thing.

But this tree was real and the scent of spruce gave the living room the fresh fragrance of the outdoors. The ornaments were a jumbled lot, most of them obviously handmade down through the years by the Murdock sisters and their offspring. Though nothing matched, altogether it was a tree that spoke of home and family and gifts given in the spirit of love, not wealth.

"The only thing that's left is the angel," Mary Jo told him. She fetched the ornament from the couch and offered it to him with an eager smile. "Would you like to sit her on top?"

The angel had been handmade, too. A piece of white cloth formed her robe, and small pieces of cardboard covered with aluminum foil served as her wings. A tiny piece of wire also wrapped with foil formed a halo above hair made from yellow yarn. Most people would've considered the angel a ratty replica, but Mary Jo was holding her with a reverence that touched a soft spot in Oren.

Silently, he took the angel and fitted her on the very tip-top branch of the tree, then glanced at her for approval.

"Perfect," she said, eyes gleaming. "I think the whole thing is beautiful."

She was beautiful. On the inside where it counted the most. He wasn't exactly sure when he'd come to that conclusion. Maybe after he'd heard the love in her voice when she'd spoken of her mother or the pain and humiliation when she'd talked of the twins' father. Or it could have been the sweet, giving way she'd responded to Oren's kisses that had convinced him she was innocent through and through. The thought of how close the two of them had come to making love still burned in his mind like an ember just waiting to burst into flame.

Doing his best to tuck away the provoking memory, he gave her a little grin and said, "I guess I'd better shape up if I expect to find any packages under this tree on Christmas morning."

Mary Jo's laughter was suggestive. "Better make it a fast shape-up. Christmas is only a few days away now."

And once the holiday was over, she would most

likely be heading back to Aztec. At one time, that notion would have filled Oren with relief. Now he wasn't at all sure how he felt about Mary Jo leaving the ranch. The only thing he knew for certain was that he would miss her. In all the ways a man could miss a woman.

"Uh—have you eaten yet?" he asked.

She shook her head. "I've been too busy. What about you?"

"I was too tired to stop by the bunkhouse and eat with the hands. I'd planned on just eating a snack here at home. But that's not a very hospitable way to repay you for all the work you've done with the tree."

"I don't want to be repaid. The tree was my gift to you." A sudden idea brightened her expression. "I'll fix us some supper. Do you have fresh things in the kitchen, like eggs and bread?"

As soon as he nodded, she turned and headed out of the living room. Oren followed on her heels.

"Mary Jo, this isn't necessary. You need to get off your feet."

"So do you," she told him, already digging items from the refrigerator. "Why don't you go wash up, then come back and talk to me? I'll have it on the table in no time."

The invitation was too appealing for Oren to turn down. Without further protest, he left the kitchen, then returned a few minutes later wearing a clean flannel shirt and the smell of horses washed from his hands.

He took a seat at the table, where she'd already set out plates, silverware and napkins. Over on the cookstove, smoked bacon sizzled in a black iron skillet, while the nearby coffeemaker was gurgling to a finish.

Oren watched her slather thick slices of bread with butter, then plop them down on a hot griddle. Her small, capable hands moved with quick efficiency and confirmed that she was a woman completely at home in the kitchen.

"I take it you've been out riding today," she said as she broke eggs into a neighboring skillet.

He glanced around the room while wondering why her presence should make it feel so different. Just the sound of her voice and the lingering lure of her perfume filled him with an odd sort of contentment.

"Six hours' worth. Me and some of the boys were hunting a strayed bull."

"Did you have any luck?"

"No. We think he's gone south. Over the mountains. We started to head that way, but the weather got to looking too rough. Tomorrow we'll start the search again. If the snow doesn't get deep."

She flipped the bread, then ladled the eggs and bacon onto a platter. Carrying it to the table, she said, "My mother used to sing a little trail song about a cowboy staying in a line shack during the winter, riding the fences and fighting loneliness. What makes you men want to do this hard work, anyway?''

As she placed the food in front of him, her hair dipped forward, hiding her face. Oren was suddenly overcome with the urge to grab a handful of the red-blond strands and tug her down onto his lap. He wanted to savor her soft mouth and draw in the sweet lilac that scented her skin. He wanted to cup her full breasts in the palms of his hands while the weight of her body warmed him. Tempted him.

He glanced away from her and drew in a much needed breath. ''Because it's bred in our genes,'' he explained. ''Ranching isn't just a job, it's a way of life, a connection with nature that goes so deep we couldn't survive doing anything else.''

She glanced at him, but didn't make any sort of reply until she'd returned with the toasted bread. ''You mentioned that your dad taught you to ride at a very early age. Is that how you grew up? Learning how to handle horses and ropes and branding irons and all the other things cowboys do?''

The mention of his father momentarily cooled his thoughts, and his mouth twisted to a wry line. ''Bill Lassiter taught me all those things and more. Like drinking, cussing and womanizing.''

She went after the coffeepot. Once she'd filled their mugs and returned the carafe to its hot plate, she took a seat across from him.

''I didn't add those last things, you did,'' she said with a teasing smile.

He gave her a halfhearted grin, then his expression sobered. "My old man was an expert at such things. So I guess you could say I had a good teacher. Fortunately, I didn't really follow in his footsteps. At least not in those departments."

Mary Jo studied his face as he sprinkled several drops of Tabasco over his fried eggs. From the moment she'd opened her eyes after her fainting spell and seen this cowboy standing at the foot of her bed, she'd been intrigued by him. And with each passing day since, she longed to know more about him. Like how he'd lived before the Bar M, what made him happy and sad, and most importantly, why he couldn't let himself love.

"Where are your parents now?" she asked. "Anywhere close?"

Oren shook his head. "They divorced a long time ago. Dad still has the ranch near Deming. Mom remarried and moved to California. I rarely ever see either of them."

He sounded regretful, but at the same time resolute.

"Your dad never remarried?"

Oren snorted. "No. He's too damn opinionated and bull-headed for any woman to put up with on a long-term basis. He ruled us kids with the same iron hand he ruled Nadine, our mother."

"So you don't blame your mother for their divorce?" she asked curiously.

"No. Not for the divorce, just for leaving us kids

behind. Me and my sisters were all teenagers when she skipped out. We needed her—but I guess she needed to get away from Dad even worse.''

His voice was strained, as though the scars of his past made it hard to swallow, much less talk. The notion made Mary Jo want to reach across the table and squeeze his hand. She wanted to tell him that she knew what it was like to feel deserted and unloved. But touching him at will wasn't a privilege he'd given her, so she tried to commiserate with only her words.

"When I was a very young teenager," she told him, "I used to wonder why I couldn't have a father. I almost resented my mother because she wasn't married like my friends' mothers. But I was too young to fully understand about adult needs back then. Now I'm glad she didn't saddle herself with some man she didn't love just to give me a father."

Her admission distracted him from thoughts of his own family and he looked at her curiously. "I've noticed you've never mentioned your father. Where is he?"

Without warning, a fragment of thought or memory zinged through Mary Jo's mind. Her brows drew together in a frown as she tried to pull it back, but the impression was too fast and fleeting to grasp. It was the first and only indication that the missing parts of her trip here to the Bar M might be coming back to her. Why couldn't she hold on to it? she wondered desperately.

Shaking her head, she pressed her fingertips against her forehead as if to will her mind to repeat the lost thought. Across the table, Oren studied her with concern.

"Mary Jo? Are you all right?"

The sound of Oren's voice snapped her back to the present and she looked at him with utter defeat. "I—I'm sorry. I was—something went through my mind just then. I had this sudden feeling that I was going to remember...something about coming here to the Bar M. But it's gone now."

He breathed out a sigh of relief. "Try not to force it and it might come back to you. Maybe it was something about your father. I'd just asked you about him."

Mary Jo's frown deepened and she shook her head again. "It wouldn't have been about him. I didn't know him or much about the sort of man he was. My mother said that he died about the time I was born. She didn't talk about him very often. I think it hurt her too badly."

"You mean because he didn't marry her?"

Mary Jo shook her head. "No. Because she loved him so much."

She watched Oren shift on his seat, as though the word *love* made him uncomfortable. Maybe he'd never felt the emotion, she thought. Or maybe he had and knew all about the pain of losing it.

"Well, I guess some people find their soul mates

in life and some don't,'' he said after he'd swallowed several bites of the eggs and bacon.

"Did you?"

The question came out before she could stop it, and Mary Jo half expected him to tell her to mind her own business.

Instead, he surprised her by saying, "When I got married I thought so. But that was when I was very young and naive."

"I didn't realize you'd been married."

The surprise in her voice twisted his lips to a dry semblance of a smile. "Yeah. For five years. I figured Chloe had probably already told you."

Mary Jo shook her head. "Chloe doesn't gossip."

He shrugged. "Well, she knows the story. Heather realized that I wasn't going to be anything more than a poor rancher. She found me boring and the life boring. She divorced me and took the land, house and cattle that I'd worked so hard to acquire for the both of us."

Mary Jo's mouth fell open. "My word, what was left?"

"Nothing. She got everything."

"How did she manage to do that? Surely your lawyer—"

"Couldn't fight the judge, who just happened to be good friends with Heather's parents. On top of that she testified that most of the time I stayed drunk and abusive. That was her main reason for wanting the divorce and why she refused to give me children.

It was all a pack of lies. I did take a drink or two now and then, especially after things started going bad between us. But I was never drunk or abusive.''

Riveted by his story, Mary Jo stared at him in disbelief. ''Did she really refuse to have children?''

Oren took a long swig of coffee before he answered. ''Yes. That much was true. But her real reason was selfishness. She didn't want the tiresome job of being a mother. You know, changing dirty diapers, washing bottles, getting up in the night. Just the mention of having a baby turned her cold. She had too much to do and enjoy to be saddled with kids.''

Mary Jo let out a long breath. ''I'm sorry, Oren, but I can't see how you could have married such a woman.''

Oren grimaced. ''I was only nineteen when I met her, and was still pretty messed up from my parents' divorce. She seemed crazy about me then and I lapped up the attention like a starved alley cat. She swore she'd love me forever, and I was so wet behind the ears I wanted to be a shining knight and give her the moon. We married before I was twenty.''

Mary Jo tried to imagine him so driven by passion. ''Were you still living at home at the time?''

He nodded. ''After we married I moved out and got a job as a welder's helper. Which cut the rift between me and my dad even deeper. He didn't like to think I could make it without him, and he sure didn't like the idea of me working outside the ranch. I guess part of the drive I had back then came out of wanting to prove him wrong. Whatever the reason, I hung tough and eventually made enough money to put down on a piece of land with an old house on it. Slowly, during the next five years, I stocked it with a few cattle and restored the house. Every extra dollar I earned went into that place. Then she divorced me, and like the snap of your fingers, I suddenly had nothing.''

Mary Jo slowly shook her head. It was no wonder he couldn't trust women. In ways, Heather had Jeremy beaten by a mile in the cruelty department. He'd only been selfish and indifferent to Mary Jo, whereas Heather had been downright vengeful to Oren.

"So you've never…wanted to remarry after all that?''

He let out a caustic laugh. "Would you?''

She frowned at him. "Jeremy didn't exactly treat me like a queen, you know. But that doesn't mean I'm going to let him mess up the rest of my life. It would be nice to have someone to love. If I met the right man, I would marry him.''

He appeared to mull over her words, but whether he approved or disapproved of her feelings on the matter was something he kept to himself. His eyes strayed from her to the glass patio door to their left.

"You'd better eat up,'' he told her. "I need to drive you back down to the ranch before the weather gets worse.''

This time Mary Jo couldn't stop herself from reaching across the table for his hand, and though he gave it to her, he slanted her a look that warned her not to push.

She didn't allow it to intimidate her. The way she was beginning to feel about him was too important for her to back down now.

"You're still afraid of me, aren't you? Afraid of this thing between us."

His lips thinned, his nostrils flared. "There isn't anything between us," he said flatly.

Before tonight his words would have hurt. But now she understood that the fear of being hurt was guiding his tongue.

"You know that isn't true," she said in a low, husky voice. "The other night, you wanted me. We—"

She broke off as her cheeks blossomed with color. Oren closed his eyes and looked away from her. He had to or else he might just go around the table and pull her into his arms.

"You don't have to remind me about the other night. I've been trying like hell to forget it."

"Why? Because you think making love to me would be lowering your standards?"

His eyes flew back to her face. "Don't be stupid!"

She gripped his hand. "I'm not being stupid, Oren. There has to be some reason that you don't want me. I think I deserve—"

Before she could finish, he cut in, "You know damn well that I want you! But I—right now you don't need me messing up your life, Mary Jo. You need a husband. Not a lover!''

He couldn't have said it plainer. He wanted to make love to her, but he didn't want to marry her.

Still gripping his hand, she rose from her chair and walked around the small table. His gaze followed her other hand as it settled on his shoulder.

"Chloe said that if you wanted a woman you wouldn't let two babies stand in your way.''

He glanced up at her, and for a moment she glimpsed a sea of anguish in his eyes. "Chloe talks too damn much.''

Determined not to let him know he was hurting her, Mary Jo thrust her chin out. "Then I was right all along. You would never want a woman with twin babies.''

Like a shot, he was up from the chair and both his hands were gripping her shoulders. "Dear God, the fact that you're pregnant has nothing to do with it! You deserve more than me. You deserve to be loved.''

He was so close the heat of his body was seeping into hers. The unique scent of him was spreading through her like a hypnotic drug. Trembling with need for him, she slid her arms around his waist and closed the last fraction of space between their bodies.

"Oh, Oren,'' she pleaded, "don't shut me out.''

The memory of how it felt to kiss her began to blur with the sight of her soft, gentle features and upturned lips. Before he realized he was giving in, he was bending his head and pressing his mouth over hers.

For long moments, his lips devoured hers as his hands roamed her back and pillaged her hair, making the long tresses fall to her shoulders. Beneath the thin flannel of his shirt he could feel her small hands sliding ever so slowly up his chest, warming him, tempting him. She wanted him. God only knew why, he thought miserably.

The likes of him didn't rate such a giving, innocent young woman. If he made love to her tonight, he might not ever be able to give her up, and that could be disastrous. He was too jaded, too ruined by all he'd been through to make her happy. He'd tried marriage once and failed. If he tried it again, what kind of hell might he be putting both of them through?

That question froze him with fear and gave him the strength to tear his mouth from hers. "We can't do this, Mary Jo," he whispered in a choked voice. "Not tonight. Not ever."

Confusion skittered across her features as she stared up at him. "Oren, why are you—"

"Don't ask why," he said bluntly. Then, before he let himself be tempted to change his mind, he turned her back to him, then nudged her in the direction of the living room. "Go get your coat. I'm taking you back to the ranch house."

With wounded eyes, Mary Jo glanced over her shoulder at him. "Is that what you want?"

Something inside his chest was tearing, sending fissures of pain right toward his heart. Looking away from her, he said, "One of these days you'll understand that people like you and me don't get what we want, Mary Jo. We get what's dealt to us."

"And one of these days you'll realize you're ruining your future by living in the past," she said, then hurried out of the room and away from the sight of him.

Chapter 7

Outside, beneath a small overhang that sheltered the front entrance to Oren's house, Mary Jo tightened her fleecy muffler against the stinging north wind.

In front of her, the enormous wooden deck that served as a porch was covered with rippling drifts of snow. Directly behind her left shoulder, Oren said, "You should go back in and let me heat up the truck first."

"No. I'll be fine," she said stiffly.

He murmured something unintelligible, then reached for her gloved hand. With it safely ensconced in his, he wrapped his other arm tightly around the back of her waist.

She followed his slow, measured steps, each one taken carefully to avoid all danger of her falling. His gentle concern was so at odds with their clash in the kitchen that she felt herself melting like the snowflakes against her warm face.

Tears silently stung her eyes as she realized she didn't want to be angry with this man. She wanted to ease his pain, take away his doubts and make him smile with happiness. She was in love with him. Totally and irrevocably.

The realization stunned her and she blinked rapidly against her tears and the force of her newfound feelings.

"Are you going to get in? Or keep standing here in the snow?"

Oren's voice penetrated her thoughts and she realized he'd opened the door and was waiting for her to make a move to climb into the truck. But she didn't follow his prompt. Instead she grabbed his arm and twisted her face around toward his.

"Oren," she said with anguish. "A minute ago— in the kitchen—I shouldn't have said some of those things to you. It's wrong of me to try to give you counsel when I can't even get my own comings and goings straight in my mind. But I only wanted you to see—to know how much I want you. How much I want you to give us a chance. Don't hate me for that."

He looked down at the dark blue woolen cap covering her hair and outlining the white oval of her face. Snowflakes were catching rapidly on the material, while others landed on her cheeks and her trembling lower lip. Her green eyes were wet, and as he looked into them, he thought about all that she'd said to him, all that she'd done for him. And deep in his heart, he knew it was too late to worry about keeping his distance from this woman. She'd already opened up his heart and walked right in.

"Oh, Mary Jo, it would be impossible for me to hate you. In fact, I'm not even angry with you. Only at myself."

Turning, she framed his face with her gloved hands. Between them, the babies turned one way and then another, as though they knew their mother was about to take an irrevocable step.

"Why?" She breathed the word, then held her breath as she hoped, prayed he would take her in his arms.

"Because I'm too much of a coward to even try to give you what you want. To take what I want."

"Don't say that, Oren. You've been hurt. So have I. But that doesn't mean it will happen to us again."

The slanting rays of the yard light illuminated his face. Mary Jo's heart thumped with anticipation as she watched his shadowed expression soften, watched desire burn in his eyes.

Seconds later he was bending his head, kissing her with a hunger that bordered on roughness. Mary Jo clung to him as she desperately tried to convey her love through her lips and her hands. By the time he lifted his mouth from hers, she was gasping for breath, but her eyes were twin flames, daring him to take more.

This time Oren couldn't resist her silent invitation. He slammed the truck door shut, then carefully lifted her in his arms and carried her back to the house.

Mary Jo clung to him tightly until he set her down in the middle of a big bed. After that he didn't waste time with words. Nor did she. They both quickly shed their heavy outer clothing, then moved on until the floor was littered and they were both down to their underwear.

When he reached to pull her into his arms, Mary Jo snuggled against him, shivering with longing. "It's a good thing it's dark in here," she murmured against his strong shoulder. "Otherwise, you'd probably be running right now."

His hands began to slide over the silky smoothness of her warm flesh. "Oh no. I can see you, Mary Jo. And what I see is too gorgeous for me to touch. Unless you want me to," he added thickly.

The hand on her breast slipped to the warm V between her legs. Already she was aching for him there. And somewhere in the back of her mind, she realized a part of her had been aching for this man ever since she'd laid eyes on him.

She reached up and slid her fingers into his thick, dark hair. "I've never wanted anything more," she whispered.

Oren bent his head and kissed her lips, and as he did, it slowly dawned on him that he was shaking, trembling with fear at the thought of taking the pleasure she was so generously offering him.

Anxiously, he whispered, "The babies—"

"Are safely cocooned," she assured him.

Gently, reverently, his hand moved over the mound of her stomach, as though he considered the two little lives growing there to be far more precious than anything he'd ever had or wanted. The notion burned her throat with a ball of emotion.

"I won't hurt you, Mary Jo," he promised huskily. "I could never hurt you."

Her arms moved down around his back and drew him closer to her and the babies. His body was a heated furnace, scorching her in all the places it touched.

"I believe you, Oren. If I didn't, I would never be here like this."

"Oh, Mary Jo. My sweet—my little darling."

She raised her parted lips up to his and he closed the short gap between them with a groan of surrender. Then with slow, agonizing pleasure, he began to make love to her. And as Mary Jo's body began to move with his needy thrusts, all she could think was that her heart had finally found a home and it was here in Oren's arms.

Mary Jo woke the next morning before daylight to find herself alone in Oren's bed and the smell of freshly brewed coffee drifting in the air.

Flinging back the covers, she hurriedly dressed,

then made her way to the bathroom. She'd finished with the necessities and was brushing her hair when she heard Oren's footsteps out in the hallway.

Figuring he was looking for her, she opened the door and called to him. "I'm in here, Oren."

Moments later he appeared in the doorway wearing nothing but jeans and a devilish smile. The sight of him made her heart begin to thump like a happy puppy's tail.

"Good morning," she said.

"Good morning," he drawled back at her.

She breathed deeply as memories of their lovemaking washed over her in glorious waves. Never had anyone made her feel so loved, so wanted.

"You let me go to sleep instead of taking me back to the ranch. What will Chloe and Wyatt think?" she teased.

Grinning, he stepped into the small room and took the hairbrush from her hand. "Probably that I've come to my senses."

Before she could make any sort of reply, he turned her so that her back was toward him, and began to stroke the brush through her long hair. "You have beautiful hair, Mary Jo. Promise me you won't ever cut it."

The tender affection she heard in his voice and felt in his touch choked her with emotion. Last night he'd not spoken the words *I love you*. But she'd felt them just the same.

"I won't," she promised huskily.

He pushed the silky curtain of hair to one side and kissed the back of her neck. She closed her eyes and smiled.

"I've made coffee but not breakfast," he said.

"If you keep doing that you're not going to make it to work, much less breakfast."

With a low chuckle, he slid his arms around the back of her waist and pressed his hands lovingly against her rounded stomach. "Do you know how it makes me feel to have you here like this?"

Urgent now, she turned in his arms and cradled his face with her hands. "Then you don't regret what happened?"

He pressed his cheek tightly against hers. "No. No regrets."

She sighed, and he eased his head back and gave her a reassuring smile. "We'll talk about it tonight, okay? I'll pick you up before supper."

She nodded and he patted her cheek.

"Right now, I've got to get ready for work, or Chloe's going to be up here hunting for the both of us."

Mary Jo took the brush from his hand and pushed him out the door.

Daylight still hadn't quite broken when Oren dropped Mary Jo off at the ranch house. The place was quiet, and she decided Wyatt must have already left for his offices in Ruidoso. As for Chloe, she'd left a note pinned to the refrigerator door.

It read: Mary Jo, I'm off on a fast trip to Roswell to look at a prospective race horse. I'll be back by midafternoon. Justine and Rose are coming over at that time to help get things together. Remember we're having that little birthday-Christmas party for Ethan and Penny's twins tonight. You don't have to dress up, but you can if you want to. Oh, and be sure to tell Oren he's to be there. Little Jake and Jase think he's the grandest cowboy to ever walk.

Love, Chloe

Smiling faintly, Mary Jo headed toward her bedroom. It was probably a good thing Chloe wasn't here this morning. Not that Mary Jo was embarrassed about staying the night at Oren's. She was a grown woman, and Chloe could see for herself how much she cared for the man. But the other woman would no doubt be eager to ask her questions about the future. And Mary Jo wasn't prepared to answer them. Oren hadn't yet discussed any long-term plans with her and she hadn't pressed him. But she wanted to believe last night was the beginning of a lifetime with Oren.

After a warm, leisurely shower, she dressed in a pair of black leggings and topped them with a white, oversize sweater. As she passed in front of the dresser, the image of her casual clothes made her pause to wonder what she could possibly wear to little Jake and Jase's birthday party tonight.

Even if she were home and able to pick through her closet, it wouldn't help much. She'd never had the money to buy dressy clothes. She did have a few classic pieces that were slightly better than her everyday wear. But she was too pregnant to wear them even if she had them with her.

Crossing the room, she searched through the things she'd hung in the closet. There was a crisp, holly-green shirt that would work. She could wear it with her better black slacks. Now if she could find the silk scarf to tie around her neck—the one with the tiny skating snowmen that Chloe had given her the other day...

At the bottom of the closet were two soft travel bags she'd used on her trip down here. Thinking she might have put the scarf in one of them, she carried them both to the bed and began to search through the zippered compartments.

She found everything but a scarf, and was about to look elsewhere when she noticed the corner of an envelope tucked behind a plastic flap inside the bag.

The scarf momentarily forgotten, Mary Jo curiously pulled the large manila envelope from its resting place. As soon as she turned it over in her hands, her heart began to bang against her ribs with unexplained trepidation. The envelope was addressed to her mother in Raton, New Mexico. The postmark was a date twenty-seven years ago, several months before Mary Jo had been born. There was no name on the return address, but there was a Ruidoso post office box number. Who had her mother known from this area and why had she kept this correspondence for so long?

Quickly, Mary Jo opened the envelope to find a photograph. It was a horse racing photo, shot from the winner's circle at Le Mesa Downs in Raton. A handsome paint horse, its neck blanketed with red roses, was at the center of the picture. Atop the horse was a jockey wearing bright red silks with a green *M* on the sleeve. On the ground holding the horse's bridle was a big burly man in Western boots and hat. Mary Jo assumed he had to have been either the trainer or the owner. Although she didn't recognize him, there was something about his face that seemed oddly familiar.

In the bottom left-hand corner in black type, the statistics of the race were given, including the date, the length, the winning time, along with the names of the jockey, the horse and the trainer-owner.

Mary Jo's eyes suddenly froze on the last bit of information. Trainer-owner: Tomas Murdock! This was Chloe, Rose and Justine's father! What had her mother been doing with this picture?

Frantic for answers, her gaze switched to the background, where several people were standing in a semicircle at the left edge of the photo. As her eyes scanned the faces, her hands began to shake, her mind to whirl. The woman with the blond hair looked amazingly like her mother. It had to be her mother!

Mary Jo flipped the picture over and was shocked

even more as she read the bold handwriting scrawled across the back. *To Josie, with love, Thomas.*

This had to be the Tom her mother had sometimes spoken about. The man who raised horses. The man who had fathered Mary Jo!

Oh dear heaven, she silently moaned. This had to be why she'd driven here to the Bar M. Had she been planning to show this photo to the Murdocks? Was it possible she actually was Tomas Murdock's daughter? Surely one photo wasn't enough to come to that conclusion.

Gripping the envelope, she jumped to her feet and began to pace around the room. When had she found this photo? And how had she connected it to this ranch? Someone who knew the Murdocks would've had to have told her.

Still pacing, she tried to retrace the days before she'd found herself here on the Bar M, to form a picture in her mind of how all of this had happened. But after a few minutes of deep concentration her head began to pound and a cold sweat popped out on her forehead and upper lip. Frightened she was making herself ill, she lay down on the bed, closed her eyes and willed her mind to go blank.

But the minute she tried to stop thinking, memory jolted through her like a sudden injection of stimulants. Jess Hastings! Her friend and the undersheriff of San Juan County. She'd found the envelope with the photo in some of her mother's old Christmas cards and had taken it down to the sheriff's office in hopes that he could help her identify the person who'd written it. Incredibly, Jess had known Tomas and the Murdock family. He'd gone on to question Mary Jo about her birth certificate.

Mary Jo sat up on the side of the bed and cradled her pounding head in her hands. Clearly now, she remembered as a teenager how she'd once snooped through her mother's important papers and discovered the document. "Father's name" had been listed as Tom Murdock. But at that time, Mary Jo had not made any connection. She'd believed him to be a man who'd raised horses out in California, and since her mother had told her he was dead and had no other offspring, there hadn't been much reason for Mary Jo to dwell on the matter.

Dazed, her head still pounding, Mary Jo made her way to the bathroom and splashed several handfuls of cold water onto her face. As she dabbed her cheeks with a hand towel, she studied herself in the mirror. Green eyes. Red hair. The Murdock trademarks. And she was carrying twins. With two sets already in the family, hers would make it a third!

Don't be crazy, Mary Jo, she told herself. *Your twins will never be a part of the Murdock family. You'll never be a part of the family. Josie obviously understood that. Now you must, too.*

Chloe, Rose, Justine and the whole family had been forced to deal with the fact that Tomas had fathered Adam and Anna out of wedlock. Sure, they'd accepted that he'd been lonely and dispirited over his wife being ill and fragile. They'd forgiven him his transgression. But how would they feel if they knew their father's philandering hadn't been confined solely to the twins' mother? It might crumble the very foundation of the family! And they'd been so good to Mary Jo. So generous and warm. She couldn't spring such a thing on them. They might even think she'd come here to make some sort of demands on the Murdock estate!

That horrible thought had her mind instantly springing to Oren, and a sense of loss welled up inside her, so deep and painful she could scarcely breathe.

From the very start he'd believed she'd come here for some ulterior motive. She'd tried very hard to earn his trust, to convince him she wasn't a greedy person. But now... Once he learned the truth, he would surely decide that she'd been lying to him all this time. Everything they'd shared last night would be tarnished with suspicions. Everything they might have had together in the future was over. It didn't matter that she loved him. He would never believe that she'd only come to this ranch out of a need to find her family.

Urgent now, she hurried to the closet and began to jerk down her clothes. She had to get away before Chloe returned. As for Oren, he would be out riding all afternoon, searching for the stray bull. He would never see her leave.

* * *

Oren and his two right-hand men, Lucky and Red, were riding in the far south section of the ranch when Lucky's cell phone shrilled from inside his jacket.

Red's horse, spooked by the sound, jumped sideways and gave a hearty buck. While the cowboy tried to wrestle the horse back under control, Oren cursed. "What in hell did you bring that thing for?" he demanded. "This is a ranch, not an office!"

Undaunted by his boss's outburst, Lucky reached for the phone and answered it. After a few clipped words, he handed the small instrument over to Oren. "It's for you and it's Chloe. I think you'd better take it."

Concerned now, Oren pulled up his horse and jammed the phone to his ear. "What's wrong, Chloe?"

"Oh, Oren, thank God Lucky had the sense to take that phone with him. You've got to get back to the ranch. Pronto! Mary Jo is gone!"

Chloe's words struck him like a fist. "Gone? Where?"

"I don't know. Just get back here. You've got to find her!"

Chloe hung up and Oren tossed the phone back to Lucky.

"Come on, boys, we've got to ride," he said, then spurred his horse in the direction of the Bar M.

Once Oren reached the ranch house, he found Chloe in tears, which was a disturbing sight in itself, since the woman was always as strong as rawhide. Wyatt had obviously been notified, and he'd hurried home to console his wife.

"Have you heard from Mary Jo?" Oren asked hopefully.

Grimly, the rugged oilman picked up a piece of paper from the coffee table and handed it to Oren. Nearby, Chloe dabbed at her eyes.

"She left this note," Wyatt told him. "But nothing else that we could find. I wanted to call Ethan and have him send out a bulletin to have the authorities stop her on the highway, but Chloe refuses."

"She's pregnant, Wyatt! I don't want to upset her any more than she already is!"

Oren read the note:

Dear Chloe and Family,

Please forgive me for leaving this way, but something has happened and I have to get home. Someday I will repay you for all the help you've given me. That's a promise. Everyone on the ranch has shown me more kindness than I've ever had in my life. Please tell Oren that I will never forget him.

Love, Mary Jo

Oren was so stunned, so cut up with pain, he scarcely heard the phone ring. As Wyatt went to answer it, he stared at Chloe.

"Why did she do this?" he growled harshly. "Is she trying to hurt me—"

"Oren," Wyatt interrupted. "You're wanted on the phone."

"I don't want to talk to anyone now!" he barked.

Wyatt looked apologetic. "Sorry, but I think you'd better speak with this man, Oren. He says he's the undersheriff of San Juan County."

Jess! He'd know something about Mary Jo!

Oren was still on the phone when Justine and Rose arrived. By the time he hung up, the three sisters had surrounded him, their expressions somber. Oren looked at them all and wondered how they were going to react once he told them the story that had just been shared with him.

"Has Jess heard from Mary Jo?" Chloe asked quickly.

"Not today," he said grimly. "But there's something you all need to know."

The three women and Wyatt all looked at him with raised brows. Slowly, Oren repeated all that Jess had just told him about Mary Jo coming to his office, showing him the photo, her birth certificate, and his advice to her about driving down here to meet her family.

"So you see," Oren went on to explain, "his call was just coincidental. He'd just gotten back into town yesterday and decided he'd see how things went between Mary Jo and you Murdocks."

Obviously amazed, Justine asked, "You mean she really didn't know who her father was?"

Still dazed himself, Oren shook his head. "Apparently not. She voiced to Jess that she was concerned about her being the only family her twins had. If something happened to her, she wanted them to at least know they had other relatives who could tell them about their roots."

"And then she had amnesia. Poor thing," Rose murmured.

"What a shocking way for a young woman to learn about herself," Justine said. "She was probably so scared about meeting us that the whole thing must have given her a mental block."

"And Daddy," Chloe said with a stunned shake of her head. "This means he wasn't just cheating on Mother, he was cheating on Belinda, too!"

"It looks that way," Justine agreed with a solemn nod. "He must have met Josie Bailey when he was racing up at Le Mesa Downs in Raton, and had an affair with her! I sometimes wonder if we knew the man at all."

Rose dabbed at the moisture brimming in her eyes. "He wasn't a bad man, really. He was just weak in some ways. I think Mother realized that and loved him in spite of it."

"Well," Wyatt intercepted with wry humor, "whatever the man was, he's given you another sister."

The three women looked at Wyatt, then swapped

glances between them. Oren was trying to gauge their expressions when suddenly all three began to laugh and hug each other.

"We have a new sister!" Chloe exclaimed, then rushed forward and grabbed Oren by the arm. "What are you waiting on? Go get your bags packed! You've got to go after her and bring her back!"

Six hours later and three hundred fifty miles north, Oren drove head-on into a blizzard. All evening he'd been listening to the weather report on the truck radio and expecting it to turn nasty before he reached Aztec, but he'd not planned on snow of this sort.

Northwest winds were driving the particles of ice straight into the windshield, turning the curvature of glass into a blinding white sheet. The highway was packed and frozen, forcing him to reduce the truck's speed to a frustrating crawl. With each mile that passed, he searched for the sight of Mary Jo's compact car stranded on the side of the road, but so far, to his relief, the only thing he'd come across was an old van and an expensive sports car.

Having several hours head start on him, he'd been praying she'd been able to make it home safely before the storm had hit. She and the babies could never survive in weather like this. And for the past hundred miles there had been little or no traffic, in case she might have needed to flag someone for help.

The nightmarish thought made Oren curse under his breath, and for the hundredth time since he'd started driving tonight, he asked himself why she'd run away. After last night, he'd been convinced she loved him. Like a fool, he'd already had visions of the two of them growing old together. Raising the twins together. But now he had to ask himself if last night was all she'd ever intended to give him.

Mary Jo rubbed her back. It was aching, and she berated herself for driving straight through and not stopping on the road and staying in a motel before she became too tired. But she'd been afraid to stop. Afraid she might be tempted to turn around and head back to the Bar M. Then afraid, too, that Oren or the Murdocks might be following her.

As if they'd want to find you, Mary Jo.

Frowning, she tried to ignore the little mocking voice inside her. In all probability none of them would want to find her, and even if they did, her address here was no secret. Any Aztec phone book could give it to them.

Her heart heavy, she pushed back the bedcovers and shoved her feet into a pair of fuzzy slippers. Maybe a little warm milk would help ease her back. It was a cinch she wasn't going to be able to sleep for a while.

She was lying on the couch, sipping the milk, when she noticed a flicker of headlights through the windows at the front of the house. Seconds later a knock sounded.

Uneasy that anyone would be at her door so late

at night, she stood, then paused and called out, "Who is it?"

"Oren."

She rushed to the door and jerked it open, half expecting to see that she was hallucinating and had only conjured his voice in her mind. But he was there on the threshold, snow clinging to his hat and coat and boots.

A sudden surge of emotion robbed her of words. She stepped to one side, and he quickly entered the house and closed the door behind him.

"What are you doing—"

"Why did you—"

Realizing they were both speaking at once, Mary Jo stopped and shook her head. Oren took her by the arm and led her over to the couch. Except for a small lamp, the room was dark. He could see she was dressed in a nightgown. The neckline was scooped low and exposed the soft cleavage of her breasts. Her long hair was tangled, her cheeks flushed. She was the most beautiful thing he'd ever seen in his life.

"Did I get you out of bed?"

She shook her head again. "I couldn't sleep. I kept thinking—oh Oren, why are you here? In this weather!"

"I barely made it here," he admitted, then because he couldn't control himself any longer, he grabbed her by both shoulders. "What in hell made you run off like that, Mary Jo? Didn't last night mean anything to you at all? Or is that why you left? Because you decided I wasn't what you wanted, after all?''

She was so stunned by his accusation, her mouth fell open. ''No! I didn't think that at all. Last night...'' Heat suddenly filled her cheeks and her gaze drifted shyly to the middle of his chest. ''It was perfect, Oren. Surely you know—'' She stopped, sucked in a deep breath, then lifted her eyes back up to his. ''Surely you could tell that—I love you!''

He'd not expected that much from her and for a moment he was too overcome to speak. To be loved by this woman was a gift. A precious gift that he wasn't sure he deserved.

Oren cleared his throat, but still his voice came out rough and raspy when he said, ''Running off is not a good way to let a man know you love him, Mary Jo. In fact, it's flat-out stupid. Do you know how terrified I've been, thinking you'd probably wrecked your car somewhere on this ice and—''

''But Oren,'' she interrupted miserably, ''I had to leave. I knew that when you found out that I'm—''

Seeing she couldn't get the words out, Oren finished for her. ''That you're Tomas Murdock's daughter?''

Her head flew up. ''You know. How?''

''Jess Hastings called me at the ranch. He'd gotten back to town and learned at the diner that you were still gone. He wanted to find out how the meeting between you and the Murdocks went.''

Defeat made her shoulders sag. "So he told you everything?"

Oren nodded. "What happened back at the ranch? Did your memory return?"

She sighed, knowing that no matter how she explained herself it was going to sound lame and farfetched. "This morning I found the photo in my bags. After that it was like my mind started taking these giant leaps and I couldn't stop it. And then, after I began to realize I was Tomas's daughter, I knew I couldn't hang around. I knew you'd think I'd gone there for money and the Murdocks probably would, too. I don't want anything concerning their estate, Oren! I went there because…" She shook her head helplessly. "I only wanted to find a piece of my family," she added in a choked whisper. "If something happened to me, my twins would have no one."

He didn't say anything right off, and taking his silence for disgust, Mary Jo rose to her feet and walked across the room to where a row of windows looked out at the snowy night.

A cold draft seeped around the windowsills and peppered her skin with goose bumps. In the back of her mind, the thought struck her that she should go find her robe, but she suddenly felt so tired and defeated, it was an effort just to breathe.

For nearly three weeks, she'd experienced a life that had been too good to be true. In spite of everything, she'd somehow known all along that it would have to end, but even the knowing hadn't prepared her for the pain.

Mary Jo's misery was so deep she didn't hear Oren walk up behind her. When his hands settled on her shoulders, she reacted with a jerk.

"I think you should know that the Murdocks are crazy with worry about you. Chloe and her sisters ordered me to come after you."

Like the wings of a wounded bird, hope tried to flutter inside her. Even if Oren hated her now, maybe the Murdocks wouldn't shut her out completely. "Do they...resent the idea of me being their half sister?"

"They're so happy they're jumping up and down on their heels."

Unexpected tears rushed to her eyes. "And what about you, Oren? How do you feel knowing that I'm a Murdock?"

Suddenly his lips were pressing kisses along her bare shoulder. "I'm sorry, Mary Jo," he whispered. "So sorry that you felt you couldn't trust me with the truth."

Her heart pounding, her expression incredulous, she whirled around to face him. "You mean, you believe me?"

His groan was scored with raw pain. "I think deep down I've always believed you were a good and admirable person. But at first I tried to pretend, to make myself believe otherwise, so that I wouldn't fall in love with you." A rueful grin twisted his lips. "It didn't work."

A thrill of joy shattered the cold shadows around her heart. "Oh, Oren! I've been so...it was killing me, thinking that you would turn your back on me once you found out why I went to the Bar M." Laughing and groaning at the same time, she stepped forward to slide her arms around his waist, but suddenly her movements came to an abrupt halt and she stared down in horror as the front of her gown became soaked with amniotic fluid.

"Oh no! No!" she gasped.

Not yet realizing what was happening, Oren anxiously clutched her upper arm. "What is it, sweetheart? What's wrong?"

"The babies! My water has broken!"

The panic in her voice chilled him with fear, but he tamped it down and tried to think rationally. "Does this mean you're going into labor?"

Trembling now, her face white, she shook her head. "I don't know. My back has been aching. I thought it was because of the long drive, but now I'm not sure."

"We'll call your doctor," he said.

He helped her to the couch, then found her a towel and fresh gown. While she attempted to clean herself, Oren snatched up the phone and punched in the numbers she repeated to him.

Halfway through, he realized there was no dial tone, and he slammed the receiver back on its hook. "The line is dead. The weather must be doing something to your telephone service."

"I have a feeling we shouldn't waste time with the phone, Oren."

He glanced over to see there was already a grimace of pain on her face. Fear such as he'd never experienced raced along his veins.

"I think you'd better get me to the hospital."

More than an hour later, after slowly slipping and sliding their way to the hospital, Oren was pacing around a small waiting room, wondering what could possibly be happening to Mary Jo and the twins, and wondering, too, how he would ever survive if he lost them.

Because of him, she'd driven an arduous number of miles under a burden of emotional strain. If something bad happened to her or the babies, it would be his fault. He shouldn't have been so thickheaded! He should have told her long ago how much he loved her, trusted her!

Deep in silent prayer, Oren scarcely heard a light knock at the doorway to the waiting room. Lifting his gaze, he found a young, dark-headed woman wearing a white lab coat over a pair of dark slacks studying him with a mixture of curiosity and empathy.

Even though no one else was in the waiting room except him, he asked, "Are you looking for someone?"

"Are you Oren Lassiter?"

He nodded numbly, and she began to walk toward him, her hand outstretched. Oren politely shook it.

"I'm Victoria Ketchum," she introduced herself. "I'm Mary Jo's doctor."

Like a punctured balloon, his lungs lost their air. A faint, rushing noise sounded in his ears. For a second he thought his legs were going to collapse.

"What's happened? How is she? The babies?"

Seeing his distress, she quickly patted his arm. "Mary Jo is fine. Very exhausted, but she's doing well, considering."

If possible, his face turned a whiter shade of gray. "Considering! Considering what? Has—?"

"Mr. Lassiter," she gently interrupted, "Mary Jo gave birth to identical twin girls about a half hour ago. The babies were surprisingly large to be born this early, both a little over five pounds. And I'm pleased to say both are very healthy."

Happy and confused at the same time, Oren blurted, "But I thought—even Mary Jo thought on her way over here to the hospital—that if the babies were born now they would be premature."

"Their arrival was a little early, which is a normal thing with twins. But I suspect there was a miscalculation in their due date, which means Mary Jo was probably further along in her pregnancy than we'd gauged her to be. That's not unusual when a woman doesn't have regular cycles." She flashed him a reassuring smile. "Would you like to see them now?"

Weak with relief, Oren barely managed to nod.

Moments later, a nurse ushered him down a wide, quiet corridor, then into a private room. Once the woman had shut the door behind her, he moved toward the bed, where a pool of muted light illuminated Mary Jo's face and the two little bundles, one nestled beneath each arm.

"Oren."

His name whispered past her lips like a reverent prayer. Tears stung his eyes as he bent to place a kiss on her forehead.

"Are you all right?" he asked in a choked voice.

A tired, but happy smile tilted the corner of her lips. "I'm fine. I hope you weren't too worried."

He'd been out of his mind. But she thought she was getting herself a tough cowboy, and he didn't want to disillusion her. Maybe later, after they'd been married thirty years or so, he'd tell her how terrified he'd been at the thought of losing her.

"Naw. I made it okay," he said, then allowed his gaze to drift to the two babies. He couldn't see much more than tiny, red, scrunched-up faces, but that was enough to melt his heart and swell his chest with emotion.

He gently touched the peach-colored fuzz on both their heads, amazed that anything could be so soft and delicate, so precious.

Swallowing hard, he said to Mary Jo, "These two little girls are going to need a daddy. Are you going to give me the job?"

She didn't answer and he looked up to see tears

glistening on her cheeks. He bent over and kissed away the salty drops until she was laughing softly and clasping his face between her hands.

"It'll be a tougher job than keeping the crew on the Bar M in line," she warned.

"I think I can do it," he said with a grin. Then, his eyes full of love, he added, "That is, if you'll marry me and love me for the rest of our natural lives."

Her sigh was brimful of joy. "Just give me the chance."

"Do you think you and the twins will be able to travel in the next few days?"

She nodded eagerly. "I'm sure of it. Victoria says the three of us will be out of here by the day after tomorrow."

He caught both her hands and drew the backs of them to his lips. "Then we'll head down to the Bar M and be married there during Christmas. Surrounded by your family. What do you think?"

Love that knew no bounds glowed in Mary Jo's eyes as she looked from him to their new daughters. "I think you didn't have a clue that Santa was going to put this sort of gift under your Christmas tree. I wonder how he'll ever be able to top this one?"

Oren grinned slyly. "With twin boys?"

Mary Jo's soft, loving chuckle was enough to assure him she'd give it her best try.

Epilogue

On Christmas Eve the ground was still covered with snow, but the sun was bright as the whole Murdock family and neighboring friends gathered at Our Lady of Guadalupe Church to see Mary Jo and Oren married.

Several days had passed since Mary Jo had given birth to the twins and her waistline had already shrunk dramatically. Enough to fit into the beautiful ivory-colored wedding dress that Chloe, Rose and Justine had bought for her.

The old church was filled with Christmas candles, and beneath an arbor of red roses, just like the ones on Tomas Murdock's winning horse, Mary Jo and Oren repeated their vows of love.

Afterward a reception was held at the Bar M ranch house. Family and guests spilled from one room to the next as cake and punch were passed around and photos were snapped of the bride and groom and their twin girls.

"I've never seen this house so full of people," Oren remarked to Mary Jo as the two of them finally managed to find a quiet corner in the kitchen. "I think everyone is happy about our marriage. Especially your family."

"My family," Mary Jo repeated, as though she still wasn't used to the fact that she was no longer alone. "I can't believe the way the Murdocks are treating me. Just like I was really one of them."

Oren leaned over and kissed her forehead. "You *are* really one of them, darling. And they're all very glad. But I'm even more glad that you're my wife, Mrs. Lassiter."

Her eyes shining with love, she reached up and touched her husband's face. "For a long time I didn't know what had brought me to the Bar M, but now I know it wasn't just to find the Murdocks. I was sent here to find you. You're the most important thing in my life, Oren. You and our children."

He was pressing a kiss against her lips when Wyatt called to them over the swinging bat-wing doors. "Hey, you newlyweds, there'll be time enough for that later. Right now everyone is waiting for you two to come see what Santa just left for you under the tree.''

Laughing, they left the kitchen hand in hand and made their way through the crowd until they were at the head of the room where a huge Christmas tree with hundreds of twinkling lights towered all the way up to the twelve-foot ceiling.

Beneath the branches of the blue spruce, in a double infant seat, were Mary Jo and Oren's baby girls. They were wearing identical red velvet dresses with tiny green bows perched on the top of their fuzzy heads. Attached to the front of each dress was a giant name tag. Mary Maureen Lassiter and Margaret Jo Lassiter.

"Two little angels," Oren said proudly. "A man couldn't get a better gift than that."

Those close enough to hear Oren's words all agreed, and Wyatt invited everyone to toast the new babies.

As glasses were lifted high, Ethan called out from the back of the room, "Just be glad they're girls, Oren. Instead of chasing little angels around for the next five years, you'd be like me and Penny—chasing two little rascals!"

While everyone laughed, Mary Jo went up on her tiptoes and whispered in her husband's ear. "They don't know I've promised to give you a set of boys soon.''

He looked down at her, his brows arched with amused curiosity. "Soon? How soon?"

Smiling, she slipped her arm around his waist. "Well, next Christmas is only a year away!"

* * * * *

Look for Stella Bagwell's next book in May, from Silhouette Romance. Also, don't miss the next short story from Stella Bagwell in GOING TO THE CHAPEL, a special 3-in-1 collection available in July from Silhouette Books.

**Take a walk on the dark side of love
with three tales by**

MAGGIE SHAYNE

WINGS IN THE NIGHT

For centuries, loneliness has haunted them from
dusk till dawn. Yet now, from out of the darkness,
shines the light of eternal life…eternal love.

Discover the stories at the heart of the series…
**TWILIGHT PHANTASIES
TWILIGHT MEMORIES
TWILIGHT ILLUSIONS**

Available December 2001 at your favorite retail outlet.

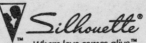

Silhouette®

Where love comes alive™

Visit Silhouette at www.eHarlequin.com

PSWIT

Silhouette

SPECIAL EDITION™
Emotional, compelling stories that capture the intensity of living, loving and creating a family in today's world.

Silhouette®

Desire
A highly passionate, emotionally powerful and always provocative read.

Silhouette®
Where love comes alive™

Silhouette®

INTIMATE MOMENTS™
A roller-coaster read that delivers romantic thrills in a world of suspense, adventure and more.

Silhouette Romance
From first love to forever, these love stories are for today's woman with traditional values.

Visit Silhouette at www.eHarlequin.com

SILGENINT

Silhouette —

where love comes alive—online...

eHARLEQUIN.com

shop eHarlequin

♥ Find all the new Silhouette releases at everyday great discounts.

♥ Try before you buy! Read an excerpt from the latest Silhouette novels.

♥ Write an online review and share your thoughts with others.

reading room

♥ Read our Internet exclusive daily and weekly online serials, or vote in our interactive novel.

♥ Talk to other readers about your favorite novels in our Reading Groups.

♥ Take our Choose-a-Book quiz to find the series that matches you!

authors' alcove

♥ Find out interesting tidbits and details about your favorite authors' lives, interests and writing habits.

♥ Ever dreamed of being an author? Enter our Writing Round Robin. The Winning Chapter will be published online! Or review our writing guidelines for submitting your novel.

All this and more available at
www.eHarlequin.com
on Women.com Networks

SINTB1R

If you enjoyed what you just read,
then we've got an offer you can't resist!

Take 2
bestselling novels FREE!
Plus get a FREE surprise gift!

Clip this page and mail it to The Best of the Best™

IN U.S.A.
3010 Walden Ave.
P.O. Box 1867
Buffalo, N.Y. 14240-1867

IN CANADA
P.O. Box 609
Fort Erie, Ontario
L2A 5X3

YES! Please send me 2 free Best of the Best™ novels and my free surprise gift. After receiving them, if I don't wish to receive anymore, I can return the shipping statement marked cancel. If I don't cancel, I will receive 4 brand-new novels every month, before they're available in stores! In the U.S.A., bill me at the bargain price of $4.24 plus 25¢ shipping and handling per book and applicable sales tax, if any*. In Canada, bill me at the bargain price of $4.74 plus 25¢ shipping and handling per book and applicable taxes**. That's the complete price and a savings of over 15% off the cover prices—what a great deal! I understand that accepting the 2 free books and gift places me under no obligation ever to buy any books. I can always return a shipment and cancel at any time. Even if I never buy another book from The Best of the Best™, the 2 free books and gift are mine to keep forever.

185 MEN DFNG
385 MEN DFNH

Name	(PLEASE PRINT)	
Address	Apt.#	
City	State/Prov.	Zip/Postal Code

* Terms and prices subject to change without notice. Sales tax applicable in N.Y.
** Canadian residents will be charged applicable provincial taxes and GST.
All orders subject to approval. Offer limited to one per household and not valid to current Best of the Best™ subscribers.
® are registered trademarks of Harlequin Enterprises Limited.

BOB01
©1998 Harlequin Enterprises Limited

SOME MEN ARE BORN TO BE ROYALTY.
OTHERS ARE MADE...

CROWNED HEARTS

A royal anthology featuring,
NIGHT OF LOVE, a classic novel from
international bestselling author

DIANA PALMER

Plus a brand-new story in the MacAllister family series by

JOAN ELLIOT PICKART

and a brand-new story by

LINDA TURNER,

which features the royal family of the upcoming
ROMANCING THE CROWN series!

Available December 2001 at your favorite retail outlet.

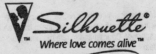

Where love comes alive™

Visit Silhouette at www.eHarlequin.com

PSCH